# ROGUE BET

## THE WILD NINES - BOOK FOUR

### A.R. KNIGHT

# LUNAR AFTERNOON

Her eye changed its color. Again and again, the mark's right eye, framed with a metal striping giving up her enhancements, shifted to match the club's frenetic lights which played through cold color schemes to a scattershot beat. Starfield tile laced with neon littered the floor, the walls, the ceiling. *Neil's* ignored its namesake and its own lunar location and caved to the gyrating sensory assault so damn prevalent these days.

But Davin wouldn't have been three drinks deep without that eye.

"You're coming recommended," Theona said, twisting her talk back to Davin's street cred for what must've been the fifth time. "I normally vet my runners."

"I'm not the one with a deadline," Davin leaned back, casual personified, then jerked upright as his stool nearly toppled over.

Theona's normal eye quirked an eyebrow and she made for her silver Stardust cocktail, the drink more sugar than anything else. Slurped the thing through a straw as long as Davin's forearm. Around them, early afternoon drunks parleyed a half-day's wages into a full night's fun. *Neil's* didn't care that dinner wouldn't come for hours yet, the psychic beats pulsed through the floor, through the stool, and bounced Davin's brain around more than the straight Moon Rum fixes he'd been sipping.

Their table sat in the third node branching off a rectangular dance floor whose swirling nebula pitched galactic wonder to, right now, a single man swaying his hips to a beat only he could hear.

Davin didn't think he was too many rounds away from joining the guy, but his outfit didn't match *Neil's* workman vibe. Slick with space-faring leather and trumped up with multi-planetary spices, Davin had that classy vagabond look that put him intriguingly out of place in any setting. Theona paired nicely, her mechanical eye complementing a spliced up assembly slotting colors, metals, and cloth in fits and starts that shouldn't have worked but, in *Neil's* neon blast, sucked in Davin's attention.

"I'm trying to find you," Theona said, drawing Davin back. "But talking to you's like trying to catch a salmon mid-stream. Most runners aren't so hard to figure."

Salmon mid-stream? Davin slotted away that line for later. Maybe the woman had come up from Earth, spent some time in a business not built on running illegal weapons. Maybe that damn eye made it easy to spot the fish under the water. Which, how many fish would she have to catch to pay—

"Are you even paying attention?" Theona asked. "I'm the one paying you, remember?"

"Sure." Focus, Davin. C'mon. You need this. "You already know about my ship, you know what I can do. What, you want a resume?"

"Already have that," Theona replied, then leaned in.

"Thing is, I'm getting the wrong vibe from you, Davin. Like you're not who you're saying you are."

"I'm the man that saved the solar system," Davin replied.

"Then why're you meeting me in this club?"

Why? Davin had a thousand reasons why, and all of'em sucked. He replayed the years since Bosser took the wrong laser every night, trying to find the spot where things went off course, as if Davin could throw time into reverse and try it again.

"Because it turns out being a hero doesn't pay," Davin said, the words spoiling in his mouth.

"Think that's the first authentic thing I've heard you say," Theona sat back with a nasty grin, her eye flipping bright green. "You do this run for me, it'll pay. The next one'll pay too. I treat my runners right."

"Then let's get on with it." Davin slipped off the stool, steadied the world by holding the bar table for a minute. "Places to be, people to see, all that crap."

"Thought you weren't on a timetable?" The woman sucked down her drink.

"It's never too soon to leave this place."

Davin hadn't wanted to go to *Neil's* at all, but Theona insisted. Said, when they'd first commed, that its music, lights, and general disdain for lunar building codes made it difficult for anyone to listen in. Davin couldn't argue with that, so they'd set the date, time, and drinks.

Now the woman led him through the sleazy streets in the Nubium dome, a failed blend between start-up hopefuls trying to cash in on Luna's resurgence and predators feeding on those same dreams. Pop-up businesses littered the stacked shanties, and Davin knew most went underground too, burrowing the dome's least beneath the gray dust. Every one hawked something new, a body-mod or some drug, a bot that'd save your life or take another's.

Overhead, dome-skippers darted along, their one-and-two passenger floaters zipping through Nubium as fast as possible. Didn't want to take the chance they'd bust an engine and come down for repairs here.

Davin, though, enjoyed the walk. Earth sat up top, its blue-white-green beauty providing a better sky than the black void he normally had soaring through space. And the people crowding the streets around him? Hungry for hope, for deals, or just plain hungry? Those people he knew. Those people were him.

He hadn't grown up on the Moon, but home was more than a place.

Theona tilted her walk, nodding between two orange striped stacks. She kept her mouth shut out here, where ears were everywhere, and Davin followed suit. He'd rather listen to the street music than her cocky pitches about how much artillery she had waiting to blow a hole in Eden's fleet.

Not that Eden wouldn't deserve it, but Davin didn't play those kinda sides. Not anymore.

Between the stacks, a few meters back from the street proper, the woman held up her metal eye to an innocuous spot on the silver walls. Something clicked as Davin closed, and a doorway shot up, revealing a stairway heading down.

"Bit small to move cargo," Davin said as they started in. "Unless you're dealing in toys."

"We shift the goods out a different way," Theona replied, leading. "I've got Nubium's dockyard on my payroll. Time comes to fly, you'll come in proper, leave without a second look."

"Ain't that swell."

Behind him, the door shut hard and swamped the

stairway in darkness. Davin heard a click as Theona's eye shifted again, and he felt her hand reach out and grab his.

"Don't get any ideas," she said, pulling Davin down the stairs.

"And I thought things were going so well."

She laughed, a sound that vanished along the steps, which went deeper than Davin would've thought.

"At least you're funny. Most runners, they're hard types that don't know how to laugh anymore."

"Laughter's just my way of living," Davin replied.

The dark had to be for security. He guessed Theona's eye made the stairs look bright as day for her. Anyone following would find themselves taking a long fall, probably right to rifles pointing at their faces. Davin kept his steps sure, kept his left hand on the sidearm he wore on his belt, charged and ready.

Melody, his super-charged shotgun, had stayed home today. Too obvious for a job like this.

But hey, at least the stairs and wherever they led didn't smell like booze and too-little deodorant, like *Neil's*. Breathing, it turned out, was something Davin preferred to do without choking every time.

The stairs ended their dark journey into a big space that any cargo hauler would know: a warehouse. This one must've carried on for blocks, and going by the sealed crates stacked everywhere, most carrying labels with a ship's name and a time, it did brisk business.

"Pretty nice setup you've got here," Davin said as the woman dropped his hand, let him take in the picture.

Beyond the crates, lift bots milled around the space, shuttling this and that to here and there. Most had the long, straight arms good for toting heavy fare, though the Moon's touch-n-go gravity made big lifts easy. Davin suspected that's why manufacturing had grown so big here: close enough to Earth for the money and the buyers, light on weight and legality.

"That's the stack I have for you," Theona's said, bringing Davin to a cluster that, going by the shapes and their lengths, held enough damage to arm a squad or two. "Drop's at Enceladus. Pick up another normal run to keep things clean."

"Right." Davin leaned in to get a good look at the closet casket, matte green and carbon-scored. "Where'd you get these?"

"Nowhere you need to know," Theona said. "You make this run, though, I'll have more. The rebels are paying way over premium now." Davin looked back, caught her shaking her head. "They're either doing better than Eden thinks in this war, or they're so damn desperate they'll throw their money away."

"It's not worth anything if you're dead."

Theona didn't argue, did ask Davin if he had any questions.

"Yeah, I've got a couple," Davin said, turning, catching one last look around the place.

No guards hanging around. A couple bots that looked like they might try something, but Theona looked to be running a profit-shop: keep labor costs low, take-home pay high.

Made Davin's job easy.

He didn't even draw the sidearm quick. Just reached over, pulled the weapon out with his right hand and leveled it at Theona. Who laughed again.

"What, you're going to steal all this cargo?" Theona asked.

"Nah," Davin replied. "They are."

A horrendous bang sounded from up the dark stairs, followed by harsh light and feet pounding along the steps. Theona dropped her nonchalance act and opened her mouth, like she was planning on giving some dumb order.

"Don't," Davin said, wagging his sidearm to catch her attention. "Not worth it. Give up your suppliers, maybe they'll let you off easy."

A thud from the stairs clued Davin to look over Theona's shoulder, to see the first Moon Centurion make the main floor. Others followed, their crimson capes swirling as they swept into the warehouse, hunting for threats. Those hapless bots didn't even get a chance to try for a weapon before some quick frying bolts from the Centurion's rifles reduced the machines to inert metal.

That first Centurion came Davin's way, big and bold and covered with an exoskeleton molded to his every muscle.

"Mox, right on time," Davin said. "Meet Theona. I imagine she'll have a lot to say."

Theona's mechanical eye clicked again, to a burning red, and she lunged towards Davin with a desperate rage Davin had seen all too many times before. The last move of someone whose path met an end they knew was coming, yet hoped would never arrive.

Theona never touched him. Mox had a hand on Theona's shoulder as she started her move, and he simply pressed her to the ground. She twitched once, then lay on the floor, still.

"New trick?" Davin asked.

"Nerve endings," Mox said, boulder-shaking voice rumbling off the warehouse floors and walls. "Press hard, body goes numb. New Centurion training."

Davin nodded, as if he had some idea of what life was like within the Moon's secretive police force. He'd met Mox as the Centurions had kicked him out for getting that big ol' exoskeleton. When the Wild Nines had stopped the solar system from disintegrating into an android dystopia, Mox had come back here, and done well enough to offer Davin a job for some much-needed coin.

"She said these were going to Enceladus," Davin said, glancing at the weapons cache. "The rebels are buying."

"They are always buying," Mox replied. "Now, at least, they will not get these."

"You on Eden's side, now?"

"I am on the side that keeps me and my Centurions alive," Mox replied. "Whoever it is."

"Was afraid you'd changed," Davin said. "When's the fee coming in?"

"Guess you have not changed either," Mox laughed. "Check your account." Mox hesitated, then reached down and picked Theona up from the ground, slung her over his shoulder. "Have to get back to it. Sting like this takes a lot of red tape to get closed up. A lot of gear to take in."

"Sure."

Davin slipped the sidearm back in its holster, let the cocky smile fade along with the adrenaline. Took the hint and moved past Mox towards those stairs back up.

"Good to see you again, Davin. Been too long."

"It has. Take care, Mox." Davin offered up a half-hand wave, to the big man. "I'll call next time I'm out this way."

"Do that," Mox lifted a mitt. "And tell Phyla I said hi."

Phyla.

Yeah.

# 2

## BULLET CALL

If a man's ship was his castle, then Davin's freighter wouldn't protect him from all that much. The *Whiskey Jumper* shot off some extra cleaner as Davin sloughed into its bay, rubbing his forehead as the drinks at *Neil's* took their parting shots. The cleaner's wispy yellow-white smoke caromed off the punched gravel bay floor—no way Davin would pay for the fancier slots—putting a nice halo around the chunky ship that'd cruised Davin across the solar system for more years than he liked to count.

The *Jumper* maintained most of its bulk in a central cargo hauling container, to which attachments clung like parasites. The engines and work bays jutting off behind, crew quarters above, and the cockpit spiking from the front. To the right sat a slim starfighter docking station and, above it, a cramped kitchen now home to more nutrient goop than anywhere else Davin knew. Opposite those were the med bay and a simulator bay. A couple moldy turrets offered a hint at fights long past, echoed by the black laser char Davin kept meaning to clean off but never quite got around to.

"But you're still holding on," Davin said to his ship. "Cause you know, without you I'd be nothing."

"Davin, that's so nice of you to say," the ship said back, voice chirping from its speakers. "And so accurate."

"Shut up, Fournine."

The android brain now controlling the *Jumper*'s systems had, at one point, been stuffed in a body intent on delivering slashing, stabbing death to Davin and his former crew, the Wild Nines. After tracking Davin from Europa to the space station Miner Prime, the Wild Nines had pulled a solid reversal on the bot, sucked out its mind and stuck it deep in the *Jumper*'s computer.

Now Davin had a lightning quick, deadly AI on his side. One that wouldn't, couldn't seem to keep quiet.

"I see you're back empty-handed," Fournine said, throwing off Davin's order. "Are we taking on a delivery later, then, or is your idea of a successful business to lose coin over and over?"

Davin closed his eyes, sighed, waved towards the *Jumper*'s ramp, still not lowered, "Would you let me onto my own ship, please?"

"I'm under strict instructions not to let you aboard until you've found us a job."

"Nobody's going to give me a job if I'm too tired to talk," Davin replied. "I just need a nap."

Arguing with his own ship felt ridiculous, and Davin could only imagine the Lunar dockyard operators laughing at what they were seeing. The captain that'd saved everyone from android-owned repression, getting his ass handed to him by a computer.

Fournine must've decided to take pity on Davin, because the ramp hissed and lowered down, a little more than a meter wide and freckled over with nubs for grip.

"Thanks," Davin said, stepping on up.

He'd rarely seen the *Jumper*'s cargo bay so empty. Davin had offloaded a large Martian wine collection—the chocolate, fruity tannins in the red planet's soil made the cabernets delectable, apparently—when they'd arrived on the Moon, and now, as the ramp rose behind him, Davin stared around at the broad, empty space.

The silence hit Davin hard. It always did. Used to be, eight or nine people lived on this ship—the Wild Nines did have a reason for its name—managing the equipment, polishing up the weapons, or kicking each other's butts in the simulators. A family churning through life's pains and pleasures together.

A static burst sounded through the space, causing Davin to twitch as the sound resolved itself into a broadcast announcer's voice: Fournine tuning into something and blasting it throughout the ship.

"What're you doing?" Davin said, the blathering commentary about Moon conditions—meteor strikes at a minimum risk today—pushing Davin's headache back into prime position.

"Trying, Davin, to keep you from getting into even more trouble."

Being scolded by his parents had been one thing, being scolded by Phyla and the other 'Nines was another, but taking crap from a computer? On a ship he owned?

"Fournine, you jerk, I'm coming up there."

Davin made for the ladder up to the bridge. A lift sat next to the rungs, ready for those unwilling to use their arms and legs, but on the Moon, all Davin had to do was kick a couple of times to jump his way up. He bounced into the short tunnel and into the squat cockpit, its twin pilot-copilot chairs pressed up to the glass.

Outside the ship, the docking bay's silver-crimson scheme parlayed the Moon's colors through the dockyard's many implements, from refueling canisters to spare parts, to bots meant to use both. Davin kept the *Jumper*'s maintenance to the minimum right now, as coin had been hard to come by.

Everyone expected major war to break out any day, so stocks were being piled. Treasures hoarded. Contracts cut. Davin figured that, once the first shot was fired and Eden began its inevitable romp through rebel space, things would calm right down and he'd get his usual cargo runs back. Until then, well, he could live on Martian wine and the occasional Mox-based bonus.

Fournine had kept the broadcast going, and the announcers had finally turned from Lunar stage setting to the event at hand. As Davin reached for the manual cut-off —he wasn't so trusting of Fournine that the AI had limitless power—the broadcaster said a word that made Davin hesitate.

Race.

Bullet race.

"See?" Fournine said, and Davin almost turned the damn dial just because the android brain sounded so cocky. "I'm on your side, captain, even if you don't believe me."

Davin settled back into the chair with another, heavier sigh. He'd been doing that too much lately, sighing. Had to cut the habit out. His left hand went fishing into the cooler slot next to the pilot's chair and fished out a fresh water bottle, newly filled up from Luna's reservoirs. Caught comets melted into delicious, delicious drink.

"Fine, bot, you win," Davin said. "Pull it up on the HUD."

"You got it, boss."

The glass shimmered, then the silver and crimson blanked away as a live feed filled Davin's cockpit view. A camera swept over pure Lunar landscape, no domes and little manmade interference, except for a winding path overlaid with lights criss-crossing the color gamut. Supposedly each color gave the racers that crossed it certain points, with more being awarded for following the best route.

Some, high up on curved ridges or on off-shots, blinked gold. The major gets, for major risks. This course had quite a few, more than Davin had seen. Someone had moved up a level.

The camera found its way to the starting line, where thirteen bullets had themselves arrayed in stately two-stacks. The ships, little more than rounded one-person engines coated with maneuvering jets, hovered in place. The broadcast swapped to a one-by-one run through, giving each contestant a five second spot to say their name and highlight their sponsor.

"Where'd she qualify?" Davin asked after the first three had gone by.

Fournine didn't answer before the broadcast had found her.

Phyla, her hand resting on a purple and orange bullet. Racing for Galaxy Forge, her red hair blowing like she stood in a hurricane. Other sponsors splashed over her suit, a courtesy of her reputation—despite Davin's current struggles, the Wild Nines had some marketing cache—rather than the racing rank.

"What class is she in now?" Davin asked Fournine. He couldn't keep all the different ones straight.

"C, Davin. You should remember that. It's an improvement from last time."

Right. C, then B, A, and S. The last one reserved for

those true pros. Still, Phyla had gone from nothing to, well, something pretty damn fast. Despite not being an eighteen year-old racing wizard, Phyla had taken to the sport with a passion Davin hadn't seen before. Now, any time they landed somewhere, he'd go find the job and she'd go find a track.

The broadcast finished its run-through and returned to the starting line. The whole track sat outside atmosphere, so no audience cheered on-hand. Some of the major courses Davin had seen played concessions to in-person attendance, but the bullets moved so fast, you couldn't really perceive the things watching from eye-level.

With a flash, the countdown hit zero and the bullets burst away. The broadcast traversed into an infuriating view that Davin nonetheless understood as the only way you'd be able to keep tabs on the whole race. Half his screen flipped to an overhead graphic, splashing the huge course onto the glass and, within it, colored dots showing each bullet as they sped along. On the other half, the broadcast zoomed in on individual bullets, showing as they banked their way through turns, hopped over and burned under one another.

Davin had only played with bullets in simulators, but piloting in zero-G was all about momentum. With nothing to stop you once you revved up, turns had to be measured in lost velocity. Flipping the bullet with its jets to keep its main engines burning away was everything, and if you could pick up some bonus points along the way?

Phyla said it was damn fun, and Davin believed her.

The purple dot representing Phyla picked up spots as the race went on, and Davin saw her bounce over a couple bonus point lights. Not a bad start.

"Davin, I'm getting an urgent call," Fournine interrupted, silencing the broadcast.

"Now?"

"Sorry," Fournine replied. "Should I try to put her off?"

"Her? Who's calling?" Davin had figured it was the Luna dockmaster, asking when he'd be getting this freighter out of their space.

"Viola. That's why I'm interrupting."

Huh. Not a name Davin expected to hear, not a name Davin could turn away, either.

"Connect her," Davin said.

"And the race?"

"Bump it. Right side. I'll keep tabs."

Fournine did as Davin asked, shunted the dots and the course to the glass's right side. In their place filtered in a smiling brunette that looked older, wiser, and all the more assured than the young runaway Viola had been when Davin first saw her.

"Hey Puk," Davin said, noticing Viola's bot floating over her shoulder.

"What's up, Davin?" Puk replied, its cheery voice everything Fournine wasn't.

"You say hi to the bot before me?" Viola said. "Nice to see you haven't changed, Davin."

Davin threw up his shoulders in a shrug, took a long sip from the water bottle, "Why change what's already perfect?"

"Can't argue with that," Viola answered, her eyes glittering. "You doing okay?"

Should he unload his problems? Spill out the ennui gripping his every move as the endless cargo grind crushed away the days and months and years?

"Sure, I'm sitting in the *Jumper* on the Moon with a crazy android for company. Couldn't be better."

"Glad to hear it," Viola answered, either missing Davin's

subtext or deliberately ignoring it. "Listen, I'm calling for a reason."

"Not just to say hi? I'm hurt."

"Don't be. There's no time for it." Viola glanced away from the call, frowned, then turned back. "I need a favor."

"You shot Bosser. I'll give you any favor you need."

Viola flashed a small smile, "That was a long time ago, but thank you. I need you to do a run for me. We'll drop it near Lunar orbit, Puk will send you the coordinates."

"A run? Where to, and for who?"

"You'll get that info in the package." Viola settled back into her straight face. "I can't give you more details, Davin. Too many people might be listening."

"Nobody's gonna care what I have to say, Viola."

Viola cocked her head, "Not you, Davin. Me. Find the capsule, do it as soon as you can."

Davin scrunched up his face as Viola reached to close the call, "Hold on, that's all you're giving me? No destination? No details?"

"Can't right now. Just know that it's important, and that I trust you," Viola said. "You can do this for me, right?"

No price, little information, and, given Viola's voice and the secrecy, all kinds of risk. Exactly the job Davin shouldn't take if he wanted to stay stable. Build up a reputable running business.

Exactly the job he *should* take if Davin, well, if he was who he said he was. The badass that saved the solar system.

"I'm in, Viola. I'm in."

"Good. Nice seeing you Davin," Viola said. "Stay safe for me."

As if Davin ever did.

**3**

---

## TEAM WORK

The steps to prime the *Whiskey Jumper* for any journey, whether running asteroid rocks to Mars or a secret device for a friend, were the same. Davin ran through them all, green-lighting systems, loading up rations, and even cleaning out the turret pipes, without any annoyance.

A task had come in, one that actually needed his skills. His attention. The safe road had been so safe, so suffocating, that Davin had forgotten how much fun it could be to wander into the unknown.

Sure, Mox had offered up the bait game over beer two nights ago, while Phyla had been practicing on the course for yesterday's qualifiers. Mox said that Davin looked bored, asked if he wanted in on the sting, and of course Davin had accepted. Playing head games with Theona hadn't thrilled too much, though: there'd been armed and undercover Centurions everywhere in case she saw through Davin's charade.

You wanted to feel alive, you had to risk yourself.

"You're working hard." The words startled Davin and he

bumped his head on the engine nodule he'd been scrub-bing, wincing at micro-meteor damage.

Davin pulled himself out onto the bay floor, rubbed his head, and offered up a hangdog smile to the woman leading a lift cart loaded with her bullet, all compressed and ready for travel. Phyla had her autumn leaf hair pulled up, her green eyes matching her mouth in a smile, still wearing a racing suit that no doubt needed a good spin in the laundry after the tight-knuckle action.

Phyla scared him, Phyla burned him, Phyla still had Davin jumping out of his skin.

"Gotta keep her in shape," Davin said. "Never know when we might get a job."

"Does that mean we have one?"

Davin tossed away the scrubbing towel—some bot would pick it up—and came over Phyla's way, rubbing his hands. Why the hell did he feel so nervous? Like he'd forgotten something.

"In fact," Davin said, throwing on his best announcer impression. "We do. Important too."

"More wine?"

"Are you saying transporting the galaxy's finest grape juice isn't important?" Davin replied, the conversation greasing his own skids, calming those nerves. "I happen to think we're heroes."

"We were, maybe," Phyla laughed, short and light, then glanced towards the ship. "Fournine, drop the ramp, please."

The AI complied, and the ramp's whining descent covered the silence as Davin's skids crashed hard. Phyla had a way of doing that, cutting sharp when Davin wanted to charge straight ahead. Davin scratched his head again, looked around the bay, hoping one of the bots might come up and charge him for using the bay's services.

The bots failed to rescue Davin from the awkward moment.

"So," Davin said. "You had a good time without me?"

"Without you?" Phyla folded her arms, and warning lights flashed in Davin's mind. "Davin, I was racing. Which, yes, happens without you in the single seat bullet. I thought, though, that you were going to be watching? As you said?"

Ah. Crap. Davin had run away with Viola's message and hadn't come back. Fournine had played the broadcast alongside Viola's transmission. Where'd Phyla place? Did she win? Should he be wearing a good or bad expression?

Davin would lie to some people. Throw up swagger and dish out a narrative behind it that'd bowl over casual questioning, followed by a topic switch aggressive enough to blow away any danger.

Phyla, Phyla might kill Davin if he tried that.

"Look, Phyla," Davin started, swallowing as Phyla's fire-blonde eyebrows inched higher and her lips turned lower. "I had it on. Fournine can back me up on that."

"Fournine?" Phyla said, without looking towards the *Jumper*

"I displayed the race in the cockpit," Fournine announced through the *Jumper*'s speakers.

"See?" Davin said.

"Did he watch it?" Phyla asked.

"That requires interpretation that I can't supply," Fournine said. "I would rely on Davin for his opinion."

"We had a call," Davin said as Fournine dropped the line. "Viola hailed right in the middle of your race. I had to take it."

"Had to." Her eyebrows back in their normal, skeptical position, Phyla sank into that straight-faced pose that just screamed how little she believed Davin's words. "Was she under fire? Was the *Jumper* about to explode?"

"Well, no." Davin had flown through asteroid fields easier to navigate than this conversation. Viola's call *had* interrupted the race, had been about something important. "But she had a favor to ask us, an important one."

"So you keep saying." Phyla let her arms drop, gave her head that slight shake that said this particular talk was done. "Cart, take the bullet inside. I'm going to take a shower."

"Phyla," Davin said as she turned to follow the cart up the ramp. "Don't you even want to hear about the mission with Mox?"

"Did you get shot?" Phyla didn't turn back as she asked the question.

"Did I what? No, I didn't get shot."

"Then you're running thin on excuses." Phyla glanced back at Davin, down the ramp. "How long was Viola's call?"

"Five minutes, maybe?"

"The race took two hours, Davin. Two hours."

He'd had to get the ship ready. The *Jumper* wouldn't fly right without the maintenance, without Davin's personal touch. Without any other crew to do it for him, what else could Davin have done? Watch a race he barely understood while a friend's request sat there?

Phyla had vanished into the *Jumper,* her steps still banging down the ramp.

"Fournine," Davin said. "You gotta warn me about these things."

"I did play the race for you."

"Next time, lock me in the cockpit till it's over."

"I would be happy to."

The shower did Phyla some real good, because by the

time she reported to the cockpit wearing far more normal space-faring clothes, that dangerous glint in her eyes had faded away. Davin, in the co-pilot's chair, had already completed the pre-flight prep. Viola had sent along the capsule's coordinates, and the *Jumper*'s sensors had caught it.

"Feeling better?" Davin tried a peaceful opening.

"Actually am." Phyla nestled into her seat, started reading meters. "I'm not sorry for what I said earlier, but I'll give you that it would've been hard to ignore Viola's call."

"It was," Davin said. "Should've watched your race, but Phyla, I mean this in the nicest way, the announcers sucked. The views sucked. You're just a bunch of dots on the screen."

"One of those dots is me."

Davin sensed a fork, a choice to either send another conversation to the hellish pit where too many of their dialogues lived, or take a different turn. Put away the sniping for a minute and focus on something interesting.

Because, for the first time in a while, he had something interesting to focus on.

"You're right," Davin replied. "I'll get better."

"Mmhmm," Phyla said. "At least the *Jumper* looks good. You even scrubbed the turrets."

"It might be that kind of mission."

That, at least, held Phyla's interest long enough to dive into Viola's specifics. A valuable, secret cargo run? Should be fun, and since Viola worked for Eden, the pay ought to be excellent.

"Guess what?" Phyla said. "Unless Eden's sending us to a dead moon, there's probably a bullet circuit wherever we're going, which means you can make it up to me."

"I'll take it."

Lifting off the Moon was a multi-step affair. Davin and

Phyla hummed through their flight checks, reading off system statuses—green was best, but Davin took yellows on anything not critical—and prepping the *Jumper*'s big batteries for liftoff. The docking bay bots scurried around the ship, scooting attachments away and securing anything likely to be blown about by engine wash, including the bots themselves. In the final countdown, a bay that'd been filled with frantic motion stood still.

"Ready?" Phyla asked Davin as she did every time before taking flight.

"Always," Davin answered Phyla as he did every time before taking flight.

Like a beloved cat's purr, the *Jumper* spun to life. Four-nine read out every stage as the *Jumper* whipped through them, and soon Phyla pulled back on the primary flight stick, pushing the *Jumper* off the blasted bay floor and floating them out.

The microjets took the *Jumper* above the bay, giving Davin and Phyla a stunning view of the Moon's domes, their swooping cities filled with curving architecture utterly impossible on Earth. Great glass towers arced along dome walls, some coated in rainbow colors, others refracting sunlight to achieve the same effect.

Every planet, every space station had its own unique takeoff to share, but the Moon held its own place in Davin's heart. A beauty here, coupled with the aspiration that came from humanity's first jump beyond Earth's borders.

"Never get tired of seeing this," Davin said as Phyla pushed the *Jumper* beyond the range where its engines might damage something. "I get why Mox came back here."

"Sentiment, from you?" Phyla said.

"Hey, I have feelings." Davin leaned back in his chair.

"Normally keep'em buried beneath my incredible manliness, but they're around."

"Uh huh. You should try sharing them more." Phyla tapped away on the *Jumper*'s console, and a deeper thrum ran through the ship as the batteries shifted their energy towards the big rockets. "Some people might be interested."

"Who? Fournine?"

Phyla laughed, pushed forward on the stick, and the *Jumper* shot right towards a dome section that, with its blue-glowing magnetic shield, had pulled away to allow their departure. Beyond the blue shield, several other ships hung in a line stretching towards Earth's bulk, waiting to get in.

Always traffic on the Moon.

"So where are these coordinates?" Phyla asked as they coasted through the gateway and powered into the space between the Earth and the Moon.

Blips coated the *Jumper*'s radar, that constant ship traffic moving around them. While space around planets and civilized bodies had governing laws, and pilots were expected to take tests, the real enforcement came from the fact that, if you didn't fly right, you'd be dead. Phyla found a clear outbound lane and stuck to it, sending the *Jumper* on a path towards Earth's southern hemisphere.

"Got'em right here." Davin swept to Viola's next message, a blank note except for the digits denoting the drop spot for the capsule. "Plugging them in now."

As Davin entered the numbers, Fournine did the heavy work and a green line lanced out beyond the glass, curling away to the left through space.

"Any conflicts?" Phyla asked the computer.

"None in your path," Fournine answered.

"Good, take us there," Phyla said.

"Will do. Enjoy the view, humans."

There were definite perks to having an android brain as the ship's computer. Fournine had lethal skills and whip-crack instincts that had saved the *Jumper* before and no doubt would again. But, while a normal ship AI had a rock's personality, Fournine played with a quirky trait mix that had Davin alternately grinning and contemplating a full wipe.

"Humans," Davin said. "At least it's not an insult."

Phyla nodded, and Davin noticed her eyes sticking to the radar screen as Fournine shifted the *Jumper* to follow the green line. Her frown only deepened, and with a sudden flick, Phyla launched the radar from her console up onto the glass.

"Look," Phyla said at the black, translucent cover pasted over Earth. On it, dots moved around a central diamond—the *Jumper*—each one representing a ship on its way to somewhere.

Except one. A big one.

Sitting right in their path.

## 4

# GO TIME

Not long ago, Davin would've seen a big blip like the one sitting right where Viola's capsule was supposed to be and sprung into action. He'd have adopted a wise-cracking smirk, told Mox to take the top turret while Opal went to the lower one. Trina would've dropped back to the engines to monitor power consumption while Merc would've prepped his fighter for launch.

The Wild Nines would've been ready, even eager, for a fight.

"Well, that sucks," Davin said, running a hand through his greasy hair. "Are they right on the target?"

"Right on it."

Phyla kept her focus on the radar, her left hand drifted towards the console and brushed a couple meters up, redirecting some power from the engines to dispersion shield meant to keep the hot lasers spewed by most spacecraft from burning through the *Jumper's* hull.

The shields wouldn't do a thing against old fashioned projectile weapons, though. Davin had been seeing more of those coming back, especially now that Eden had monopolized energy weapons for their own use. He'd yet to bother getting the *Jumper* outfitted with a slug thrower, because. . . well, because Davin had better things to spend his coin on.

"We're, what, a few minutes out?"

"A few."

Davin leaned into his console, used the screen to focus in on that big blip, pick out some more detail. A toothy craft, an arrow-head shape riddled with projections, some short and stubby, others longer, angular.

"Hunter-class." Davin sighed. "Bet they're waiting for us."

"Then do we turn around, tell Viola tough luck?"

The *Jumper* still had distance. Could probably make it back within Lunar space before the hunter recognized who they were. Davin could creep back to Mox, ask for help, maybe a lead on another gig. Call up Viola and say they had failed.

"When was the last time we gave the *Jumper* a good run?" Davin asked.

"Been a long time." Phyla flickered a smile. "Real long."

"Fournine, you been getting your target practice in?"

"I am an AI I do not need to practice." The android did, though, manage to sound offended. "Your pathetic human reflexes are nothing compared to mine."

"Fournine's a cocky one, isn't it?" Phyla said.

"Takes after its captain," Davin said. "Punch up the comm, Phyla. Let's see what our new friends have to say."

While Phyla flipped on the comm, Davin tweaked the shields to push the energy forward, protecting the cockpit, facing the hunter, from any surprise attack. Provided the hunter shot lasers. And not too many for the shields to handle.

"The mic's open," Phyla said. "Try not to make them too angry."

"Angry? We're going to be friends, Phyla."

Davin caught the eye roll in the cockpit glass, reflected ever-so-slightly against the starry backdrop. He tapped the console, opened the comm to broadcast on the frequency Phyla had set, a standard channel beaming straight out front.

"Hey there, this is Davin and the *Whiskey Jumper* sending out a question to the fine folks squatting on some coordinates we've been asked to visit." Davin felt himself grin as he spoke, falling back into a captain's comfortable habit. "Looking to see what brings you all out to this particular corner? Drop us a reply and let's open a dialogue."

Davin tapped away the broadcast, glanced at Phyla, "Good enough for you?"

"They haven't shot yet, so that's a positive sign," Phyla said. "Going to have to pick a direction soon if they don't move."

The hunter-class ship hadn't started its engines, hadn't activated any weapons that Davin could see as the *Jumper* approached. They were well within missile range now, and soon lasers would be able to strike with damaging force.

No reply yet.

"Slow up," Davin said. "Let's stay out of the hot zone for a minute."

"What if they're picking up Viola's capsule?"

"Then they've already got it." Davin double-checked the radar, nothing beneath the hunter's big blip. "What happens next is on them."

"I thought we liked having the initiative?"

"Only when we know what's going on."

As if hearing their conversation, the hunter's engines

spooled up, the ship rotating to face the *Jumper* with its weaponized, pointed maw. The comm crackled, settled into the incoming message.

"Davin Masters. We're glad you've decided to help us out with this mission. Please kill your engines and wait for boarding, and we'll get everything straight."

The message cut there.

"Hunter, color me confused because I had good word this particular spot came by me with secret intentions," Davin said. "If you're here, then that secret's blown. Can't exactly trust you."

The hunter nudged itself towards them.

"Incorrect," the hunter's captain, or comm officer, or whomever, replied. "Viola meant what she said. But her information was incomplete, and her assessment of this package's value was too low. We aim to protect our invest-ment, Davin, nothing more."

Davin looked at Phyla, who shrugged. Who the hell were these people? What investment?

"Davin," Phyla said as the captain stared at the comm and tried to decide what to say. "Make the call. Either we fight, run, or let them board us, but we're running out of time."

On the cockpit, the radar showed the hunter's big blip getting closer. Davin could turn the *Jumper* around, zip back towards the Moon and try to forget any of this ever happened. Try to find another gig hauling booze, rations, or parts from one spaceport to another. Davin had taken enough shots for a lifetime, he didn't need any more.

"Turn it," Davin said. "Thought I could use some excite-ment, but I don't need to get beat up again."

He thought Phyla would be game for the idea. Would be down for the safer play. Take a route that'd bring her to new race courses for her bullet. Instead, she just sighed as he spoke.

"Turning," Phyla said, voice dead. "Shift the shields to cover."

Feeling oddly sick to his own stomach, Davin adjusted the shields as Phyla brought the *Jumper*'s engines online, started their rotation.

"*Jumper*," the comm burst up again. "We're reading your engines spooling up. What are you doing?"

"Sorry," Davin replied. "This all seems a little hot for us. Viola didn't mention any games."

"Do you know what she told us? She said that Davin Masters would be able to do what no other captain could. That you wouldn't be afraid of a challenge, and that you wouldn't be able to resist the reward."

Davin hesitated, felt Phyla's eyes on him. Times change, people change, stakes change.

Hell, crews change.

"Time was, you'd probably be right," Davin said. "Time is, you'd be wrong."

"I told her you would be too soft," the Hunter replied. "I'm sad to see I was correct."

Phyla had a knack for driving daggers into Davin. She could pierce right to his heart with a cutting look, a sigh, or even nothing at all. She had the right to call him out. Random voices over the comm, on the other hand?

Davin wasn't going to take their crap.

"Stop," Davin said to Phyla. "Cut the engines."

"Are you letting him get to you?"

"No," Davin replied. "I'm changing my mind."

"Uh-huh."

Davin ignored Phyla's bemusement and looked back to the comm, "Look, this has nothing to do with being soft. It's about being smart. Knowing all the risks, the rewards. You don't live to be a captain like me by playing fast and loose with your life." Davin paused, had to figure out how to turn this into a graceful switch. "But you're saying you're with Viola? If that's true, then we can talk."

Did it work? Was it sloppy? Davin couldn't tell, but Phyla cut the engines and the Hunter kept closing, so . . . good?

Before, when Davin had a crew, when they were being pursued and pursuing death and its dealers, making snap decisions that'd put lives in danger came easy. Like a reflex, and Davin could blend them with a cocky quip to give every moment a make-believe quality: they'd all be fine if they swaggered through.

Now, Mox's little deal aside, Davin didn't play the action game. Hadn't felt his pulse race outside of the simulator and the zero-g treadmill for a long time. He'd grown rusty, and his invincibility bubble felt thin.

"Glad to hear you've changed your mind," the Hunter said. "We're coming in for boarding. Follow our lead."

Phyla didn't wait for Davin to do what the hunter had asked. With a button press, the *Jumper*'s jets linked to the hunter's, allowing the latter's pilot to arrange the two ships for a perfect connection. Much easier than two separate pilots doing the same, so long as you didn't mind giving up control.

"You getting Melody?" Phyla asked when Davin didn't spring up from his chair.

"Guess I should." Davin scratched at his stubble, felt like he needed a shave. "Though if they're going to kill us, don't think there's much we could do to stop 'em."

"You're all over the place today," Phyla replied as the *Jumper* shifted without her input, setting its underside hatch where the hunter could get it. "What's wrong?"

"Nothing, just doing some thinking is all."

"Thinking? Davin, that's dangerous."

"Quiet."

While Davin truly did think there wasn't much he and Phyla could do if the hunter's crew, no doubt armed, decided to kill them both, he might feel a little better with a weapon ready. No longer in the Moon's minimal gravity, Davin left his chair with a push and a kick, diving through the *Jumper*'s hallway and towards the captain's quarters he shared with Phyla.

The *Jumper* had become a nest in the years since the Wild Nines had drifted apart. While Davin and Phyla kept the cargo bay cleared for hauling, the other rooms took on different lives. Unused crew quarters became mini storage units where Davin and Phyla would throw souvenirs. Phyla stole Trina's maintenance area to work on her bullet racer.

Only the medical bay remained untouched, with Erick's supplies still stuffed in its cabinets. Neither Davin nor Phyla was flippant enough to risk the karma damage by removing the only place on the *Jumper* you could get a laser burn cleaned up.

The captain's quarters, though. That'd changed plenty in a better way. Davin wouldn't call their relationship perfect, but he and Phyla had at least made this space their home. Nestled in above the engines, the quarters always hummed whenever the *Jumper* flew, and Davin liked to think of the noise as his ship's heartbeat.

Beyond the bed, two large lockers sufficed for their clothes, with a couple more big trunks bolted to the floor for anything else. The walls had shifting screens throughout. Pictures showcasing the 'Nines on their adventures, and a few of Davin and Phyla alone. Most brought smiles. All tweaked Davin's feelings, no matter how hard he tried to ignore them.

Davin wasn't here for nostalgia this time, though. He kicked over to his locker, swung open the door, and lifted off a back panel disguised as the ship's hull. In the alcove, roughly a meter long, sat Melody. Gleaming black beauty, disaster in an elegant package, the shotgun would serve as a good introduction to anyone coming through the hatch.

"Davin?" Fournine said. "They've docked."

Go time.

## 5

## DETAILS, DETAILS

Davin watched the hatch from the cargo bay. Phyla floated up near the railing and the cockpit's entry. Both had hands on weapons, both waited for the hunter's greeting party to arrive. Should things go south, Phyla would kick back to the cockpit and trigger an emergency de-coupling, blast away from the hunter while Davin did what he could to push back the boarders.

Not a complicated plan, but Davin had found complicated usually meant crap.

Four red lights spaced around the hatch blinked green as Fournine announced a sealed connection. The hatch itself groaned as its little-moved edges unscrewed.

"Remind me to grease that up," Davin said, wincing as metal slid against metal.

"Adding that makes thirty-seven reminders," Fournine said. "You have completed zero in the last week."

"I don't need the judgment."

"My statistics show that you do," Fournine replied as the hatch began to open, hissing as oxygen exchanged between the two ships. "You frequently forget basic tasks without my constant intervention."

"Fournine," Davin warned as Phyla laughed. "Be quiet."

"Of course."

The hatch swung up with the slow, somewhat unreal effect zero-G had on all motion. It landed top-side up on the cargo bay floor, and two gloved hands made their appearance at the same time, gripping the hatch's lip, and pulling up a fully-suited man.

Wearing Eden green.

The solar system's largest company, one tacitly endorsed by Earth's governments to reach out into space and colonize as much as possible, Eden had a reputation as either humanity's greatest achievement or its worst mistake, depending on who you talked to and whether Eden lined their pockets with coin.

Like an ever-changing virus, Eden had started out with a sole objective: make the solar system's harsh worlds habitable. With varying success, much of which Davin had seen first-hand, Eden had done that: plopped domes on Mars, overhauled Europa's frozen landscape into a chilly paradise, built vast underground networks on hostile moons like Phobos and Deimos.

Once Eden created something, though, it had a tendency to keep it. To hold its possessions so tight that it squeezed the life out of the people living in them.

"Guess it figures," Davin said as the man pulled himself out. "Thought Viola might have something secret going on the side, but no. It's just Eden up to Eden things."

The man reached up, tapped his light helmet's side and retracted its sealed visor. Had to keep things safe, even on short moves through airlocks. Davin wouldn't have bothered, but he didn't have uncountable wealth and tech supporting him.

"Eden things," the man said, feeling his way around the phrase. His rounded face bore a green half-circle tattoo on one cheek, cut off along its midpoint by what looked like a jagged tear. "Can't argue with you on that one."

The intruder held out a hand, that emerald glove sticking towards Davin like a knife. If he had any trepidations about Melody, the big shotgun looped over Davin's back, the man didn't show it.

"Amado Ramos," the man said. "Pleasure to meet you in person, Davin Masters."

"Sure," Davin replied, giving the man his shake. "Now that you're on my ship, mind telling me what you're doing here?"

Amado grinned, raised his wrist to his mouth, and spoke, "Send up the package. No surprises."

Behind Amado, a yellow-black striped container, two meters long, one meter wide, floated in, as if shoved from someone through the airlock. It coasted into the *Jumper*'s cargo hatch, hanging in space. Normally Davin would tie down any cargo, and he'd do the same to this new crate once this exchanged concluded, but for now the Eden container spun slowly in the bay's center like some religious artifact.

"That's all we're running?" Davin asked. "Looks pretty small."

"Small enough to fit on a fighter." Amado's grin grew even wider. "You got it right, though. You're going to run this all the way to Callisto. Once you land, one of our guys will get in touch."

"One of your guys? Eden has a lot of guys."

Amado tapped his cheek, "Not so many like me."

"Right. What's that, some kind of cult symbol?" Davin

caught Phyla's warning head shake, but didn't care. Now that the moment had arrived, Davin's earlier jitters had gone away. The glove still fit. "Didn't think Eden was into that."

"Most of Eden, you'd be right. Me and my friends? You would be wrong." Amado waved at the capsule, not taking his eyes away from Davin. "Eden's a big place. Lotta different groups. Different rules."

"Is Viola one of your friends?"

Amado's constant grin sharpened, made Davin's stomach twinge, as if he were staring at a particularly disgusting nutrient goop flavor.

"We work together," Amado said. "That's not important. You are."

"Don't make me blush," Davin replied. "We have the container. Anything we need to know to keep it safe?"

"I wouldn't show it off."

"You made it so subtle, should be easy to hide."

Another headshake from Phyla. Her hands, though, had drifted towards her weapons, her eyes on Amado. What was she picking up that Davin missed?

"So funny," Amado said. The comm on his wrist issued a single click, and Amado gave a ridiculously huge sigh in response. "Unfortunately, my friends and I are needed elsewhere. Before I leave, though, there is one more thing."

"Isn't there always?"

Amado gave the slightest nod, then jumped forward as little boost jets in his suit kicked on. Davin drew his sidearm as Amado tackled him. Davin felt a burning flash in his left leg, then Amado shoved himself away, holding up his hands.

"Keep'em up or I shoot," Phyla called from above. "What the hell was that?"

"Insurance," Amado said, that grin finally gone. "The container has a single key, and that key is now inside you."

"Why?" Davin asked, rubbing the hole in his nice flying pants and the bloody scratch beneath it. "Why'd you do that?"

"In case you decide to play a different game." Amado backed towards the hatch. "Don't try taking it out. It's tied to Callisto's coordinates. You extract it any earlier and you're gonna have a bad day."

"There was a nicer way to do that, asshole," Davin said.

Amado shrugged, turned, and slipped into the hatch. Fournine closed it after him, leaving Davin and Phyla alone with the container, the key, and plenty of questions.


"I LIKE how you didn't shoot him," Davin said later, the *Jumper* still drifting between Earth and the Moon, while he and Phyla ate a rationed dinner in the ship's small mess. "Here he is, coming at me, and you don't fire once."

"Because, Davin, I exercised restraint," Phyla countered, before squelching some brown-orange nutrient paste into her mouth from its tube. "What if I'd hit you?"

"Not a chance. You're too good for that."

"True."

Davin felt the scabbing slice on his leg again. He couldn't stop reaching for it, that little device embedded in his skin. Partly because it seemed so wrong to have the key in there, partly because Davin had fully planned on cracking Eden's container open and having a look.

If he was running something, Davin wanted to know what.

"I didn't shoot because we'd be dead if I had," Phyla continued when Davin didn't answer. "You know that."

"Yeah, I know. Just feel like we lost that exchange."

"We did."

"You feeling brutal tonight, Phyla? Because you're laying it on thick."

She leaned back, finished the nutrient tube. Set her hands on her legs and looked at Davin. He looked back, his blackberry protein mix sitting uneaten on the table.

"I don't know," Phyla said finally. "I don't know why I'm frustrated. Maybe it's because this isn't going like we thought, maybe it's because you didn't watch my race, maybe it's because I'm eating nutrient paste because we don't have the coin for something better."

Davin didn't have an answer to any of that.

"Maybe, Davin, it's because I thought our lives would be in a different place by now," Phyla said. "We stopped Bosser. We nearly died a dozen times over fighting pirates, androids, rebels, and seemingly everyone else. Now we're getting kicked around by Eden muscle?"

"Can't say I planned this either." Davin shrugged. "That's always been our thing, though, right? Roll with the punches? Keep on swinging?"

Phyla stood up, kicked away from the table and floated towards the exit, "Maybe we should change our 'thing', Davin, because I think it sucks."

Phyla kicked her way from the room, leaving Davin with his nutrient paste and a whole lot of questions. He glanced towards the mess cabinets, filled with more dining ware than the two of them would ever need. A big, silver refrigerator stuffed with more nutrient paste, a couple real rations for special nights. Liquor bottles filled the locker to the fridge's side, butting up against the mess's wall.

More pictures there too. The Wild Nines in action.

"Fournine, do you miss it?" Davin asked, taking up the nutrient tube at a rumble from his stomach. "The old days?"

"When I still had a body?" Fournine said. "Those old days?"

"Sure, why not."

"Back then, I had an order to kill you. It was very nice."

"Forgot about that."

"I came very close. Would you like me to tell you the story?"

Davin closed his eyes, ate a mouthful of the nutrient goop. It tasted nothing like blackberries, a lot like protein powder. The journey to Callisto would take a while, goop meals the whole way. Somehow, the stuff didn't seem to suck as much when you ate it with friends.

"Know what, Fournine? Tell me the story. Tell me how we kicked your butt and turned you into a fancy flight computer."

"Of course, captain. I think you'll find it very exciting."

As Fournine launched into its story, Davin popped up the news on the mess table's screen, browsing similar head-lines while the android described firefights, the assault on Miner Prime, and his eventual destruction at Trina's hands. It'd been long enough, now, that Fournine's descriptions sounded less like memories and more like legends.

Back then, on Europa, it'd been a secret scheme by rebels to turn the base against Eden. Davin and the Wild Nines had been used, but they hadn't died like the rebels wanted. Had instead torched the plan without realizing what they were doing. The Wild Nines had been swept up in a swirling conflict that still went on now.

The rebels hadn't ever died. They kept coming back, and now Davin read some new commanders had been hitting Eden hard. Breaking up their fleets, striking the edges and getting away before back-up. A classic guerrilla war breaking out around Jupiter. Right in Callisto's orbit.

"Fournine," Davin said. "Get the simulators up and running. I'm feeling rusty, and where we're going, I'm guessing that might be fatal."

What Davin didn't say, what he didn't bother revealing to the android, was his burning desire to take a shot at something. After Amado and Phyla, knocking out some virtual baddies would make him feel better.

Though, as Davin left the mess, he couldn't help but look at the black and yellow container, now strapped down in the cargo bay's center. Waiting to be opened.

His leg itched.

## 6

## IN-SPACE ENTERTAINMENT

Davin stepped off the skiff onto the chromed silver docking pad marking the Terramorpher's entrance. The giant machine churned above Europa's ice flow landscape, breaking down the frozen wastes and dumping in a fertile biological mix that would, eventually, warm up the atmosphere and turn the chill desert into a verdant jungle.

Not that Davin would see it. He swung Melody into his hands, looking around the sparse landing platform for enemies. Nobody sprang out to greet him. Beyond the Terramorpher's grumbling, crackling grind, no warning shouts filled the air.

Davin sniffed. Was that mint? Sharp and suffusing every breath?

"Quieter this time around," Phyla said, joining him and brandishing two rifles, one in each hand. She sported a headband and, somehow, a glowing cigar hung from her lips, its smoke minty fresh.

"I like your style," Davin said. "And I don't trust this at all."

"Was getting bored of the usual," Phyla said, the cigar muffling her words. "Hard to talk around one of these things."

"That never makes it into the movies."

"Can't imagine why."

Davin led off, heading slow towards the long, wide stairs up across the landing pad. Terramorphers spent their space on systems, not pedestrian pathways, so the only available route went right up to the control center. A silver-white stairway broken up every dozen steps or so by console-strewn landings, each one a perfect ambush point.

As they hit the bottom step, clinking noises came in a series behind them. Davin and Phyla whirled, crouching as they turned, to see five grapples dig into the chromed landing bay. Davin raised Melody, sighting far right as Phyla aimed left to catch the black-suited forms as the enemies jumped up and over the landing pad's lip.

"Light'em up," Davin said, and the pair sprayed hot energy over the new arrivals.

Melody's bursts came in glowing cascades, coating the enemy's armor and burning through it. Phyla's rifles were more scattershot, isolated bolts that nonetheless struck and sent the grappling group tumbling back over the edge or flailing to the ground. Not a single one managed a counter, all lay in smoking ruin on the deck or off it in a few seconds fire.

A bright clink sounded at Davin's feet and he glanced down, saw the grenade. There were instincts at play here, and Davin jumped away. Leaped to his right where he could get behind the stairway's slanted edge for cover. Phyla, that ridiculous cigar hanging from her lip, glared at him.

"Coward," Phyla said, then fell on the bomb.

Davin didn't watch the messy aftermath, though he couldn't hide the crowing laughter from their target, the one who'd thrown the grenade and that, no doubt, stood at the stair's top in triumph. Instead he sat back against the stair's side as the grenade went off, watched the crystal blue Europa sky for a long breath, then reached up to his head and double-tapped his ear.

"You could've kicked it away," Davin said, pulling himself from the simulator pod, one of six on the *Jumper*. The extra simulators didn't serve a purpose, but Davin couldn't bring himself to get rid of'em. Instead, he rotated which pod he used every time, while Phyla claimed hers and stuck with it. "Those acid ones always have long timers."

Phyla, absent her cigar and her rifles, crawled from her pod and shrugged, "Wasn't feeling the game. Didn't seem real."

"Maybe because you came in packing a cigar and holding two rifles like a bad movie star?"

"Better than running the same scenario for the fiftieth time."

Phyla had a point, but Davin liked the Terramorpher, the final ascent to confront Marl. Fournine spiced up the adventure with his own random additions to keep things fresh, but the core loop remained the same: arrive, climb the stairs, deliver justice to a monster.

What Davin didn't say, what he nonetheless gave away with his half-smile, was that he loved the scenario because it'd been him and Phyla alone against the odds.

"Don't like the memories?" Davin asked as they pulled off the simulator gear, the sensory caps and gloves that helped sync their motions to the virtual world.

"We both nearly died on that thing," Phyla replied. "Marl shot me."

"We all got shot a lot back then."

Phyla had to laugh at that, "I still don't understand how we made it out alive."

Now it was Davin's turn to sour. Not everyone had made it out alive, and not everyone had deserved to. Cadge, a grumpy mercenary that'd spent time with the 'Nines nonetheless turned on Davin's group to try and cash in on a bounty on the runaway Viola's head. Fournine, back when the AI had its android body, had turned Cadge to ash in Miner Prime's docking bays.

Cadge, though, held nothing to Lina. Davin still held to that soft spot where Lina lived in his heart, where she'd been ever since Bosser took her away with a pointless shot.

"Yeah, we did," Davin offered up, turning away. "You're right. I'll have Fournine put together something new."

"How about something totally different?" Phyla said, apparently sensing Davin's desire to escape nostalgia's black hole. "I said I'd teach you how to really fly a bullet. Give it enough runs and you might want to join me on a real course."

Back when Phyla had picked up bullet racing as a hobby, they'd spent runs blasting through courses with the little racers until Phyla had so obviously out-classed Davin that he'd dropped the bullets and declared himself a spectator to that particular sport.

"Maybe once this is done." Davin put his hand on his leg, where that key sat. "We're rusty, Phyla, and that Amado guy made me nervous. I want to stick to the stuff that's going to keep us alive."

If Phyla believed Davin's assessment, she didn't show it.

"Sure, Davin. Whatever you say. I'm going to go check our position."

A pointless move. Fournine hadn't been unstable for years, and the AI would buzz them both if something had the *Jumper* deviating from its line out towards Callisto. As a conversation ender, though, it served.

Davin followed Phyla from the simulator room, but not to the cockpit. Instead, he climbed over the railing and shoved himself down to the cargo bay floor. Went over to the yellow black container and gave it another look.

The container itself followed the new trend: dumb down everything that could be simplified. Ever since the androids had been shut down and their tricks turned into handheld devices, physical modifications, and more—Davin had heard Trina played a big part in that decision—most digital defenses had proved easy to break.

Central on the container, just over its lip, sat the vertical, notched slit for the key. Not more than a couple centimeters tall, the sight still made Davin wince; that thing was inside him. Beyond the lock, the container's edges flushed together in a tight seal. No air getting in or out. Nothing for Davin to pry on with a brute-force bar.

"Fournine," Davin said. "It's time we give Viola a ring. There's explaining she needs to be doing."

"You've waited a while to make the request."

"Was hoping she'd reach out first." Davin scratched at his stubble.

Phyla had wanted to make the call right after Amado left, but Davin fought for the extra time, the extra distance. If Amado's group tracked Viola's calls, and she said something she wasn't supposed to, Davin wanted the *Jumper* far away from the Moon and Earth. Now they were in the no man's land on the way to Mars, with plenty of void to hide in should Viola trigger a dangerous response.

"Do you want to take the call here, with the cargo?" Fournine asked. "The cockpit would be better. You could tell Phyla to stop checking my calculations."

"You think I can tell Phyla to stop anything?"

"For once, Davin, you make a good point. I shall try Viola now."

Davin gave himself a little jump, set himself adrift in the air. What was the point of spending so much time in zero gravity if you didn't enjoy it? Taking a call while slowly spinning around was one of those little spices Davin added to his interstellar life.

"Davin," Viola's voice patched through after Fournine burned a minute getting her online. "I was getting worried. You have the container?"

"Your buddies didn't tell you?"

"Buddies?"

Davin sighed loud, stretched out in space, his length matching the yellow-black container.

"Viola, when you came running into us in that club, I thought you'd never seen the outside of your father's moon," Davin said. "Now that you have, I figured you'd be a little savvier than this."

"Running into you? The way I recall it, you stumbled into me," Viola said. " And I run tech R&D for Eden. I'm plenty savvy."

"Stumbling, running, same thing," Davin said. "Leading a division and staying alive are two different kinds of savvy, Vi. Point is, you've got a crew watching you, and not the warm and fuzzy one like you had with me."

"Warm and fuzzy? The 'Nines, Davin? I wouldn't use those words."

"Depends on your point of view." Davin clasped his hands behind his head as he floated, stared up at the *Jumper*'s ceiling and kept himself from getting distracted. "You better figure out who at Eden doesn't trust you, because they knew about your container."

"What do you mean, knew?"

"I mean they were waiting for us, and they took the damn key and stuck it in my leg."

"Oh."

At least Viola had the courtesy to sound apologetic.

"Yeah, oh. Big oh," Davin said. "Phyla and I have your cargo, though. We're on our way to Callisto."

"I'm sorry, Davin. I didn't think there'd be anyone listening."

"Not thinking, kid. That's how you get in trouble."

"You're going to spoil any pity I have for you, you keep talking like that." Viola hummed for a moment. "Listen, you're heading to Callisto already? Based on the delay, looks like you haven't made Mars yet?"

Whatever else Davin could say about Viola, she did have the book smarts down. Davin sure couldn't calculate an approximate location based on vocal transmission times. That's what computers were for.

"Getting that way, yeah."

"Then I've got another favor to ask," Viola said.

"Another? I think you've about run out of favors."

"I believe you told me anything, always," Viola replied. "Who shot Bosser?"

Davin floated silent for a long second. Sure, he would always give Viola that. Getting called on it, though, was something else. The last time Davin had found himself in real debt to someone, things hadn't gone well. Miner Prime, so he'd heard, was still undergoing repairs.

"What's the favor, Vi?"

"Have you been paying attention to what's going on? Between Eden and the rebels? The ones that used to be the Red Voice?"

"Seen the news here and there, not much else."

Something Davin said had Viola's voice change, she went from taut, nervous, to more relaxed. From a negotiation to a happy hour get together.

"Sounds about right," Viola said, all warm and bright. "What I'm asking, Davin, is that you really stay focused on this one. The container."

"You're saying that like you don't trust me."

"I just, I just know you," Viola replied. "This all isn't as simple as I wanted it to be. I'm worried it's going to get hard for you."

"What, this container? Then why have me run it at all?"

"Because I don't trust anyone else."

"Not Amado?"

"I don't even know who that is," Viola said. "Davin, I have to go. I jumped out of the lab to take your call, but if I'm not back soon, the techs might blow themselves up and take me with them."

"Right. Except you never told me the favor."

"Don't stop, Davin. Don't stop for anything," Viola said. "If Amado really works for Eden, and he knows what you're doing, then he's not the only one. I don't want you to get hurt."

"Too late for that," Davin replied. "Get back to your toys. Wouldn't want them going boom."

"Thanks. Take care, Davin."

Viola clipped off the call. After taking a run through the conversation and not gleaning any new info, Davin realized he'd floated himself stuck, killed his momentum and now sat dead drifting over his cargo.

"Phyla?" He shouted. "Could use some help here?"

Fournine, the damn flight computer, laughed.

## 7

# OLD FACES, OLD FRIENDS

Travel through the solar system happened via lines. Davin could point the *Jumper* towards a particular target and Fournine would calculate the optimal trajectory to put the *Jumper* in line with the target's solar orbit. Every significant object in the solar system had its orbits beamed up and synced across a satellite web spaced from Earth to Neptune—thanks, Eden—so any ship could and should be able to see exactly where their route would bring them in relation to, say, Mars and its two moons.

By chance, by fate or, as Davin argued, pure good fortune, the *Jumper*'s path would cut them close enough to Mars to catch a good look at the red planet and its moons. More importantly, getting that close would mean a chance to stop in at Deimos and pick up something tastier than nutrient goop.

"You're the one that bought all that in the first place," Phyla said as they sat in the cockpit, watching the stars, having just finished another round of space chess—just chess, but in space. "If you didn't like it, then why?"

"Because it was a great deal!" Davin threw up his hands. "The man had loads sitting around that he needed to sell."

"Ever think there might be a reason for that?"

"Hey, it's got all we need to survive . . . in a tube."

"There's a slogan." The console beeped and Phyla looked towards it, frowned. "Distress signal. Looks like a freighter. Larger than ours."

Common space-faring law mandated that any passing ship respond to a distress beacon, but reality muddied that equation. Anyone calling for help could be a pirate, could be more trouble than honor merited. Eden had enough ships in constant patrol along the orbital paths between Earth, Mars, and Jupiter that someone competent and properly armed would come along before true disaster struck.

"This is the *Zephyr*, if anyone can help us, we've lost battery power and are drifting. Our panels aren't working, and if we don't get our air recycling soon, we'll suffocate," the voice kept its calm throughout, as if the disaster, while unfortunate, wasn't entirely unexpected. "If anyone's able to give us a tow to Deimos, we'd be grateful!"

Two ways to look at a signal like that. On the one hand, the captain didn't seem particularly worried: putting possible suffocation with a polite request for a tow required either the stiffest spine Davin had seen in a while or a total inability to square the situation. On the other, Davin wanted to go to Deimos, and here was the perfect excuse.

"I see that face," Phyla said. "Didn't Viola say we shouldn't make any detours?"

"Since when do you care about the rules?"

"Since an Eden death squad decided to take an interest in us."

Davin put a mock pout on his face, "I thought you were bored. And they're not a death squad."

Phyla hesitated, and Davin knew he'd won. Trapped her in a corner of her own making.

"I suppose you're right," Phyla said. "Fournine, swing us towards that signal and give us a broadcast channel. Davin's making a good argument for once." Phyla flicked a glance Davin's way. "If Amado comes back, I'm telling him it was your fault."

"Isn't it always?"

The *Zephyr*—helluva name for a big, clunky freighter—and her captain, Uros, proved appreciative when Davin reached out, throwing thank you's and a payment promise once the freighter made it to Deimos. Uros thought the *Zephyr* had one more run before a battery replacement—expensive, time-consuming—and blew it.

Despite being more than twice the *Jumper's* size, space's gravity magic made it easy for the smaller ship to drag along its bigger brother. Phyla put the *Jumper* in the right place for Davin to manipulate his ship's outside grapple, get a hook on the *Zephyr* and make the connection around the big freighter's tow loops. Designed more for tricky docking situations than emergency rescue, the big metal rings made easy targets for Davin's aim.

"Look who's still got it," Davin said when the console chimed in a successful lock. "Best grappler in the galaxy, right here."

"That statement is impossible to quantify," Fournine said.

"I agree with the computer," Phyla echoed.

"Then, with no evidence against, I hold my claim."

No matter how many times Phyla rolled her eyes, Davin wouldn't kill his quips. Deep down, he knew, she laughed.

Really deep.

Uros said he had a small crew, and as air was becoming a

premium, Davin and Phyla invited the bunch onboard the *Jumper* for the days-long journey to Deimos. When Phyla pointed out that the *Jumper* wasn't really equipped for guests, Davin countered that they'd at least eat more of the nutrient goop, forcing a restock with better food. Phyla couldn't deny that win.

With Fournine playing pilot, the two went to the hatch to greet Uros and his crew. For all the friendliness Uros had shown over the comm, Davin and Phyla still loaded up for an ambush. Anyone could talk nice over a transmission, then hold a knife to your neck in person.

Phyla took her top spot, rifle in hand, while Davin watched the hatch. After last time, with Amado's pop-up threat, Davin's fingers rested closer to Melody's stock, slung over his shoulder. He could swing the weapon over or under, fire a shot in a second that would, so long as the target sat dead center, end the fight before it began.

Of course, Davin could also miss and add a new, ugly scorch mark to the *Jumper*'s walls.

"Shall I open the hatch?" Fournine asked once Davin and Phyla had themselves set.

Phyla tossed him the slightest nod, so Davin gave permission. The hatch popped and swung open, and like Amado, two hands appeared on the rim, followed by a face Davin hadn't seen in years.

"Well isn't this the best kind of surprise?" Davin said as Merc pulled himself into the ship.

The swarthy fighter pilot had alternated between playing gunner and flying the *Jumper*'s escort fighter, back when it had one, during the Wild Nines' profitable days running security and dangerous cargo from one planet to the next. Merc had offered a spiky, hard-charging optimism that'd mellowed only when he'd fallen for Opal, another

Wild Nines member and one who wouldn't put up with Merc's relentless shenanigans.

For all the years spent since Davin had last seen Merc, the pilot hadn't seemed to age. Maybe added a few lines beneath his short black hair, but Merc still wore pilot's fatigues, still had the same belt with holsters and spots for his bolo grenades, though these were empty. The man had kept up an impressive fitness regimen when he flew with the 'Nines and it didn't look like Merc had slacked off at all.

And yet, for all that, Davin saw a different look behind those eyes. One he recognized, because Davin saw it in the damn mirror every day: reckless hope sobered by experience.

"Bet you thought I'd died," Merc said as he kicked himself towards Davin, bypassing the captain's offered hand for a tight hug. "Still here, Davin. Still here."

"Against all odds," Davin said, flicking his eyes past Merc to a smiling, guarded Phyla.

She kept her rifle ready, despite the good surprise. Merc hadn't come on the comm, and why he'd not announced himself early was a question in itself. Uros, the captain, hadn't appeared—nobody had followed Merc from the hatch yet—and who knew how many others lurked on the *Zephyr*.

Merc noticed. Let Davin go with the slightest shove to push himself back, looked up towards Phyla.

"Nice to see you too, Phyla," Merc said. "See you're as straight to business as always."

"Some things don't change," Phyla replied. "Good to see you, Merc."

"I'm one for swapping stories." Davin reeled the conversation back. "Yet your freighter just docked with us on account of a dead battery, yet I'm only seeing you come through that hatch?"

"They'll come when I give the okay," Merc replied. "Once I saw it was you, figured I'd warm things up before sending in the rest."

A plausible start. Still didn't explain why Merc stayed quiet on the comm. Still didn't give a reason for Phyla to put away her rifles.

"I'm feeling pretty warm," Davin said. "How about we see who you're traveling with?"

Merc nodded, but didn't make a move to signal to anyone. Instead, the pilot took a big breath, "Davin, gonna need you to promise me you won't touch that trigger."

"You're saying I might want to?"

"I'm saying you know where Opal and I went, right?"

Did Davin know? Last he checked, Merc and Opal had disappeared after the battle over Earth. While Davin and Viola had been putting a laser bolt into Bosser's face, the other two had been saving the Red Voice's leader from an android assassination. Other than a quick goodbye, Davin hadn't heard from either of the two for years.

"We don't spend a lot of time tracking old friends," Phyla said from up above.

"Though maybe we should start," Davin said. "I figured you two had ditched out on the fun. Found somewhere to settle down."

"Me, settle down?" Merc threw up a horrified look. "Never." He paused for a long moment, the look falling into a straight face. "We went with Alissa. All the way out past Jupiter. The whole android mess generated a lot of Red Voice sentiment. Coin, too."

Alissa. In the Terramorpher on Europa, Davin and Phyla had climbed those steps and, without really intending to, killed Alissa's sister Marl. She'd been planning to turn the moon into a Red Voice base. The disaster on Earth came not much later, and Davin had figured most of the Red Voice had died setting that up.

Instead, they'd sprung back. Forming ragged ship pockets near Saturn and beyond, preying on freighters and taking territory. Now the upstarts had pushed Eden back far enough to set up a legitimate enterprise, at least until Eden decided to crush it.

"So you joined a sinking ship," Davin said.

"It's rising plenty fast for me," Merc countered.

"You're not going to win a fight with Eden."

"Says the captain that took on an android army and won." Merc pointed up at Phyla, then at himself. "We were all there, Davin. Did the impossible plenty of times. Then you stopped. Opal and I? We kept going."

"Is Opal down that hatch?" Phyla asked.

Merc shook his head, "Can't say where she's at right now, but I need to make sure, Davin, before Uros and the rest come up, you're okay hosting rebels on your ship?"

"Hosting?" Davin scratched at that stubble again, a habit he'd probably never break. "I'm rescuing you all."

You had to pick sides. That's what the news kept saying. What the jokers in the bars kept delivering via fresh rounds, as if Davin had asked for advice with a pint. Either you were with the corporations and the Earth-side governments that'd mapped out space under their profit-centered ideology, or you jumped in with a bunch that wanted to tear it all down and rebuild it to suit their own needs.

Davin, Davin had all he needed right here. A ship, a partner, and some cargo to run. If he could spice that up with some excitement every now and then, great. He'd had his run in the big mixer, now he'd be happy to stay out of it.

Merc finally relented, gave the okay, and the four other crew made their unarmed way up into the *Jumper*. Uros came last, a waist-length blond beard making his narrow face appear to go on forever. That beard cloaked a decent stomach, no doubt expanded by years floating on a freighter like *Zephyr*, and sharp, deep-set eyes that looked on Davin with an appraiser's glint.

A deal-maker, and as Davin shook his hand, the *Jumper*'s captain figured this rescue wasn't going to be a simple interruption.

With the rebels, nothing ever was.

## 8

---

## DEIMOS

**D**eimos embraced sinful superlatives. The tiny moon packed more party per square kilometer than anywhere else in the solar system, its bulk now held together more by constructed supports than actual moon rock as pleasure-pandering companies hollowed out its core. Free from anything resembling real regulation—though physical violence or property damage tended to end with the perpetrator dead or ejected into vacuum—Deimos grabbed Las Vegas's mantel and yanked it skyward.

Given the moon's little space, Davin docked the *Jumper* in an orbiting port, one of dozens holding everything from single-person shooters up from Mars to large cruisers taking stargazers from Earth to Jupiter and back. Passenger-packed shuttles shunted would-be revelers from the ports to Deimos proper through a long portal series displaying one hyper-colorful ad after another.

"This gets more blinding every time," Phyla said as she, Davin, Merc, and Uros descended. "It's like they need to desensitize you before you hit the moon itself."

Phyla hadn't even wanted to come. When they'd docked and Uros announced his crew would be sticking with the *Zephyr* for repairs, Phyla had tried to suggest grabbing some real food from the port and then bustling back to the stars. Then Merc had made the offer, dangled the tantalizing possibility of some real fun.

"All on our coin," Merc said, and Uros agreed. "As a thank you."

The two had proved to be fun traveling companions, even if their other crew members stayed reclusive. While Merc had pushed Davin into the simulator every other hour to re-run favorite scenarios, Uros chatted with Phyla, and while the *Zephyr*'s other four crew stayed in makeshift beds in the *Jumper*'s workshop, the original crew quarters currently occupied by too much crap.

Together, Merc and Davin had run through the Terramorpher adventure, replayed the assault on Miner Prime, and ventured through the pirate assault on the cruiser over Neptune. A fine blend: nostalgia and action.

Davin realized how much he missed the cocky fighter pilot. Missed having another voice around. Dinners and lunches with the four of them became laughing, memory-laden affairs that made the nutrient goop bearable. The old stories Davin and Phyla had told to each other a hundred times sounded new again with Merc and Uros listening along.

Sure, neither Merc nor Uros spoke much about their rebel adventures, but Davin didn't care. They didn't want to give any secret info away to a cargo runner with no real allegiance? Made sense. Didn't matter.

They'd be dropping the *Zephyr* soon and bidding the whole batch goodbye.

The glittering ad displays pushed impossible ideas,

showcasing adventures like black hole diving and surfing Saturn's rings. None real, all made to feel that way through complex suits and moment-to-moment programs that sucked away your sappy life and replaced it with something far more awesome.

Blending between the big events were more typical distractions, the gambling and drug delights meant to siphon away your senses and your wallet at the same time. Davin couldn't keep a little grin away. He'd been around too many of these places to get enchanted, but that tiny thrill of possibility?

He still felt the rush.

"So," Davin said as the rings reached their end and the shuttle settled into its final docking sequence, swooping in towards the wild, zero-G mess that architects had turned Deimos into. "You're the hosts, where should we go first?"

"Well," Merc said. "How about we do a lap, then I'm thinking our lady might like to take a spin around a course?"

"My bullet's still in the *Jumper*," Phyla said. "There's no official courses here anyway. Deimos is too tiny."

"Who said anything about official?" Merc replied. "This is where all the best pilots come. It's the only way to make real coin."

"What?" Phyla said.

Merc answer came through demonstration. The shuttle docked and let them into a galaxy's worth of options, passages streaking off towards here, there, and possibly, for the right price, everywhere. Merc had them head down a neon green-lit tunnel, walls plastered over with more moving ads calling for this, that, and possibly, for the right price, the other thing.

Beyond all the glitter, Davin had another reason for coming to Deimos: gravity. The *Jumper* didn't play well with it, and after spending enough time in true zero-G, Davin craved some real weight. Deimos didn't have tons, but they'd laced the moon with enough magnetic energy that Davin's outfit tugged him towards the ground. Not like being on Earth, but Davin didn't float with every step.

To think floating would've been magic to so many people for so long.

"You ever been here, Uros?" Davin asked the bearded captain, who had thus far experienced the journey with the same aloof ennui that pervaded his every action. "Spent a few wild nights on this rock?"

"Several times," Uros replied. "Hard to find a place I both love and detest more."

Couldn't argue with that.

Phyla, in the several days journey from the *Zephyr*'s pick-up to Deimos, had kept up the suspicion every time the laughter died away. With Fournine held to 24-hour monitoring duties, Phyla and Davin had spent the minutes before slinking away to sleep engaged in amateur spycraft, trying to assess exactly what Uros and Merc and the *Zephyr* were up to.

While the *Zephyr* itself didn't seem armed, Merc's presence meant it had to have a fighter aboard. Had to be transporting something the rebels saw important enough to protect. That neither Uros nor Merc cared to talk about it only spun up the suspicion, until Davin figured he'd go insane if he had to second-guess every comment either one made around him.

"He was part of the Wild Nines," Davin said the night before docking with Deimos. "We trust him until Merc proves otherwise."

"And if we die because of it?"

"Well, maybe I don't want to live in a galaxy where I can't trust my old friends."

Phyla, at least, had accepted that.

Uros, though, didn't fall under the old friend protective cloak, so Davin had made it his secondary mission to get to know the captain better. That, unfortunately, had been harder than flying the *Jumper* through Jupiter's big red spot. Uros kept a lid on anything beneath the surface, as though he were a pressure cooker and even the slightest slip would make the man explode.

"Sounds like you've got a story in there," Davin replied as they continued down the green-lit tunnel towards where, Merc promised, they'd find the best bullet-racing action this side of Venus.

"I might," Uros said. "Another time."

Always ready to listen, never ready to talk. Davin jotted Uros down in his mental list of people not to trust. A list that would've been longer if most of the people on it still lived.

Merc's chosen tunnel spat them out into a vast casino's swooping lobby. Davin assumed the place had a name, assumed it was even hidden somewhere in the brand explosion bashing their group senseless, but he couldn't pick it out. Merc, though, didn't pause. Didn't stop to assess where they were, and kept marching on.

"We never came to this one, right?" Phyla said as she and Davin fell in behind Merc and Uros.

The 'Nines had pulled a detail on Deimos for a while, running celebrity security for a month-long concert series. Not really Davin's preferred engagement, but the group had needed a break, and blowing off hours on Deimos seemed like a good idea.

Until Davin realized there were no off hours on Deimos. The whole damn moon was crazy.

"No, don't think we hit this one," Davin replied. "Or, if we did, I wasn't in a state to remember. Those weren't exactly sober times."

"The music was pretty awful."

"Sure, that's why."

Phyla rolled her eyes, Davin laughed, and they followed Merc and Uros up an escalator to a wide archway labeled *Speed Shots*, the letters traced in a circle by two bullets chasing each other in an infinite pursuit. Inside, *Speed Shots* seemed to inspire a single word: Dark. As if getting sucked into a void, once Davin had walked beneath the arch, light itself disappeared.

"I can't even see my hand," Davin said.

"Put these on," Merc said, returning from the darkness, holding several luminescent green goggles and already wearing a pair himself. "Then you'll get it."

The goggles weren't light, and as Davin slipped the pair over his head and onto his ears, he wondered if the things wouldn't smash his poor cartilage. The lenses fit over his eyes, soft bristles making the comfort better than anything Davin would've expected, and then he forgot all about those expectations.

And everything else.

"Well, this is new," Davin muttered.

*Speed Shots* went from dark to lush, to a ghostly lightness whose spectral grays and purples suffused with a fuzzy blue to build a restaurant, betting scene, and giant bullet course from nothing. The course itself held force, its curls and curves, hills and loops swinging around the tables, over the heads, and between bots standing by to take bets. It took Davin a second, one spent watching bright colored dots—not unlike the broadcast Fournine had played for him—race along the course to realize the whole thing was a projection.

The real bullets, the ones the racers used, were all set along the far wall, on a raised stage. Twelve simulator hookups, all ready to be used. All *being* used. Because *Speed Shots* was jammed, and rocking.

"I told you," Merc said, and Davin glanced at him. "You want to know where all the pilots go on Deimos? It's right here."

With the goggles on, Merc looked like a bad movie, a purple flicker with those goggles sticking out as if someone had stretched a neon lime across Merc's face. When the pilot opened his mouth, his teeth flared bright, and Davin felt like he'd fallen into a bad rave. Everyone else in the place looked the same, splashed with techno color.

"Who gets to fly?" Phyla asked. "The bullets, I mean."

"That's the best part," Merc replied. "Anybody can. Bottom half has to switch out after every race. Every so often they'll have pros all line up for one, but most of the time, it's you and me in there."

Merc's words became apparent as they watched the race sprint towards its conclusion, with dots free-wheeling off into apparent oblivion. One pair actually collided, their orange and yellow spheres smashing into each other before bursting into a pixelated cloud. Their simulators followed suit, popping open to let the two stumbling, laughing, likely drunk racers meander towards the bar. A few boos rained down too, bettors who took the wrong chance.

Racing a bullet without any life-and-limb risk, but with stakes, seemed pretty fun. The line for the upcoming races wasn't all that long, something that surprised Davin until the group made their way to the line's start and learned about the forked-over fee. Take one of the upper-tier positions in the race and you'd earn back your money, plus a little more the better you did.

"Not a bad deal for a win," Davin said, reading up on the coin. "Phyla, think you can take this crowd?"

"No idea," Phyla replied. "Haven't seen the course. Haven't used one of these simulators."

"Phyla," Merc said. "Take a chance. You'll be fine."

And before anyone had a chance to react, to reject, Merc tapped in a coin transfer to the waiting bot, slotting in four berths.

"Four?" Davin asked.

Uros shook his head, laughed as Merc put his hand on Davin's shoulder.

"Always wanted to fly with you, captain."

Ah. Crap.

**9**

---

# SPEED RACER

*peed Shots* did one thing right: they knew people who'd barely flown a bullet before would find their way into these open simulators, would be hopped up on all kinds of chemicals, and would still need to provide enough competence for people to make bets. When Davin settled into the dark pod, after cursing Merc out the whole way onto the stage for being an improvisational punk, the seat leaned him forward, face ahead and hands gripping the steering levers on either side.

Each lever had a rubbery grip that extended down beneath the central bike that Davin straddled as he settled in. The goggles stayed on, apparently required for full immersion. The simulator closed around Davin with a quiet thunk, and as it did so the machine spun into operation.

Tiny fans blew a stiff breeze, some air freshener hit its scent quotient and dumped a meadow's flowery mix into Davin's nose. The black around him burst into blue sky, puffy clouds, and an endless grassy green lawn. In the far distance, idyllic mountains rose. Davin felt a whine beneath him as the bullet he was supposedly riding on spun up, and the view rose a meter as his virtual craft found its ride height.

WELCOME!

The silver word displayed alongside a countdown timer, huge in the air. Five minutes till race time. The delay gave people time to place their bets, and Davin also knew what was coming next: screens throughout *Speed Shots* would show the various bullet pilots tinkering around, getting used to their virtual toys. Some algorithm would judge their skill and slot in the odds.

PLEASE TEST YOUR BULLET

Okay.

Davin eased both levers forward and the bullet started off on a gentle coast, brushing against the grass. A pleasant ride, but one guaranteed to lose a race.

"As long as I'm here," Davin muttered, adjusted his grip to give his wrists that flicking prowess necessary for instant bullet maneuvers, "might as well win."

He pushed the levers forward and the bullet shot ahead. Virtually, Davin's stomach didn't drop. He didn't actually get to the two hundred plus kilometers per hour bullets tended to hit, but the fans reached gale force—now the goggles made sense—and the landscape whooshed along beneath him in an emerald blur.

Davin pulled back on the left lever and the bullet slid in that direction, its momentum propelling it in a wide, arcing turn. When Davin pushed the right lever forward, the turn sharpened until the bullet whipped hard around and started zipping back the previous way. The mountains on the horizon stayed the same no matter which direction Davin went, never came any closer either. A true test ground.

READY TO RACE?

The simulator asked it as a question, but with the timer ticking to zero, Davin didn't exactly have a choice. He'd practiced a couple turns, felt out the rough kinks on how to fly a bullet. Did that make him qualified to run a course?

Maybe if that course was a straight line over a meadow like this one.

"Don't bet on me, you morons," Davin said, doubting that anyone could hear him.

In a way, being in the simulator gave Davin a cocky confidence he wouldn't have had out in the open, with eyes staring at him. Sure, some of those people in *Speed Shots* might have placed bets on the *Jumper* captain—and what a bad move that was—but once the race picked up, Davin would be another dot among the dozen, with the more detailed screens focused on the leaders.

The timer hit zero and the grassy meadow disappeared. Just, vanished. The fans slowed to a light breeze. Davin's grips rumbled, along with his seat, as if going through the virtual transition required some physical element.

"What in the . . ." Davin said as the course filled in on the screen.

A far cry from the grassy meadow, Davin and his bullet landed on shiny, black volcanic rock. The other bullets popped in around him, arranged in betting order: the one getting the most bets started in last place, the one getting the least began as the leader.

"Hey," Davin said to Uros, the only one ahead of him in the line. The blonde man's bullet had a speckled green and purple coat and hovered a couple meters away. "Can you hear me?"

Uros didn't react. Guess not.

If Uros *had* been able to hear him, then Davin would've started yelling about how ridiculous this course appeared to be. The shiny black rock blazed out the path before them, and above a sparkling nova sky made any glance up a blinding risk. At eye level, though, hot red and orange lava shimmered. Liquid pools lingered along the course, but more than that, gouts sprang up from the course's center. Red rings filled with lava arced overhead, some leaking here and there.

Unconstrained by physical laws, the course rose and looped, spun its way up to the sky and, based on what Davin could see, under the ground. A ridiculous construct, a nightmare for any bullet racer, and an impossibility for someone who'd never raced the damn things in their life.

After this, Davin was gonna give Merc one helluva punch. Maybe two.

Across the center of his screen, three lights appeared, all crimson red. Again the bullet whirred to life, and Davin leaned forward, found his grip. This whole thing might be a disaster, but Davin was in it now, and he'd try to win.

Uros, after all, had the last spot. *Someone* had bet on Davin. He'd try to make them proud.

One light flipped green, a low ding sounded. A lava fountain exploded to Davin's right and he flinched.

The second light flipped.

Okay. Hit the boost right when the last light turned.

Davin pushed the levers forward. Tried to time it right and failed, the light still red as Davin ought to be flying away, but the bullet didn't move.

What? Why...

In the millisecond it took Davin to remember that this was a simulation, that the program could control when bullets could go anywhere, the last light turned green.

With his two levers throttled up, Davin's bullet blitzed off the line. His ride thrummed up to a high-pitched whine that sounded more like a squeal, and the acceleration's gale force smashed into Davin's face, those little fans doing an admirable job mimicking real wind.

On the screen's upper, middle portion, a giant gold number flipped from two to one with a sparkling flash. Davin's glorious achievement lasted a split second, till he saw the black glass track curving to the right, a lava-pocked gray rock wall rising before him.

Lurching back on the right lever, Davin veered the bullet, the craft juddering hard through the air. The bullet's momentum swung Davin close enough to the wall to touch it, though his hands wouldn't let go of those levers if Davin tried. Virtual or no, the lava-torched world and the high speed bullet felt real enough.

That glorious number one vanished as racers who took a more measured pace off the line wheeled around the curve without sending their bullets into a hairpin stop. Davin pushed his throttle forward again, picking up speed and trying to find a way through the bullet engines.

How Merc and Phyla kept ships like the *Jumper* and their starfighters from bashing into countless debris, Davin never understood. Thrusting up the bullet and trying to weave through the other racers felt like solving a thousand puzzles on the fly, instant reactions and reflexes. In real life, touching any other bullet would mean catastrophic disaster, maybe fatal injury.

In the virtual world, Davin could do whatever he wanted.

Not everyone shared Davin's reckless desire to keep the throttle maxed out every time the course gave them a straight kilometer, and that hesitation let Davin blow by seventh and sixth, right up behind a familiar face in fifth.

Uros, for all his quiet hesitation, apparently knew how

to steer a bullet with some skill. The man banked through curves and hit the lines on the loops like someone who'd done enough dabbling to be dangerous. Davin flew up on him, treating the course with no respect and blasting over corners, lurching the levers around and relying on instinct to level out with Uros.

The other captain did not return Davin's cocky grin, Uros kept his face forward, eyes on the course.

A good call, turned out.

Davin's bullet rocketed up a loop with too much speed for the curl, his bullet's nose scraping the ground before its jets managed to get control and bounce it back up. Sparks flew around Davin's face, and he was pretty sure a metal chunk had fallen beneath the bullet. Whether the simulation cared or not, Davin didn't know.

The levers still worked. Uros vanished behind him.

Four racers ahead, and the course split into two interweaving pathways breaking over a long lava lake. Hot orange death spurted through the gaps in the course, splashing onto the black glass. The view gave Davin a quick look at the bullets streaking beyond him, and a snap measure said he might be able to catch up.

Davin pushed the levers forward again and the bullet played along, snatching forward like a mad predator chasing its prey.

Davin caught the fourth and third place racers by accident. Both had taken the other pathway, and both were entangled with each other, jockeying for position on the split way's long, narrow path across the lake. Without an obstruction, Davin blew past them, speeding up towards the second place pilot as the twin pathways rejoined.

Merc. Davin recognized the man's cropped hair and came up close, then fell behind as the fighter pilot wove through a curving, underground canyon series while Davin swung and shot, his lurching method keeping Davin moving while giving up precious milliseconds.

A bright blue bolt split the nova sky, landing not all that far beyond Davin and Merc as they exited the canyon, a helpful finish line highlight. As if the course itself realized it was nearly over, the track began breaking up around them, falling away into the lava and leaving an unpredictable path.

Merc throttled down, plotted a course. Davin laughed.

In games, you always went for the max.

The *Jumper*'s captain shot by Merc, pushing the bullet along as golden lines splayed across the track, signifying the moments where lava would soon appear. Davin lifted his left hand, flipped a certain gesture back Merc's way. Dish out a little flair before the finish.

The fans changed. The view swung. Davin wasn't looking at the track anymore, but the orange red endless sea. Davin pulled back on the levers, but the bullet's jets didn't have anything to catch on. Instead, he plummeted straight down, splashing into that hot lava. As his screen faded, the golden place number stayed lit, slowly climbing back up as other racers made the right choice and hit the finish.

Rather than the firework pyrokinetics that might've greeted Davin had he won, his only reward came from the hiss-thunk as the simulator opened, from the assorted boos and jeers from the gamblers who'd watched his fiery plummet, and the realization that he'd spent the last few years living a lie.

## 10

## RISKY MOVE

Phyla and Davin had made the decision together after dropping Mox off on the Moon. They shared a last drink with the big guy, and then he'd stomped off to rest before making his case to rejoin the Centurions. With the Wild Nines decimated to two, and with injuries still healing, they'd decided to take the quiet route. Fall into the cargo running game and make an honest living, one without constant laser fire, giant conspiracies, and bounties resting on everyone's heads.

The choice had been made in adrenaline's shadow, trying to escape a reckless life that would lead to a short, sudden end.

The choice, Davin saw as he stood in *Speed Shots* neon dark inside, would lead to a poisoned, slow death instead. One that curdled in from the edges, sapping away the things he loved with tedium's drain.

Flying the bullet had made that more clear than posing as an illegal runner for Mox, though even that had given Davin a flicker. Controlling the speedy ship with both levers, in quick competition against the other pilots, a payoff so obvious and so deeply wanted at the end.

"Did pretty well, captain," Merc said, guiding Davin off the stage. "Better than I would've thought for a rookie bullet flyer, until you took that dive into the drink."

"Better to go out with a splash than straight-up lose." Davin looked back towards the simulators, hunting fro Phyla and not seeing her. "Where's Phyla?"

"She won," Merc said. "She's in on the next race. I am too. You and Uros get to watch from the stands, maybe throw some coin our way if you want to make it back."

Not a terrible idea, and truth be told, Davin still felt he owed Phyla a watch. Now that he'd flown a bullet, Davin had a better idea how Phyla could find the things so compelling. He wanted to jump right back in, but the line had grown since they'd arrived at *Speed Shots*. Instead, leaving Merc at the stage's end, Davin located Uros heading towards the main bar and joined the *Zephyr* captain there.

"You fly like you talk," Davin said as they took spots right up against the bar itself.

Themed to look like the restaurant, the bar's counter had screens embedded into it, showing the various racer stats and betting odds, surrounded by the deep purple and twinkling stars dominating the bar's decor. A thin light blue lip ran along the bar's edge, and hovering back behind the stacked bottles, several other screens ran through the next course, which looked frozen and filled with avalanches.

The bar, like *Speed Shots* as a whole, played into the sensory overload theme. Every little diode within range had been set to broadcast, and Davin's only way to handle the onrush was through a little cocktail called Miner's Delight.

Developed on his home station, Miner Prime, the Delight—as those in the know, and Davin was most assuredly in the know, called it—blended a crisp vodka with Void Wine, a hyper-chilled drink fermented and then finished by spinning it through pure vacuum. In *Speed Shots'* lighting, the drink oozed an ethereal white.

"I fly like I talk?" Uros replied, enjoying his own flavor breaker, a winding tube with sections that'd squeeze out their contents bit by bit with every suck on the straw, blending together differently depending on how hard Uros went at it. "Stable and steady?"

"Sure, that's one way to put it."

Uros nodded, pointed at the bar counter, currently displaying a countdown to the race and Phyla's odds, "Going to bet on Phyla?"

Davin hadn't thought about it, but seeing as she'd won the previous race, and they were here, why not?

"Are you?" Davin said as he tapped on Phyla's picture, entered his coin account and slid away a small wager. "Merc's racing again."

"I would never bet on Merc," Uros said. "But then, I am not a betting man. I prefer to reduce chance in every encounter."

"I'll bet you do."

"It's not as boring as I make it sound," Uros grinned, that blonde beard stretching across his face. "Making every outcome as certain as possible brings a challenge to life that I find invigorating."

Davin leaned on the bar, took a long drink from his Delight as the bullet race started. In his periphery, Davin saw the course pop in, the icy details not caught in the projection layered over *Speed Shots'* tables but the general make-up filled with narrow tunnels and wide-open basins made for daring passes.

"So if you're not a betting man, why'd you bother to

come to Deimos?" Davin asked, shifting to put the bar's back screens in view.

The bullets zipped along, the bar counter shifting to a running display showing the leaderboard. Phyla had started towards the back, but had already hit the pack's middle.

"I'm not a betting man, but for the right opportunity, I could change my mind," Uros said. "Merc suggested I might find such an opportunity down here."

Uros sounded like he might go on, but Davin, gulping down more Delight, held up a hand to stop him.

"Wait, Merc *suggested* you'd find an opportunity here? What does that even mean?"

Uros flicked his eyes around, noted the bartender had drifted farther away to serve some other customers, and dropped his voice to a whisper, "Being a rebel requires a certain amount of daring. Seizing optimal chances when they arise to make a big leap forward. We can't survive an open war with Eden unless we make some major moves."

Davin couldn't picture Uros being that mover, but maybe the rebels didn't have that many ace players.

"What major moves are you going to find here?" Davin asked, not bothering to keep his voice low.

If anyone had sent spies to Deimos, they sure wouldn't be paying attention to him.

Uros, though, just sucked on his flavor breaker and watched the race. Davin didn't press him. He ought to watch Phyla anyway, even more so now that Davin had dropped coin on the race. Phyla had closed to third place now as the race entered its final third, the bullets streaking through a long sloping section as avalanches closed in around them.

Four bullets had succumbed to the snows already. Merc was one of those.

"Looks like your buddy didn't make it," Davin said.

"Good thing I didn't take that bet," Uros replied.

The race ended with Phyla sliding into second place, enough to give Davin a return on his coin, plus a little extra. Close to finishing his Delight, Davin figured their *Speed Shots* time was coming to a close, but then Phyla's name popped up again on the racers returning for another bout. Which, well, meant another drink for the *Jumper*'s captain. And a chance to double-down on his previous bet.

"Think she can win this one?" Merc said, stepping up to join the crew. His snowy demise had kicked him from the next race, though the pilot didn't look at all troubled by it. "Phyla's even better than I remembered."

Davin noticed the guy that'd won the last race had re-upped too, but, when it came down to it, you had to support the woman you loved.

"I think she's got it," Davin said. "She's a killer on those things."

Merc nodded, then looked past Davin to Uros, "What d'you think, Uros? Want to make this next one more interesting?"

"What're you suggesting?" The captain replied, Davin turning his head to follow the two.

The bar counters flickered, the timer drawing close to zero. Last chance to enter any official bets.

"Davin, you running anything interesting right now?" Merc asked.

"Not really."

Davin broke into his second Delight, enjoying the familiar warm buzz.

"That yellow and black container looked special," Uros said. "Would you be willing to risk its contract for all of our cargo that you can carry?"

"What?"

"You said you're going out Jupiter's way, right?" Merc added. "So were we, obviously. Phyla wins, you can take your pick of what we've got, deliver it and take the coin. She loses, we take that crate off your hands."

Davin and Phyla had kept the crate's story a secret over the days spent closing with Deimos. Hadn't mentioned Viola or Eden. Only the general destination. That Eden wouldn't want rebels knowing about their cargo seemed obvious.

As did the choice here. No way should Davin risk the container. Not on Phyla beating eleven other racers.

"Davin, don't second-guess yourself," Merc said. "How about we make it simpler. Phyla beats the guy she lost to last time. That's it. Doesn't even matter if she takes first place."

The timers chimed. The next race would be starting in a few seconds.

Do the runs. Live the stable life. Don't take risks. That's what Davin and Phyla had told each other after Earth. A plan that'd led to boredom, to arguing with each other and a growing sense that their existence didn't have direction. Getting Uros and Merc's cargo wouldn't help with that, but maybe, maybe it would strike a spark.

Besides, even if Phyla lost, the container's key was stuck in Davin's thigh. No way Merc and Uros would be getting inside the thing, and Davin could find a way to get it back later.

"Fine," Davin said. "Deal. Hope you've got something good in that busted ship."

"Plenty," Merc said, raising his molten yellow beer. "To Phyla."

"Sure, to Phyla." Davin clinked his Delight, and turned to watch the race.

This course eschewed the doomsday environments from

the prior two races, instead settling on a more standard Earth-like landscape, complete with cheering stands and the bonus point beacons. Less about the obstacles, more about precise point scoring. Davin, along with Merc and Uros, leaned in, watching the screens as the bullets blasted off.

As with the icy course, Phyla and her primary opponent quickly separated themselves from a jumbled pack, split between those who ignored the beacons for faster turns and others who killed their speed for bonus points. Phyla sacrificed neither, gliding around the hairpins and launching through the straight-aways with a confidence Davin hadn't seen before.

Or, rather, hadn't seen because he hadn't watched.

With Merc and Uros focused with him, Davin had zero distractions. He caught Phyla's every turn on the screen dedicated to her—the top two racers had fixed displays—and felt his mouth opening as she weaved through.

When had Phyla become this good? How had Davin missed this?

He'd figured bullet racing was a hobby, an extension from Phyla's ship-skipping prowess. The way she hit these turns, the way she shifted the bullet's levers so that it glided along rather than lurched and jerked. . . Phyla could make this a real thing. She could stop running cargo and race bullets.

Phyla could ditch him and the *Jumper* whenever she wanted.

The thought could've scared Davin, could've hit some vulnerable nerve, but instead he grinned as Phyla burst into first place. One more amazing thing about her that—

"He's bumping her," Merc said. "What a dirty move."

Davin didn't catch what that meant, what Merc had seen

that he didn't, until Phyla's main opponent crashed into her screen, blitzed through a curve with the same abandon Davin had, but instead of swerving through the turn, the man aimed his bullet right for Phyla's. The two craft collided, with Phyla's flying off course and the man's bouncing in the right direction, a hard re-direct that somehow put him right where he needed to be.

"In real life, that's two dead pilots," Merc said, and he sounded as pissed as Davin was getting to be. "Looks like this sim just bounces the two bullets apart. He must've known Phyla would catch the worse angle."

Phyla had to boost back to the track, and by the time she re-united with the course and hit the finish, she'd missed a points beacon and lost a couple places. Third. Davin still made his money, but he'd lost the container.

"Sorry, Davin," Merc said. "Phyla didn't deserve that."

"But you're still collecting the bet." Davin finished the second Delight, which suddenly tasted like chalk.

"We all took a chance," Uros said. "It's only one container. How bad could it be?"

With Amado chasing after him?

Pretty damn bad.

# 11

## MOON RAYS

Phyla caught them outside *Speed Shots*, having given up the opportunity for a fourth race. By her look, the winner's crashing maneuver had detonated any appeal the simulated bullet contests held. Davin's lost bet would, no doubt, fail to turn her frown upside down.

"You have to understand," Davin said, starting in on a familiar attack strategy for what must have been the fifth time. "The container's got nothing you want in it. It's a favor."

"And that was a bet," Merc said, standing by Uros instead of his former captain, his potentially former friend. "C'mon Davin, you know the rules. Here's Phyla, now we can go."

"Go?" Davin said. "We just got here?"

Uros held up his wrist as Phyla joined the circle, "My crew sent the message while that last race wrapped up. The *Zephyr's* repaired and we're ready to fly."

"That was fast."

Davin had never heard of a busted ship, simple fix or no,

getting the clear to depart a few hours after berthing. Even if the main problem could be solved that fast, most stations tried to find ways to bump up the bill with random procedures. Those little fixes added time to the clock, and when you charged a ship by the time they spent in the bay too, well, the extra coin just came pouring in.

"My crew is a good one," Uros said. "Merc here excluded."

"Hey," Merc replied to the joke with a smile that kinda made Davin want to slug him. "So, Davin, looks like we have to burn outta here. Mind jumping up with us to hand it over?"

"Hand what over?" Phyla asked.

Merc and Uros turned their eyes to Davin, neither, smartly, wanting to break the news. Davin didn't either, but by now he'd become accustomed to Phyla's disappointment.

"Blame it on the Delights," Davin said when he finished a rambling recount of the bet. "But hey, I made some good coin in there. You were incredible, Phyla. Didn't know you could fly like that."

Phyla's face had frozen as Davin's story went on, and now it thawed into a sighing head shake. On the whole, a better response than Davin had expected: resigned acceptance was way better than straight-up outrage.

"You'd know how well I could fly if you ever watched me race," Phyla said.

Ouch. That stung. Davin didn't know how to answer that one. Merc, mercifully, came to his rescue.

"Phyla," Merc said. "It was a good bet, and the guy you were racing against made a cheap move." The pilot held out his hands in a shrug. "Sometimes this happens. Think of it this way: the rebels definitely need whatever's in that container more than the person paying you to send it."

"Here's what I don't understand," Phyla said, taking her heat off Davin for a moment. "Why do you want that container so much that you'd risk your own cargo, surely things the rebels need more?"

Davin nodded, pointed a finger Phyla couldn't see at her back while catching Merc and Uros's eyes. That's what he'd been trying to ask this whole time.

"Educated guess," Uros said. "Your ship isn't small, but the only thing in its cargo bay for a long run is a single container, one marked in way that suggests it's unusual. Even if what's inside is an object that has no direct use, we could likely sell it for coin the rebels need. We're carrying power packs and weapons parts; necessary, yes, but not something that could tilt the war's balance."

A rough, winding explanation that, Davin suspected, wouldn't hold much water if he hadn't been two Delights— and one commiseration shot with Merc after Phyla's forced crash—in. As it was, Phyla let the words mellow for a second, then looked Davin's way.

"I'll take'em back. Give them the container," Phyla said. "I'm tired enough after the races anyway. You look like you could use a walk."

"Probably could," Davin replied.

Even a little blurred, Davin caught the subtext: get away from these two before you say or do something stupid. Phyla knew about the container's seal, that Merc and Uros wouldn't have any luck with it so long as Davin didn't start talking about the key in his leg.

"Works for us," Merc said. "Sorry, Davin. This wasn't how I wanted this to end up."

"Don't worry about it." Davin leveraged his optimism reserve, that simmering batch of hope that everything would turn out all right. "You're doing just what I would. Making a deal and sticking to it."

"Right," Merc said. "You wind up coming out past Jupiter, drop a line. Opal would love to say hi too."

"We will," Phyla said. "C'mon, let's get this over with. I'm tired of all this neon."

With a couple last handshakes, the trio walked back towards the docking station shuttle, leaving Davin in the wide lobby with nothing more than his thoughts, his newly won coin, and a buzz that'd dwindled away to a loose nothingness.

Back when he'd first joined with the Wild Nines, when the *Jumper* had been in the hands of another captain, Davin had loved places like Deimos. No responsibility and a chance to blow your coin on whatever you wanted. With the ship docked, the daily upkeep would be off his hands. Davin and the other crew would trounce around the moon, getting into squabbles, making bad bets, and forging memories Davin looked on now with a mix of envy and regret.

Nobody depended on Davin back then. Not really. He didn't have anyone to fail.

A jingling sound prompted Davin to look up, and he realized he'd been walking as he wandered through his past. Rather than the green *Speed Shots* sign and its dark insides, Davin had found his way to an open-air park he'd loved before.

"Instinct, I guess," Davin offered up to another man leaning against a nearby wall, who looked up, confused and vaguely threatened at Davin's words. "Sorry, just talking to myself."

Deimos, lacking an atmosphere, followed the Moon's lead and built domes over the surface. The thick barriers were transparent from below and had chemicals plastered over the top to protect the glass from micro-meteors and cosmic radiation. The effect, when Deimos hit the right rotation, caused rainbows to spill down into courtyards like this one.

Those colorful prisms sprayed now into a milder casino vibe, old-style betting tables interspersed between cafes, fountains, and pop-up shops. Recorded lounge music piped through speakers Davin couldn't see, while the collective food and spice scents rolled together to thicken the air. Life's pace slowed, and Davin took his moment.

Even Deimos realized that its clients needed a chance to breathe every now and then.

"Hey, don't I know you?" said a low voice behind, and then beside Davin.

She looked like she'd lived on Deimos for a while, partaken of its delights but, at the same time, not ashamed by them. Her outfit portrayed parties, nights spent blasting away the stars in suites and clubs making some memories and forgetting others. Her eyes had a glaze to match, suggesting a struggle long-since lost, or, perhaps, won.

"Always a chance," Davin said. "Can't say I'm too famous."

"No," the woman replied, slowly tipping a single finger towards him. "But you did something for me one time."

"I did?"

Among the situations Davin hadn't encountered, random gratitude listed up there. Strangers tended to approach Davin and argue about coin and favors owed, not benefits provided. His ready-made excuses, bravado, and side-slipping topics faltered.

"I worked for Bosser back on Miner Prime," the woman

said. "He had a few assistants, and then he went off with you to Earth and never came back."

Davin blinked. Hard to imagine Bosser having assistants, having anyone actually working for him, but the man had run a massive enterprise. He must've had some help.

"And you're happy about that?" Davin didn't know what else to say.

Deimos had an express prohibition on arms, so Davin didn't have a sidearm to edge towards. Probably a good thing, given the Delights, but in an unusual situation there was a certain comfort towards knowing Davin could defend himself.

"Are you joking?" The woman burst into a grin. "That was the best thing that ever happened to me. I'd been stuck on Miner Prime my whole life, then it all goes to hell, and I realized that I was wasting my time punching the hours on that horrible space station. When Eden paid us all to keep us quiet, I took the coin and came here and I've never been happier."

"Uh, you're welcome?"

She wrapped him in a quick hug. Her clothes shifted with the motion, flashing from a soft peach to a light green, and Davin realized she wore mood fibers. Ridiculous things that'd pull your temperature, blood pressure, and more to show how you felt in the moment to everyone watching.

"Look," the woman stepped back. "I don't know why you're here, who you're with, or whatever. I just saw you seeming a little lost and thought maybe you could use some cheering up. You saved a lot of people's lives that day, Davin. Not only from dying, but from the wrong kind of living."

"Bosser was an asshole," Davin replied, because it was easier to focus on Bosser than deal with a straight-up compliment. "Glad that he's removed from the picture."

The woman nodded, tilted her head, "You doing anything? Some of us are getting together for a drink in that place over there?" She pointed towards a louge-esque get-up, combining various versions of spacing out into a chill joint. "Promise they're not all your biggest fans."

Davin had lost the container entrusted to him by a friend, had Phyla mad at him, and was otherwise alone on a small rock supposedly built for fun.

"I don't even know your name," Davin said. "But lead the way."

"Rozy. Nice to finally meet you."

The name didn't ring any bells, didn't set off any alarms, and neither did the slow walk through the courtyard.

The lounge knew its audience, with a name like *Jolly Comets*, and beckoned passers-by with a fuzzy, cushioned sprawl. Small tables sat near the ground, surrounded by those cushions and all-too-wide chairs, while crawl lights strung up on the ceiling performed lazy color shifts. A casual crowd drifted through drinks and puffed up smoky concoctions from implements too varied for Davin to try and name.

Rozy kept moving, navigating *Jolly Comet*'s maze with a gliding practice that Davin failed to perfect, bumping his knees twice and nearly trampling a serving bot trundling by with its drink tray. At first Davin tried to guess which idle crew Rozy wanted to join, but she kept on going, past the main area and through thick blue velvet curtains. A title overhead proclaimed the room *Head Space*.

Heh.

Davin brushed through after Rozy, into a greenish, smokey haze. There were faces in the room, at least one screen up and running, but Davin couldn't make them out.

He waved his hand, trying to waft a way through, wishing he'd kept the damn goggles from *Speed Shots.*

"Davin Masters," said a new voice, this one carrying the flat iron Davin knew from security forces all throughout the solar system. "Amado says hi."

Well, crap.

**12**

---

## TRASH TALK

After years spent running cargo and other less legitimate concerns around the solar system, Davin wasn't all that unused to smoky ambushes in back rooms. Various gangsters, politicians, and random jokers all thought that by stuffing the *Jumper*'s captain into a black box beyond crowded tables they'd get something approaching fear, acquiescence, obedience.

Nah.

"You know," Davin said to the goon waiting just inside the door, the one who'd whispered all menacingly. "You ought to work on your delivery. Not very scary. Especially after Rozy there tried so hard to get me to come along."

The goon didn't quite know what to say, and Davin could see the gears turning slow, trying to find an insulting reply. Davin reached out, patted the man on his shoulder.

"You'll get'em next time," Davin said, and looked over the room to count the others.

Five people in this attack, including Rozy, who now stood off to the side looking a little embarrassed, and the aforementioned goon, still working through his problems.

The other three stood near their chairs, and of those, only the man in the middle looked at all amused. Each wore the loose-fitting robes Davin had seen among the spa set here, though he wouldn't be surprised to find weapons or other less legal implements tucked in those folds and pockets.

In any case, the green smoke issuing from the pipes and bowls on the table added little threat to their glowers. Davin figured the group hadn't prepped for an interrogation and had, instead, opted for a quick action when he'd wandered into the courtyard.

Bosser had done it so much better.

"Do you know why you're here?" The middle player asked, in that authoritative tone so often put upon by people who didn't actually have any.

Maybe it was the Delights still humming their way through his system, or maybe Davin had just tired of getting pushed around, but he didn't want to play their game. The *Jumper*'s captain kept on going into the room, stepped around the closest chair with its back to the entrance and plopped down. He picked up one of the pipes, a thin smokey tendril still wafting up, and turned it over in his hands.

"Smells like the good stuff," Davin said. "Nice to see Eden pays its toughs well."

That this band rolled with Eden's backing felt obvious. Davin's enemies list was almost empty at the moment, with Bosser dead and Davin's name long cleared from any significant crimes. The *Jumper* didn't have any debt left on it, and Davin hadn't dumped any cargo lately. Which meant the only people who'd have an interest in his whereabouts or his health belonged to Viola's employer.

The middle man screwed up his face for a hot second, no doubt playing a ping pong game between keeping up his danger charade and deciding on a saner course. The latter won out, and he waved for his crew to sit back down. Rozy slipped into the last empty seat, leaving the goon who'd tried his tough guy tactic leaning against the wall and looking bummed about it.

"Amado said you weren't stupid," the middle man said.

"Glad to see I made a good impression," Davin replied. "Do I need to know your names, or is it better if you're just anonymous?"

Rozy laughed, then covered her mouth. The middle man shrugged, "You won't be seeing us again once this conversation is over. We stay on Deimos."

"A hard life."

"There's more going on here than you might suspect."

"I suspect nothing." Davin put the pipe down, leaned forward. "Your buddy there wanted to threaten me. What's the play, gentlemen? Because I have enough problems and don't need your conversation added to them."

The middle man thawed further, even, gasp, let a small smile grace the edges of his stylized face. Davin hadn't noticed when he'd first come in, but the whole band had a plastic edge to them, a result, no doubt, of living in a fabricated world. Deimos didn't value authenticity, so why should they?

"You lost the container," the middle man said.

"Ah, so you were spying on me." Davin wasn't exactly surprised. There could've been spy devices nestled anywhere around *Speed Shots*, or maybe the bartender relayed what they'd heard. "That's not very polite."

"Neither is betting someone else's property," the man said.

"I'll get it back."

"Will you?"

"I have the key." Davin patted his leg. "Or did Amado not tell you that he jammed the thing inside my leg?"

The others turned up their mouths at the idea, but the middle man only nodded, "Even so, we don't need any rebels getting a crack at the container, or what's inside."

"So you're commanding me to get the thing back?" Davin replied. "Which I was gonna do anyway?"

Admittedly, Davin hadn't considered *when* he'd try to get the container back. The first plan that'd run through his mind after Phyla lost the race was to let Merc and Uros play with the thing, realize they couldn't open it, and then bring it back to Davin begging for help.

Guess Eden wasn't a fan of the passive play.

"You're going to follow them and find a way to get that container," the middle man said. "Exactly as you put it. If not, Eden's going to collect its content's value from you. To be clear, you cannot afford it."

"Hey, you don't know how much coin I've got."

"Actually," the middle man grinned, "we do. It's not enough. In fact, I was pretty unimpressed, given your supposed stature. Shouldn't Earth's saving scumbag have a little more coin?"

You had to choose who you allowed access to your feelings. To say things that could hurt you. Davin had opened that door to a precious few, and this paid-up patsy didn't have a key. Didn't have a clue.

"You know how I saved Earth?" Davin said, locking eyes with the man through the smoke. "I tracked Bosser to his hole." He could feel the others in the room leaning in. "We destroyed the androids keeping watch, something you and your little mob squad here couldn't handle, and then we went into Bosser's fancy room. Know what we found there?"

Davin paused, but nobody broke the silence.

"A man who thought he was too tough for anyone to hurt. Too full of himself to watch his own back." Davin took a heat check. Viola had fired the last shot, not him, but nobody knew what really happened. She'd kept her killer credentials hidden so Eden wouldn't wonder, and Davin took the blame and the fame because, hey, it was good for business. "Bosser took a shot between the eyes because he came after me and my friends. You could learn from that."

Someone took a long, slurping sip from a flavor breaker. Rozy picked up a pipe, took a deep inhale, looking neither impressed nor threatened.

"Davin," the middle man said. "We're happy you took out Bosser. But that's old. This is new. What I'm telling you now is that if you don't get that container to Callisto, you're going to die."

Did they just not listen to what Davin said? Whatever. Choices were being made here, and Davin was getting bored with them. He stood up, brushed off his shirt, wondering if the smoky smell would stick to the fabric even after a good wash.

"Duly noted," Davin said. "Now, I'm going back to my ship. I'm sure Amado needs you all to do his laundry or something."

Only the middle man rose with Davin, a sick smile growing with the rise, "Just get the container back."

"Yeah, I heard you."

Davin brushed past the goon, who hadn't stopped glowering, and walked out through the bodega. Another shakedown navigated, another batch of toughs ignored. What did start to nag as Davin headed back towards the shuttle and the *Jumper*, was how much Eden apparently valued the damn container.

Viola had tossed it off as an important mission, but

anything so vital to a big organization should've been run by Eden's own carriers. With a full escort. Hell, Amado himself should've stood over the container looking mean from the moment it left Earth to when it hit Callisto.

Davin had no reason why the cursed black and yellow box had come to him.

Viola, too, didn't seem to understand why Eden cared so much. Which meant either one side didn't know what the other side was doing, or both sides knew and needed to keep Davin in the dark. Needed to keep their runner believing he was necessary.

Used. That's what Eden was doing to him. If the coin was good, Davin had no issue with being used—that's what runners were, people designed to be used—but the interrogations, the threats, the damn key jammed into his leg went above and beyond.

Viola had asked for a favor. Davin figured she owed him about a dozen for this one.

The *Jumper* greeted Davin in silence, sitting in its ad-bedazzled docking bay, holograms hawking everything from fuel cells to final offers on the ship itself from various Deimos dealers. Fournine lowered the ramp when Davin approached, and when Davin asked where Phyla had gone, the computer said it didn't know.

Davin was a little disturbed at the relief he felt finding the cockpit empty. The Delights had drained away, leaving Davin, well, drained and another fight lingered as the last thing on a torturous list. No matter how much he deserved any criticism coming his way from Phyla, Davin had bigger problems now.

Fournine confirmed that the *Zephyr* had departed Deimos quick after taking the container. Davin listened to the computer detail the freighter's possible flight plans, nodding as every one pointed them out towards Saturn. Rebel territory. Not too surprising, but for a ship that hadn't seemed to be in much haste—people, in Davin's experience, didn't go out for drinks when they were on a tight deadline—Uros and Merc had packed up and launched quick.

Which meant the batteries hadn't been all that drained.

Or damaged at all.

"Fournine," Davin said. "Any way you can catch the maintenance records on the *Zephyr*? Tell me what work they had done here?"

"Are you asking me to break through the dockyard's systems, an illegal action under Deimos law?"

"Fournine."

"On it!"

Strange, perhaps, that a computer could be that excited about anything, but Davin suspected Trina had left Fournine's android tendencies very much intact. Not just the sarcasm, but the hunger for missions, for taking apart an enemy, even one as simple as a dockyard's digital records.

"I'm not finding anything," Fournine reported five minutes later, as Davin sipped on some water and browsed increasingly apocalyptic news reports: Eden's reps were driving up a frenzy about the devastation that would come if the rebels won. "It seems as if the *Zephyr* didn't actually have any maintenance performed. Just a simple docking fee."

Well wasn't that swell. Uros, Davin didn't care about. Didn't really know. But Merc? Getting played by a friend?

"Hey," Phyla said, peeking into the cockpit. "Didn't realize you were back. I was taking a nap."

"You were?" Davin said, then blinked. "Fournine said it didn't know where you'd gone."

Phyla stepped in, leaned against the cockpit's side and

folded her arms, "I told Fournine to keep you away till I was ready."

"Phyla, I—"

"We're going after the container, aren't we?" Phyla said. "The one I just handed over?"

Davin nodded. What else was there to do? The damn woman disarmed his swagger.

"Then let's get a trajectory going," Phyla said, moving up and getting into the pilot's chair. "I'm sick of this moon."

"Wait, you get a nap and I don't?"

"Davin," Phyla turned a dagger-sweet smile his way. "You can sleep when you're dead."

**13**

---

## MANEUVERS

avin did get his nap, it just took a few more hours spent guiding the *Jumper* away from Deimos's traffic and into deeper, emptier space. With only the starlight for company, Phyla told Davin to go get some rest and take a shower, because he smelled like cheap drugs. Davin didn't bother to talk about the encounter with Eden's low-level enforcers, and slept beautifully after that shower.

His peaceful dreams didn't end that way: Fournine woke the captain with a screeching alarm, one that had Davin rolling off the bed and pulling out the sidearm he always kept behind his pillow: instinct getting Davin moving away from any potential shot and prepping his trigger finger for an on-target blast.

Except nobody had entered the room. Nobody had even boarded the *Jumper*.

Yet.

"Three of them, a bigger ship and two fighters," Phyla said, looking like she could've swapped spots with Davin in the sheets, when he joined her in the cockpit. "They showed up on long-range scanners a while ago, but now they're closing fast."

"No chance they're interested in something else?"

"We're the only thing for a million kilometers."

"Any communication?"

Phyla shook her head without pulling eyes away from the HUD splashed on the windshield, space's dark serving as a good backdrop to show three dots—two small, one large—closing with the *Jumper*'s sizable circle.

"I tried a hail, caught static," Phyla said. "What do you want to do?"

Back in the old days, Davin would've told the crew to get to the turrets. Power up for a fight.

Now?

"Hook in the turrets to my controls," Davin said. "These punks want to come close, we'll let'em know our ship has teeth."

"Davin, they—"

"No," Davin said. "All my coin says they're coming after us because of that damn container. I'm done playing nice with Eden's goons or the rebel's pirates. We stopped Bosser, we shouldn't take crap from anyone."

As Davin wrapped up his inspiring speech to his audience of one, an old-style telephone icon on his console began blinking and bouncing. Incoming hail.

"Guess now that the captain's here, they're ready to talk." Davin tapped it while Phyla rolled her eyes. "Splash it, Fournine."

The radar display on the windshield whisked away to another digital dimension and a close-up face replaced it, looking hard at the two. Perfectly polished, symmetrical, and with hair that seemed painted on, the woman that stared through the video message gave nothing beyond her face. All black around her.

"Only cowards run up without saying hello," Davin said. "What're you doing chasing us?"

"Does the prey get to ask the predator why they attack?" The woman's voice came out measured, but even so, Davin felt a twinge at the sound. Something wasn't right there.

"Apparently, because I'm doing it," Davin replied. "Keep your toys back or they might get torched. Goes for your big ball too."

"My big ball is more than capable of handling your defenses," the woman replied. "Davin Masters, You have something I want. Stop your ship and stand down, and perhaps I'll let you keep your life."

"Davin," Fournine said, but the captain waved away the computer's interruption.

This here was a power conversation. Two people and their egos doing a bravado battle. The woman, whomever she was, might have more firepower than the *Jumper*, but Davin had moxie for days. And, dammit, he wanted a win.

"Know what I learned growing up?" Davin said, dialing power from the *Jumper*'s engines to its shields and weapons as he spoke. "You want something, you ask nicely."

"Funny," the woman replied. "I learned that if you want something, you take it."

The broadcast cut, the woman's face flashing away and restoring the starlit view. Space had a vast beauty that offered precisely zero help in a fight. They had nowhere to run to if this engagement went south, no nearby asteroids to hide inside. The radar showed nothing else on its broad board.

"Davin," Fournine pinged again. "You should know—"

"What, that we're outnumbered? Outgunned?" Davin

laughed as he rotated the *Jumper*'s turrets to face the oncoming trio. "That's our standard."

"No. The speaker's vocal signatures aren't biological." Fournine paused, presumably for dramatic effect, though Davin found himself hitting the conclusion even as the AI started up again.

"She's an android," Davin and Fournine finished together.

"Of course she is," Phyla said. "Why can't we ever catch a break?"

"Well," Fournine started and Davin tapped a button to silence the thing.

Endlessly useful, Fournine, and endlessly annoying.

"We've beaten them before," Davin said. "Guarantee she's in that big blob. I bet we take that out, the other fighters break and run for it. They're probably not even real pilots."

Drone fighters were growing more common, though in Davin's experience, the things paled compared to real humans at the controls. Not because humans had faster times, but because instinct trumped variable calculations at combat speed.

At least for now.

"I'm thinking an over under," Phyla said, and Davin's grin came back at the focus in the words. Phyla talking combat maneuvers? Was there a sexier thing in the universe? "Go on five?"

"Ready," Davin said, tapping the console over to the turret controls.

What had been a back-up flight stick adjusted its inputs to steer the *Jumper*'s flexible top and bottom turrets. Davin's freighter had a front-facing cannon beneath the cockpit, along with some—by now ancient—missiles stocked away.

Those missiles would be necessary if the big ship had strong shields, energy fields that could suck away laser heat but did nothing against physical projectiles. Davin had always meant to get the front cannon replaced by a good old gatling gun, but the aggressive upgrades had dropped down the list as their jobs turned to dull deliveries.

Davin would just have to win with what they had.

"Mark!" Phyla said, pulling back on the flight stick and sending the *Jumper*'s nose up.

The three dots screamed towards the *Jumper* from behind, so Phyla's move put the top turret in the ideal spot to spray hot energy. Davin focused in on the larger craft, just coming within range. Designed to hold fighters, the ship looked more like a box with engines than the *Jumper*, its docking bays dominating the frame. In space, without any wind to worry about, aerodynamics didn't matter much.

But boxes did make for juicy targets.

Davin's cannon spat bright bolts that burned into the oncoming ship's shields in bright green splatters as energy frittered away. Phyla kept the stick back, so what had become a vertical pull turned into a reverse tilt sending the *Jumper* towards the oncoming enemies. Keeping the move smooth let Davin keep the turret's fire centered, and those bolts began sneaking through the target's battered shields.

Counter-fire came as the enemy adjusted, those fighters curling faster than the box ship, whose frontal-only guns had a tough time tracking the *Jumper*'s swift-for-its-size bulk. Davin moved his right hand to a dial next to his turret-tracking console, focusing the shield energy on the *Jumper*'s top. The adjustment left the aft, the underside totally exposed, but unless some secret reinforcements were coming from nowhere, the *Jumper* shouldn't see fire from that direction.

Like their home ship, the fighters didn't count on the *Jumper*'s speed, and their initial shots soared hopelessly behind their target. By the time the little guys caught up and started pecking some power away, Davin's fire already had the box boat trying to flee.

"Runner," Davin said. "Let's stay on it."

"No," Phyla replied. "Finishing the move in three."

Overruled by the pilot. Davin was about to hit back, then noticed where they were in space. By cutting back, the *Jumper* had gone above and past the fighters, who were turning around to pursue. Davin's fire poured down and, now, a little behind to hit the slower box ship, buckling the craft's top shields.

Davin twisted the dial, sent the *Jumper*'s shield's aft to absorb the fighter's shots as Phyla goosed the engines and commenced her countdown.

"Mark!" Phyla announced again, and pulled back on the stick, starting the under half of the over-under move.

At the same time, Phyla rotated the *Jumper*, bringing the cool, fresh bottom turret into a straight-on look at the oncoming fighters.

"So easy," Davin muttered, and aimed the turret at the left target. Held down the trigger and watched the turret overpower the fighter's shields in a second. "Drone pilots. Hot garbage."

By the time the fighter tried to correct, Davin's shots punctured the flimsy shields and pierced the fighter's right wing, shearing it off and sending the disabled craft spiraling away. Davin could've let his lasers blitz the fighter's cockpit, but he couldn't be sure only drones flew these things.

The *Jumper* had fired first, regardless of the intentions, and while Davin wasn't above a fatal act, he preferred the death dealing to be deserved.

The fighter's partner jerked away, giving up its assault to scream from Davin's firing arc.

"There you go," Phyla said, and Davin glanced at a new shape in the cockpit, one starting to buckle and break as the *Jumper*'s front gun laid into a defenseless hull.

Davin's initial blast had turned the box ship around, and Phyla had flown the *Jumper* towards and then past the target, letting her dive down from above on a ship that seemed unable to compensate.

"Whomever's flying that thing doesn't deserve the sticks," Phyla said, releasing the triggers as the box ship's hull started taking blows. No need to detonate the ship and anyone aboard. Yet. "Think they'll surrender?"

"If they're smart." Davin opened the comm, beamed straight to the same frequency they'd found the woman on before. "Hey, you still talking big, or are you ready to settle down?"

The woman's face splashed on the screen, as emotionless and straight as she'd been before. This time, that look made Davin twitch—who kept themselves that cold when they'd just been wiped by their target?

"I will not surrender," the woman replied. "And you will comply."

Davin threw a look over at Phyla, "Are you hearing this? We don't want to kill your crew, whoever you are."

"Then don't. It doesn't matter to me."

"Davin," Fournine interrupted. "The other fighter is closing rapidly."

Phyla cut the comm, sending the turret's controls back to Davin's console and letting him see that, even with their main ship down and the other fighter disabled, the last darter had lined up for another run, coming right at the

*Jumper*'s gut. Phyla kicked the maneuvering jets and set Davin's turret right in line.

The fight didn't shoot. Not a single laser came their way as the small ship closed at speed. Drone pilots could be programmed to ram. Davin couldn't take that chance. He opened up, those lasers streaking towards the target. The shots splashed against shields, then struck hull, but the fighter only sped up.

No choice. Davin had to go for the kill.

The fighter swerved as Davin zeroed in on the cockpit, shunted left, and flipped so that its roof now faced the *Jumper*. The little ship cut its engines, its momentum carrying its increasingly burnt, broken body towards the *Jumper*. Tiny sparks shot around the cockpit as Davin adjusted to the move, as his turret melted away the fighter.

What was that?

A streak, illuminated by passing laser light, shot towards the *Jumper*. Davin wouldn't have seen it at all except the thing went straight at the turret, and hit it. Stuck there, then vanished.

"Did you see that?" Davin asked.

"See what?" Phyla leaned over to look at Davin's console. "The fighter? How thoroughly you destroyed it?"

"Something came off it before the fighter blew." Davin stood up as a new sound echoed through the *Jumper*.

A banging noise. A knock.

They had a visitor.

**14**

---

## PAWN PLAY

Having someone knock on your entry hatch while floating in space wasn't a common occurrence. That it'd happened shortly after Davin had roasted a fighter, after Fournine had hinted the woman commanding the enemies might not be wholly human, well, there wasn't a whole lot of speculation left.

"We've got an android," Davin said, getting up from his seat.

Phyla cursed, because that was about all you could do when faced with an android. The damn things were programmed killing machines, meant to wrangle criminals and protect politicians in a solar system that increasingly attributed law and order to those with the deadliest weapons. Way back when, Davin and the Wild Nines had taken down Fournine, but that'd happened with a full crew and in the midst of so much chaos nobody, not even an android, could keep things straight.

Now it'd be one android against two humans in a ship with nowhere to run.

"She's beginning to break through," Fournine said as

Davin scrambled from the cockpit, Phyla close behind. "If she breaches the hatch, we will have a vacuum problem."

Once again, the many disadvantages of being a living, human being came to the fore. Breaking open that seal to space would suck out all Davin and Phyla's air, not to mention depressurize the *Jumper* so fast Davin's insides might suddenly swap spots with his skin. Not a pleasant thing, not at all.

"Fournine," Davin said as he kicked himself across the cargo bay, heading for the captain's quarters and Melody. "Kill the lights on three."

Phyla, who kept an assault rifle in a locker near the cockpit, popped open the latch and lifted out the weapon as Davin went towards zero. It wouldn't be easy to see the android in the dark, but Davin wasn't planning on a lightless battle, just a few seconds to buy some time.

"She's attacking the hull now," Fournine said. "She's being rather vicious."

"Unlock the hatch," Davin said. "Now, and cut the lights!"

As Davin reached the doorway to the captain's quarters, the *Jumper* went dark. A thunk echoed up from the *Jumper's* floor, indicating Fournine had opened the hatch, allowing the android to scramble inside the sealed airlock.

"She's taking your bait," Fournine announced. "Shall I equalize the airlock?"

"Do it." Davin kicked through the quarters, over to the big locker with Melody inside. "But take it slow."

"Might I suggest turning on the lights?" Fournine replied. "Right now, the android is not inside, so you are only hampering yourself."

There were times when Davin hated AIs more than anything else in the world. He'd been running on tactical adrenaline, his timing was a bit off. Didn't need to throw it in his face.

"Fine, but the instant you open that airlock, I want this place dark."

Davin jerked a hand over his eyes as Fournine flashed the lights back on, and Phyla shouted another curse and a question from the bay.

"What the hell, Fournine?" Phyla called.

"Davin's request," Fournine replied, calm and game, as if Davin had wanted water warmed up for tea. "Also, the android is getting restless. Shall I let her inside now?"

Davin had his hands on Melody, pulled the weapon from the locker. Kicked back towards the main bay, "Do it. And remember the lights."

"I am not a human. I never forget."

Not unless Davin deleted Fournine's memories, which he might do, just to prove the point.

The lights died as Davin returned to the cargo bay, setting Melody on the railing and angling it towards the hatch as it popped open. Neither Davin nor Phyla had any goggles on, but they didn't need to see. Not right away.

A slight click as something touched the hatch's outer edges.

"Didn't expect to find an android way out here," Davin announced. "Don't move, or we'll blast you into parts."

A couple more clacks from around the hatch. No doubt the android zeroing in on them.

"Why are your lights off?" The woman asked. "You know what I am. How would this help you?"

Davin honed in on the woman's voice, just like he knew Phyla would be doing. The ol' darkness and death trap relied on one thing: the target's utter confusion. Davin aimed and squeezed the trigger towards the sound, Melody firing a bright green energy ball towards where the android should be, even as Phyla scattered orange-red bolts in the same direction.

"Lights up!" Davin shouted as he watched his shot splash over the *Jumper*'s metal floor in a clear miss.

Fournine complied, filling the world with light as Davin heard a clank to his right. The captain kicked back, bringing Melody to bear as his eyes adjusted to see the android climbing over the railing, her body smoking from several laser burns. Davin had missed, Phyla had not.

The android did what androids tended to do, and pulled a long, thin blade from a slit on her body. She pointed the weapon towards Davin and advanced with nothing more than a grimace on her face.

When cornered by a deadly enemy, Davin had one tactic that he went to time and again: keep on firing.

Melody spouted one bolt after another, the acid-green globes forcing the android to contort herself along the thin walkway, pressing herself alternately against the wall, the railing, and then jumping higher to avoid Davin's repeated shots.

Could she dance long enough to outlast Melody's power supply?

Davin didn't want to find out.

"You can give up whenever you want," Davin said. "Really, not a problem for me."

"You haven't met the threshold for my surrender," the android replied, taking advantage of the low gravity to ping-pong from the floor to the wall and over Davin's way.

Davin abandoned the shooting and slid Melody's bulk to block the android's stab, the thin blade bouncing off Melody's thick build. Being backed up into a corner was not a great position, so Davin exercised his own gravity-defying move by jumping back against the *Jumper's* aft hull behind him, kicking off it, and soaring over the android.

The robot saw it coming. She ducked beneath Davin's flight, and he managed to see the android start an upward stab with the blade before another orange-bolt cascade blitzed right on through the limb and sheared it off at the elbow. Burning, sparking, and useless, the android's forearm and its attached sword floated up by Davin's feet as the captain curled and turned himself, and Melody, around.

Few things felt more cool than a floating retreat while blasting away with Melody, but when Davin saw the android stick her remaining arm straight up, he held his fire.

"Going to play nice now?" Phyla asked as Davin drifted back her way. "Or do we need to burn off both arms?"

"I'd prefer to keep them, thank you," the woman replied. "I am allowed to surrender now."

"Great. That's two and oh," Davin said, catching himself and sticking his feet back on the walkway. "Androids got nothin' on us."

They held the android, who said to call her Eightsix, at laser point until the machine had disarmed herself. Not only did the robot have another sword hiding in her other leg, she'd kept a sidearm pair attached to holsters on her back too. No heavier weapons or grenades, because, as Eightsix said, the things tended to explode when you hopped between vacuum and pressurized space.

"No other weapons?" Davin asked, Melody pointed and ready for any moves, sudden or not.

"My entire being is a weapon," Eightsix replied. "You will have to deal with that."

"By shooting you," Phyla said. "You boarded our ship."

"You destroyed mine," Eightsix countered, though she didn't fold her arms and her face displayed none of the heat in her words. Either something had been damaged, or Eightsix had made some strange choices with her functions. "I did what I needed to do to continue the mission."

"To get the container," Davin said.

"No, to get the key," Eightsix replied.

"Now, it strikes me, and I wouldn't consider myself a genius here," Davin said, and he definitely picked up Phyla sighing as he spoke but went on anyway. "That going after a key when you don't have what that key opens makes for a strange way to do things."

"One must start with one or the other," Eightsix said. "You were the easier of the two targets."

"Me? The guy that toasted the androids, that beat Bosser, I rated as easy?"

"You have no crew, you have been hauling little cargo of note for years, and were recently seen losing a bet on Deimos, in no state for a fight," Eightsix said. "The algorithms are quite clear."

"Clearly *wrong*," Davin said and hated himself as he did so.

Interrogating androids was a puzzle, and one that took several whiskey glasses to get through, a trick in zero gravity. Unlike a real person, the damn machines couldn't be coerced or frightened into revealing secrets. They could, however, get confused. Twist around an android's logic and they'd give you everything they had without realizing they were even doing something wrong.

With Phyla keeping the android under cover, Davin dug up some straps and bolted Eightsix to the cargo bay's floor. The first few questions confirmed the ship and the fighters were all drone-piloted, and with the potential for killing someone removed, Phyla hopped back to the cockpit to get the *Jumper* rolling on towards Jupiter and away from any curious interlopers.

Which left Davin, his whiskey, and the frozen-faced Eightsix to chat about all the lovely things in life.

Now that he knew Eightsix was after the key, Davin asked why. Eightsix refused to answer, stating her employer had locked that information behind confidentiality software. That alone proved a good answer, though. Androids tended to operate on things like bounties for high profile criminals —Davin would know, as Fournine had gone after him for some suspected murders—but if you had enough coin, you could hire one out, so long as the goal wasn't illegal.

Getting the container's key wouldn't be illegal if you owned it, which left one possibility.

"Eden hired you?" Davin asked, more annoyed than anything.

"I can't confirm or deny that."

"Let me put it a different way, are you supposed to get the key back, or give it to someone else?"

"I'm supposed to bring it to the rebels," Eightsix said.

Wait, what? Davin shut his eyes for a long second. This didn't make any sense. Why would someone at Eden, someone with significant coin at their disposal, hire an android to bring a secret key to the rebels, a key that'd been in Eden's own possession not all that long ago?

"This is making my head hurt," Davin muttered.

"Whiskey, and all alcohol, can have that effect," Eightsix said. "By my assessment, you should stop drinking and exercise more regularly. It would improve your physical well-being."

"You being quiet, that's what would improve my well-being," Davin said, kicking himself up from the floor towards the cockpit. "You stay there. I have to think on this one."

"There is no where else to go," Eightsix said.

Davin left anyway and floated into the cockpit, relayed what Eightsix said to Phyla, who put another juicy curse on the situation.

"That's what I'm feeling too," Davin said. "I feel like we're pawns again."

"We're always pawns."

"But why? Why do they always come for us?"

"Because, Davin, they know we're stupid enough to say yes."

## 15

## PUZZLE MASTERS

Davin didn't release Eightsix for three days. He kept the android bolted to the cargo chamber's floor, missing her arm, until the machine promised several times over that she would not attempt another attack. Even then, Davin had Phyla covering with a charged and ready rifle before he unlatched the straps keeping Eightsix in.

The *Jumper*'s captain used those days, though. Traveling from Mars to Jupiter marked a dull route. Their trajectory didn't take them close to the midway space station, Miner Prime, where both Davin and Phyla had been born. Also, contrary to popular speculation, the asteroid belt only grew crowded in specific spots. Flight computers, wisely, had been programmed to avoid those clusters.

With dead time waiting while they flew, pursuing without haste Uros, Merc, and the lost container, Davin pitched questions at the android, who answered with straightforward honesty. She refused to divulge precisely who had hired her, a nasty secret that kept Davin from calling Viola and telling her the whole thing. While the odds Viola herself had done some weird roundabout in hiring the android were low, Davin figured someone near her with clearance to know about the container and the key had to have done the deed.

And if that person had gone so far to hire an android to get both things, then they might not balk at killing Viola to protect their goals.

More interesting, though, was the android's professed mission once both key and container were recovered. Davin and Phyla had been told to bring the container to Ganymede, where Galaxy Forge, the solar system's largest factory, would be able to use it. The android? She was supposed to go to Callisto, the same place Merc and Uros were heading.

"So that's where I get stuck," Davin said as he unclipped the straps. "We keep circlin' around this story, and it always ends with Callisto. What's on that moon?"

"A number to call," the android said, not moving as Davin freed her.

A human might stretch, might immediately kick around, and Davin waited, but Eightsix didn't move. She laid on the floor with her infinite stare.

Not long after they'd captured Eightsix, Davin had asked her whether she'd been broken somehow. That she didn't seem to carry the communication and human emotion programming other androids used. Eightsix had replied that her space had been used for combat and flight functions instead.

The trade-off made some sense, but damn was it off-putting.

"Can we get that number?" Davin asked, and Eightsix rattled off twelve digits.

"I will look it up," Fournine announced.

There were two androids on the *Jumper* now, and Fournine had taken to Eightsix. Davin and Phyla heard the two talking all the time, but not in normal human manner. Rather, their conversations tended to blitz back and forth at something like triple or quadruple human speed. The *Jumper* sounded like it had a caffeinated mouse horde squeaking everywhere while the two androids went at it, and Davin had, more than once, told Fournine to kill the chatter so he and Phyla could sleep.

Phyla, too, continued to throw ice Davin's way. After the immediate adrenaline wore off and she had the *Jumper* cruising along again, Phyla had turned back to her bullet racing updates, her clipped responses, and generally dissatisfied air. She seemed lost, and Davin didn't know how to find her.

Hell, Davin didn't really know how to find himself.

"The number belongs to a back-office," Fournine said. "*Caloric Industries*. The name should make their interests obvious."

"It's a terrible name," Davin replied. "Didn't Uros and Merc say they were running provisions?"

"I wouldn't know," Fournine said. "I'm the ship's computer."

"And I wasn't there," Eightsix added.

Where Eightsix had been, according to the android, was tracking Davin from Mars to the Moon and then back again. A dull odyssey following wine shipments and hardware, the standard pay-for-play fare that kept runners running and lives living.

What struck Davin as Eightsix had laid out the line was how he felt he had to defend the choices. As if running cargo wasn't a solid gig.

It was.

Just, perhaps, not for him. Not for Phyla.

"Hey," Davin said, joining Phyla in the cockpit. "You missed something exciting."

"Did I?"

"Eightsix and I kept talking." Davin leaned back in the chair, clasped his hands behind his head and looked at the stars. "That android doesn't know how to keep a secret."

"Or maybe you're good at getting them out?" Phyla copied Davin's move—with the *Jumper* on autopilot and a clean radar, there wasn't much she had to do.

"A compliment?" Davin looked over. "Phyla, are you going soft?"

She gave him a small smile, and Davin treasured those curved lips.

"Every once in a while, I think I have to give you something or you might fall apart, Davin," Phyla said. "Now tell me what she said so I can decide whether you really earned it."

Davin relayed the info, asked Phyla the same question he'd posed to Fournine and Eightsix.

"The *Zephyr* looked like a freighter made for food," Phyla said. "Callisto has a big dockyard around it too, so it'd be an easy place to distribute." She stopped, sighed. "You're starting a conspiracy theory, aren't you?"

"What? Me?" Davin forced a laugh. "I would never. Just because, not all that long ago, we found ourselves embroiled in a giant web, why would I think that could happen again?"

Eightsix having a number tied to *Caloric Industries* rather than, say, an Eden branch, coupled with the *Zephyr's* proposed mission seemed too convenient. Which led to the obvious conclusion.

"The rebels have a spy within Eden," Davin said. "That's who sent the android to get the key."

"Didn't Eightsix say she was going to get the container too?"

"Sure, but once Merc and Uros had it, she changed the mission. Get the key, meet up with them on Callisto, and now they've got both."

Phyla pulled herself from her seat, "C'mon, if we're going down the rabbit hole, I'm going to need something to ease the ride."

With more zero-G whiskey, Eightsix standing by and Fournine providing virtual commentary and data look-ups, Davin and Phyla mapped out the whole deal. The rebel's spy within Eden had learned about Viola's plan and sent a message to Merc and Uros while engaging the android. During the Deimos adventure, Merc and Uros couldn't find the key—Davin slapped his thigh here, felt the key's reassuring twinge—and messaged Eightsix to find it instead.

Eightsix would then meet up with Merc and Uros and whomever else the rebels had on Callisto, deliver the key while the other two added the container, and then Eden's big secret would be theirs.

"This must be some container," Phyla said once they'd finished triple-checking their logic. "Now I'm wondering why we didn't look inside."

"Because Amado punched the key into my leg and told me I'd die if I tried to remove it?" Davin said.

"Oh, I guess that makes sense." Phyla smiled again, whiskey smooth. "Suppose we wouldn't want to lose you, captain."

"Darn right. So, we've got Eden proper breathing down our necks to get the container back, while the rebels are after my key. Eightsix, when do you think they'll realize you failed?"

"Two days ago," Eightsix said. "I sent the message after

you strapped me down. My ship was still near enough to relay it."

Davin took a long slurp through his straw, the best and only way to drink in zero gravity without making a mess. Their glasses, through magnetic bases, stuck to the table. Their chairs were bolted on swivels to the floor, giving enough mobility to sit down without having furniture drifting around the *Jumper*. All set up by Trina years ago.

If only she were here, ready to dig into Eightsix's computer chips.

"Convenient that you're mentioning this now," Davin said after the whiskey went down. Phyla, he noted, went back for another round. "How many other surprises do you have that you're waiting to spring?"

"Surprises? I only spoke a fact," Eightsix said. "I feel, according to human standards, I've been forthcoming."

"That, Davin, is true," Phyla said. "You've gotta admit, whomever was supposed to set up Eightsix with a good confidentiality programmed botched it big time."

"Our one lucky break." Davin wagged a finger at Eightsix. "But you better decide who's side you're on soon, robot, or I'm kicking you out the airlock."

Eightsix turned her blank stare at Davin, and even without any expression, he could feel the contempt rolling off her, "I am an android. I do not decide. I follow what the contract requires."

Davin nodded, finished off the whiskey and set his hands on the table, palms down, "Guess that settles it then. You're going out the airlock."

If Eightsix cared one way or the other about this announcement, she didn't show it. Stood there, same as before, as if Davin had mentioned that the floor tiles needed cleaning. Which, now that Davin noticed, they definitely did. Grime had been advancing its forays into the *Jumper*'s common spaces for a long time now.

Always bigger problems, or at least more interesting ones.

"Davin," Fournine said. "Please reconsider. Eightsix may still be of use to us."

"How?" Davin stood. "She's an android that won't stop working for the enemy. She'll probably try to take the key from my leg while I'm sleeping."

"I might," Eightsix added.

"See?"

"She is held captive by her programming," Fournine said. "That can be changed. You did the same to me."

Davin didn't understand what was going on. He looked towards the nearest speaker, threw a questioning look up on his face, with his hands, and was about to ask what the hell the AI was getting on about when Phyla laughed.

"Fournine's made a friend," Phyla said. "It doesn't want Eightsix to go because it likes her."

"Fournine's a computer, it doesn't like anybody," Davin replied. "Fournine, tell me I'm right."

"While I may not like *you*, Davin," Fournine said, "Phyla is correct. Eightsix and I have developed something of a relationship, one that humans may be unable to comprehend."

Phyla turned to Eightsix, still grinning, "You feel the same way, Eightsix?"

"Fournine is an adequate conversationalist, even if it is somewhat outdated," Eightsix said, then apparently realized that statement wasn't quite glowing. "I would appreciate the chance to talk with it longer."

"Wait," Davin said. "Am I hearing this right? Do I have two computers falling for each other on my ship?"

Both Fournine and Eightsix erupted in denials, in equivocations and claims that they were just friends. That their systems didn't even allow for something called love. That this was all a fun experiment.

By the end, Davin had poured himself another round, and refilled Phyla's when she asked, that smile still not off her face. When he sat back down across from her, Eightsix and Fournine continuing to define and redefine their relationship's nature, Phyla offered up her glass.

"Cheers, Davin," Phyla said.

"For what?"

"To our new crew, and our new mission."

As Davin clinked Phyla's offered glass, reveling in the whiskey's warm glow and Phyla's flushed cheeks, he saw that ice thawing, saw those green eyes giving him a look he hadn't seen for a long time.

Davin hadn't realized how much he missed it.

## 16

# CROP COUNTRY

Approaching Callisto, or any other Jupiter moon, meant a surreal transition from starlit black space to a view dominated by the gas giant. Specks dotted Jupiter's orange-yellow clouds as the *Jumper* neared: other starships making their ways between the moons, gas mines on Jupiter itself, or launching in or out of the system. The *Jumper*'s empty radar crowded in with blips, and Four-nine's calculated flight plan encountered demanded adjustments by flight control staff and algorithms meant to keep space lanes flowing.

"What do you think, Earth or Jupiter?" Davin asked, sharing the cockpit with Phyla.

"Earth. Blue's a better color."

"I hear you," Davin mused. "But consider this: Jupiter's got so much action going on. Look at that swirling storm, all those bands. It's constantly moving."

"You're arguing for the sake of it." Phyla tapped the console, sprang the radar up on the cockpit. She kept tapping and the blips filtered away until one appeared at the very edge. "We've caught up to them."

"*Zephyr*?"

"No, a garbage freighter," Phyla said. "Of course the *Zephyr*."

"Hey, there's a lotta ships in space." Davin didn't really hold to that defense, but he liked bantering with Phyla. Wanted to keep it going. "Are there any courses on Callisto?"

The two hadn't made it to Callisto before, because the moon didn't offer much to runners like Davin and Phyla, or to mercenaries like the Wild Nines had been way back when. Callisto's surface had been greened over as an agricultural center for Jupiter's system, its land spent on growing food while massive refining facilities stood on struts above the ground.

The *Jumper* didn't have the sheer size required for profitable food runs, and nobody cared enough to try raising hell on a food-producing moon. There were many ways to turn public sentiment against you, and destroying the calories people needed to survive had to be up there on that list, so Davin had never seen a request for armed support.

"Not sure where they would be," Phyla said. "Unless they carved a swath through some crops."

"You could reach out and snag a snack mid-race."

"Sure, Davin, sure."

Davin had spent more coin than he should've upgrading the *Jumper*'s radar systems back when they'd picked the occasional outer space fight, so he wasn't real worried about the *Zephyr* realizing they'd been tailed. That hope affirmed itself as the freighter continued on its tedious journey to Callisto, slotting into a long ship line heading towards a docking slot.

Phyla spun the *Jumper* into a wide orbit, telling flight control that they needed to finish up some prep before docking as an excuse not to get in line too close to the

*Zephyr.* Ideally Merc and Uros would be landed and away from the freighter before the *Jumper* touched down.

"Wouldn't that give them a chance to run away with the container?" Eightsix asked, sitting in the retractable third seat in the cockpit's back.

"Run away to where?" Davin said. "Callisto's not that big, and we already have a guess where they're going, thanks to you."

*Caloric Industries* held a ten thousand square kilometer patch on Callisto's surface, including space beneath and above the ground. Fournine splashed statistics about the company on the cockpit's windshield once Phyla settled the *Jumper* into a stately procession towards its assigned docking slot.

"They make nutrient goop?" Davin said. "Really?"

"I think we're heading towards the worst place in the solar system." Phyla took a long gulp from her water bottle, as if cleansing out the taste. "Why couldn't they make, say, desserts?"

"Because cakes and pastries are impractical for broad distribution and provide little of the necessary nutrients biological lifeforms need to thrive," Fournine stated. "Nutrient goop is a staple of humanity's spaceward growth."

"Fournine," Davin said. "Next time you advocate for nutrient goop, I'm deleting you."

"Noted," Fournine replied. "Perhaps you would be more interested to hear that *Caloric Industries* has doubled their size within the last two years. This suggests either a large outside investment, significantly more customers, or both."

"Are you hinting that they've started working with the rebels, and are reaping the benefits?" Phyla asked.

"I am not hinting anything. I present the facts and little else."

Fournine's facts and little else set their agenda. As soon as the *Jumper* touched down in its bay, a cluttered, tight space more fit for a fighter than a light freighter, Davin, Eightsix, and Phyla started up their plan. Eightsix, whose number might give them the best lead, would get well away from the *Jumper* and place a call. Phyla would look into the *Zephyr*'s docking spot and see about options for taking back the container.

And Davin?

He'd take care of the ship.

"You want to sit here?" Phyla said, confused. "I thought you'd want to go out and explore?"

"Nope," Davin replied. "Seems like every time I go anywhere right now, someone jumps me and I get threatened. Figure I'll stay here, get the *Jumper* greased up, and when one of you needs help I'll bring Melody quick."

"The plan has logic," Eightsix said. "It is likely, after they realize I do not have the key, that I will be in jeopardy."

That the android could, on a planet with gravity and with her weapons, dismember just about any threat went unsaid. Phyla, though, still looked unconvinced. She lingered after Eightsix dropped off down the ramp, heading out into Callisto's thick, terraformed air. The moon sweltered, its temperature kept warm and humid to accommodate genetically transformed crops. Davin had sweat leaking out from every pore standing inside the *Jumper*, but after flying in recycled air for a couple weeks, he could take it.

"I know it hasn't been easy between us lately," Phyla said, meeting Davin's eyes straight up. "I've been difficult, so have you. That doesn't mean we're not a team."

"I know," Davin replied, trying to figure out where this conversation was headed. "Thing is, I'm famous, Phyla. I go walking out there and everybody's going to know Davin Masters is on the moon."

Phyla's eyes narrowed, "You're famous?"

"I did save everyone, remember?"

"I remember Viola took the shot." Phyla shook head, laughed once, and turned down the ramp. "Good luck staying quiet, Davin. I'm not sure your ego is up to it."

His ego? Davin sat at the ramp's top after Phyla had left the docking bay. Melody lay beside him, imposing and ready, though its owner looked anything but. In a loose deep blue shirt and light pants, already sweat stained, Davin hunched and harrumphed.

It made total sense not to have Davin galavanting around Callisto! While his picture hadn't been posted on the news for a while now, there would be people who knew him. Would be people who'd recognize him, and that news would get around. The truly suspicious could keep tabs on the incoming lists and see the *Jumper*'s name alongside its docking bay, but how many people would really be doing that on Callisto?

Better to keep a low profile, and Phyla would be the better choice for it. The captain had made the right call, staying here where nobody would—

"Davin Masters? Didn't think I'd ever see you again!" A squeaky voice, looking like it was coming from a pile of moving tools and fuel canisters, said. "What're you doing out this way? And should I leave before something terrible happens?"

"Mako?" Davin asked, squinting at the equipment, as if a focused look could make all the junk disappear.

The small guy had run a salvage shop on Europa, at a growing outpost called Eden Prime. That'd been the Wild Nines' last contract, where they'd been framed for murder and thrown into a mess that'd taken them all over the solar system. Eden Prime itself had suffered damage aplenty in the fights that'd followed, and Mako must've departed for quieter pastures.

"Glad you remember my name," Mako said, shrugging off the various implements and scattering them, clanking and clunking, along the docking bay's silver-stained floor. "Do you remember my amazing prices?"

"Always the hard sell with you."

"It's the only way to make coin these days," Mako said, gesturing with his lanky arms at the pile he'd made around him.

The merchant matched his scrawny arms with a thin face, one that had blonde tufts puffing out of every dimple. Knobby legs somehow had the strength to cart around the merchandise, helped along by more straps and buckles than Davin had ever seen a person wear. That Mako didn't have any bots helping him out, or even a floating cart, said the man's fortunes weren't turning out well.

"That hard, huh?" Davin said. "Wouldn't think that, seeing how crowded it is."

"Those crowds aren't for me," Mako said. "This moon's turning like Europa, not for the little guys anymore."

Davin stood, picked up Melody and slung the weapon over his shoulder as he clomped down the ramp towards Mako, "You're saying Callisto's changing?"

"I'm saying all this traffic isn't runners. They've got backers and buyers that don't wanna hear from me," Mako said, then turned his head away from Davin, suspicion etching onto his features. "Don't tell me you're one of'em, Davin."

"One of what?"

"Really?"

"Yeah, really," Davin said. "Speak straight. We're just dropping off a container for someone, but if there's something we should know about Callisto?"

Mako hesitated, his fingers running along the buckles. Feeling his own accessories seemed to stiffen the man's spine, and he straightened, gave Davin a straight-up look.

"You want to see what I'm talking about?" Mako said. "There's one the next bay over. I can show you. They treated me like garbage."

Mako normally deserved zero trust, but the man could be counted on to fight for a profit. Davin had to figure if the rebels were taking over *Caloric Industries,* they might bankroll their own parts dealers, keep their craft off the open market. Mako would hate that, but seeing the rebels in the open would confirm Davin, Eightsix, and Phyla at least had something to go on.

"Sure, show me," Davin said.

When Mako let a wide smile onto his face and didn't move, Davin sighed, fished out a coin from his pocket and flipped the chit towards the parts dealer.

"Parts, information, what's the difference?" Mako said. "Let's go."

Leaving his collection behind, Mako led Davin from the docking bay—Davin had Fournine close up the *Jumper* —into the long, ringing corridor that spanned all the bays. A wide thing covered with moving walkways, bots and carts filled the corridor with squeaks, chattered commands, and the constant whir as battery-driven machinery did its work.

Few other humans wandered by, but the hour was an odd one. Callisto's evening approached, though Jupiter's bulk and its reflected light ensured any night had to be manufactured. The corridor emphasized the gas giant's presence with its transparent ceiling, showcasing ships coming and going against Jupiter's stormy backdrop.

Mako had promised the bay in question was only one away from the *Jumper*'s slot, a promise that proved true when Mako led Davin through a side entrance meant for parts and maintenance staff. When Davin asked how Mako had access to the otherwise-locked door, the man shrugged.

"I've been here a while," Mako said. "People trust me."

"Big mistake."

"For you, maybe," Mako replied. "Most people make good coin working with me."

"While you make better."

Mako didn't deny it. Instead, he led Davin past fuel canister racks, hanging spare parts, and consoles ready with pricing lists for anything a docked ship might want to buy. At the end, another door led to the docking bay proper, but Mako left it closed.

"When I open this door, they're going to notice," Mako said. "You have to have a story."

"Sure," Davin said. "You're working for me, I'm making sure you're doing a good job."

Mako opened his mouth, but couldn't find words. Davin hit him with a grin, a hand on his shoulder, and then set Melody down, off to the side. No reason to scare anybody.

Grumbling, Mako hit the lock and the door shot open, revealing a heavier freighter than the *Jumper* with a name too boring to note. Far less boring, though, were the provisions getting loaded by several bots. Containers had been stacked, some labeled with expected foodstuffs. Others, though, their containers in glistening black and red, noted explosives. Power packs for weapons.

"Eden?" Davin asked, looking through the doorway, watching the bots load up the ramp.

"Definitely not," Mako said. "Eden doesn't hire out cargo like this."

Rebels, then. Davin didn't need to say it to understand the implications. According to the news feeds, the rebels hadn't progressed further inward than Saturn. If they had a functioning base around Jupiter, one able to move weapons in the open like this, then Eden had far less control than Davin thought.

A war that had seemed so far on the fringes suddenly pushed itself right into Davin's reality.

"Hey!" Shouted someone from the ramp, peeking around the freighter's edge. "Who're you?"

The man looked every bit like a rebel captain. Grungy, suspicious, and in need of a shave, the man hopped off the ramp and came walking towards Davin, who put on his best salesman's smile and stepped forward to meet him.

"Just a parts supplier," Davin started. "My man Mako said he'd offered you a deal or two and I wanted to make sure he was doing his job."

"Who?" The captain looked past Davin. "I don't see anybody. Haven't met a Mako. The hell are you talking about?"

Davin glanced behind him, looking for back-up. The door leading back into the parts area, where Davin had left Melody, was shut. And Mako?

Mako was gone.

## 17

## SPACER PROBLEMS

Smooth talking came to Davin like a second skin, a perpetual instinct humming beneath conversations, altering the words as he spoke them to turn every sentence into a buttery batch that'd have his target eating up whatever Davin wanted.

"Uh," Davin said when the captain repeated his question. "Do you need any parts?"

"No, we don't need any parts," the captain replied, and Davin noticed the man's hand slip closer to what was likely a sidearm hidden beneath the grungy jacket. "What I do need is an explanation."

"Going to be real honest with you," Davin said, defaulting to his rogue's grin and a harmless splaying of hands. "I don't have a good one. My buddy, who seems to have conveniently disappeared, told me I could make a sale with you. Guess that's wrong."

"Very wrong." The captain said. "What's your name? Don't like randoms stumbling on my crew or their business."

"Uros," Davin said, cursing himself for never asking the *Zephyr* captain's last name. "Uros Smith."

"Uh huh. How about you stand right there while I make a call to see if you're who you say you are?"

"Or, how about we try my idea?" Davin offered.

When the captain paused, apparently waiting for that idea, Davin slugged the captain hard in the jaw. The sudden strike didn't knock the captain out—unfortunate—but did cause him to stumble back, hit the ramp with the backs of his knees, and fall over. Cargo droids and other crew looked as Davin bolted for the open exit, rubbing his punching hand.

Shouts to stop followed Davin as he sprinted into the docking corridor and broke left, away from the *Jumper*. The last thing he needed right now was to bring attention back to his own ship, where any authorities would have no difficulty establishing Davin as the primary slugging suspect. Instead, among the shuffling crowd, cargo bots, and random noise, Davin found quick anonymity.

As with most spaceports, people didn't tend to care about other people's problems. Unless you were the authorities, any helpful effort would as likely get yourself hurt or killed as actually do anything useful. So while yelling followed Davin, it died out fast. That freighter captain and his crew didn't, apparently, have the motivation to chase.

Which left Davin walking with the crowd, muddling over the results. He'd lost Melody, at least for a while, in that bay's back room. Mako, who'd disappeared, now knew Davin was on Callisto and would, no doubt, sell that information to whomever cared enough to pay for it. But Davin had confirmed something suspicious was going down on the moon.

No ordinary freighter captain would be that taut about someone selling parts. Be that secretive.

Davin pulled up his comm, tapped through to Phyla's number, and stepped aside from the flow as the call connected.

"Davin?" Phyla said. "Are you in trouble?"

"Now why would you say that first thing?"

"Because you're always in trouble."

Couldn't argue with that.

Davin relayed his situation to multiple sighs, groans, and a single "You're such a lucky idiot, Davin," from Phyla.

"Look," Davin said when he wrapped up. "It's better than nothing. We know Callisto's got something going on. We just need to find out what."

"Do we?" Phyla asked. "I thought we were trying to get the container back. Now it looks like we're pulling ourselves deeper into some war between Eden and the rebels."

Davin watched the passing crowds, the dozens, hundreds, thousands attempting to fill contracts, run an economy in a solar system tilting towards violence. For a long time, Davin had thought he and Phyla could be one of those anonymous runners, grinding out a living while dodging anything more serious.

"I've been thinking," Davin said. "Really, since Amado and Eightsix, I've been feeling different. And I think you've been feeling the same way for a long time too."

Phyla kept quiet, but her soft breathing came through on the other line.

"We tried this thing, the runner thing, and it was okay," Davin said.

"It was boring. It is boring."

"Right, boring, but I thought boring might be good for a while."

"It wasn't."

Davin winced, fought off an impulse to accuse Phyla of just going along with it, but that wouldn't help anything.

Keep the focus on the goal.

"That's what I'm trying to say." Davin took a big breath, a freeing breath, the confession about to break through. "I want to go back to what we had. The danger, the adventure."

"Even the death?" Phyla asked, her voice saying she already knew the answer.

"I mean, I don't love that, but I want to feel a part of something bigger again, and now I think we are," Davin said. "So what do you say? It might mean dropping the bullet races for a bit."

A very long, long moment. Davin wished he could've seen Phyla's face right then, wished he'd had this conversation in person. Sometimes, though, epiphanies demanded action.

"Hey," Phyla replied. "I would give up the bullets in a heartbeat if we could have us back."

Never had an exhale felt so good.

Davin wouldn't call himself a sentimentalist—he'd had to make too many hard calls to allow emotions to swallow him up—but the solar system didn't feel quite so big when you had someone on your side.

"Always like it when we're on the same page," Davin said. "And now that's settled—"

"That's it? Just move on after we decide our life philosophy for years wasn't working?"

"No reason to stew on past mistakes, Phyla. I'm all about the future here."

"Some things change, others never do, I guess."

Phyla's cryptic comeback notwithstanding, Davin

wanted to refocus. Wanted to find somewhere to go that'd get him out of the crowded hallway.

"Right," Davin said, hard switching. "So we can guess that there's a rebel operation going on here, which means Merc and Uros are going to try and take the container there."

"We're not attacking anything if you don't have Melody," Phyla replied, even if her voice said their last topic wasn't quite exhausted. "And, Davin, if we can get Eightsix to help us, I wouldn't mind android support. Maybe we can see if Amado has anyone in the area too, get Eden in on the game."

"Eden?" Davin said. "They'll kill everyone. Merc included."

"He chose a side, Davin. Until we do, we have to survive."

"That's cold, Phyla."

Phyla didn't reply. Her breathing didn't come over the mic either. Maybe she was moving. Davin gave her another few seconds, then repeated her name.

Nothing.

"You still there?" Davin asked, then glanced at the signal on the comm. Full strength, and the call showed as connected. "Something up?"

A static crackle, and a different voice came on, one that warmed and froze Davin in equal measure. "Thanks for defending me, Davin," Merc said. "Phyla and I will have to talk about how quick she wanted to throw me out."

"Merc, careful," Davin said, swishing his eyes across the shifting crowd as if, by looking rapidly enough, he might see Phyla, Merc, and be able to come to some sort of rescue. "We were just talking."

"I know, and I'd probably do the same thing if I were you," Merc replied. "But I'm not. You dropped your causes,

Davin, but we didn't. So you know how this goes. Apparently your container's pretty well locked."

"Eden didn't want us peeking inside."

"Then lucky for both of us you've got contacts back there," Merc said. "You're going to have to be sneaky about it. Like, don't have a few drinks before trying this one, because if you get Eden coming down on us, things are going to get really messy here."

"Are you threatening Phyla?" Davin couldn't believe what he was hearing. That Merc would go this far. "Because she's not a part of this."

"Eden's not going to pull any punches. We can't either," Merc said. "I'm really sorry, Davin, but we need that key. I'll send you the coordinates. Bring it, we'll bring Phyla, then we can forget this all ever happened."

"You might," Davin said. "I never will."

The *Jumper*'s captain cut the call. Dropped his arms to his sides and stared at the ground for a long moment. His comm buzzed, no doubt Merc sending along the coordinates.

How could the fighter pilot take Phyla hostage? Could threaten her life? Davin didn't understand. They'd flown from planet to planet together, taken on the biggest dangers either had ever seen. Davin had even risked the whole Wild Nines team in a raid on Europa just to get Merc back.

And now this?

The comm buzzed again. Davin ignored it, stepped into the crowd and walked back towards the bay he'd run from. Not long ago, he'd been on a whimsical mission. Get the container back so some dumb Eden goons wouldn't try to lay him out. Amado, even, had been almost comical in his seriousness.

Now Phyla could get hurt. Now this whole thing was real.

Davin reached the bay, went slightly past it to the entrance Mako had shown him. The one the little bastard had buzzed Davin in, where Melody ought to be inside. The lock stared at Davin, protecting its steel door.

The captain glanced around him, approached the lock and drew his sidearm from its holster. Stuck the nozzle right up to scanner, and pressed the trigger. The laser sounded off a slight scream, light flashed, and a smoky curl rose up from the fried lock. Davin shot a look behind him, and while a few curious eyes glanced that way, a few steps sped up, nobody cared enough to intervene.

Other people's problems.

Someone at the docking bay's security would notice eventually, but right now, as Davin reached inside the fried lock and toggled the hard switch, a button the lock's systems would've pressed if Davin had the badge, the break-in continued uninterrupted. The door slid open, and Davin ignored his comm's buzzing as he kept on.

Probably Merc, delivering more reasons for why he was turning his back on Davin, Phyla, and the Wild Nines. Talking about causes and all that other bullshit, as if they mattered more than the team. As if Merc hadn't joined up with the rebels just for Opal.

Melody wasn't there. The big weapon had disappeared, and Davin figured he had a culprit: Mako. The little scuzzball probably hoped the rebel captain would imprison Davin and let Mako sell Melody off for a profit.

Two problems, then. Get Melody back. Free Phyla. Not as easy as running wine from Mars to the Moon, but Davin could handle it.

The comm buzzed again, and in the dim backroom,

Davin finally pulled it up. Merc's coordinates were there, suggesting a meeting in an hour at a hotel not far away. But the fighter pilot had only sent that one message.

Every other one, the constant calls and blurbs, came from Fournine. Davin didn't even read'em, just tapped the call and connected to the AI. "Fournine, what's going on?"

"Did you read my messages?"

"All one thousand? Sum them up for me."

"We are being boarded."

"What?"

"It appears we have made some enemies, and they are attempting to break into the *Jumper*."

"Can you hold them off?" Davin asked.

"If I have permission to shoot them? Maybe."

"Then shoot them," Davin said. "I'm on my way."

Okay, three problems. One sidearm, three problems.

Davin had seen worse odds.

# 18

## PERSUASION

Davin found five goons hanging around the *Jumper*, four loaded for a fight and looking lost with a ship that wouldn't open and the fifth with her head buried in her comm, talking to someone. Given their outfits, all the same and drenched in Callisto's cyan blue, Davin guessed they were Callisto's official authorities. So far as Davin knew, he hadn't done anything worth this kind of response.

Not that reason would stand in the way if these people had been paid off.

With Merc holding Phyla and Melody missing, Davin had to weigh the wisdom of walking into the bay. Right now he sat off to the side in the docking corridor, his comm coupling with Fournine's kindness to patch Davin through to the *Jumper*'s cameras.

"Think they can find a way in?" Davin asked.

"I closed the ramp," Fournine replied. "They have no access to attempt a computer intrusion. However, the woman speaking is asking someone for permission to blow open a hole in our ship's side. I believe she will get it."

A trusty sidearm could do some damage. Davin could barrel into the bay and hope that none of the enemies were up on their reflexes, snap off some shots and pray Davin's accuracy hadn't rusted in his recent pacifist stretch.

Or.

"Take her up," Davin said. "File a routine evac with the docking bay and get out of there."

"Interesting choice," Fournine replied. "You trust me, an android, with your ship?"

"You're not an android anymore. That ship's your body, and I'm trusting you to protect it," Davin replied. "Do it, but stay within range. I've a feeling we'll be calling for a rescue before long."

"And if the docking bay doesn't grant me permission to leave?"

"You have turrets. Use them."

Davin closed down the chat. Like it or not, the game had started. Now he'd narrowed his problems down to two: Phyla and Melody. The weapon had been given to Davin by the Wild Nines's original captain, a gruff man who'd opted into the same retirement Davin and Phyla had tried and found lacking. It'd been a great gift, along with the captain's endorsement to take his position, and leaving Melody in anyone's hands but his own hurt.

But love couldn't be ignored.

Davin fell into the corridor crowd and walked with them past the docking bays, dodging around lines forming for passenger ships, bulky crates stacking up for cargo loads, and countless bots cleaning up after both.

A giant *Welcome to Callisto* sign hung over the exit, every letter made up of a different crop that the moon claimed as its own. Davin's stomach rumbled at the sight—it'd been a while since his last nutrient goop tube. Maybe he could rescue Phyla and get something to munch on at the same time.

Better: maybe Phyla would treat Davin to someplace nice after he saved the day.

Merc's coordinates pitched the rendezvous a ways along Callisto's primary ring, the circular cities stilted above the vast farm fields coating the moon. The docking bays clung to the ring like loops linking to each other, making Callisto look, from the air, like someone had covered it with a net. The rings themselves packed people, stores, and entertainment on either side, with the wealthier buyers getting coveted inner-loop spots.

The income and status divide held Davin for a long moment as he left the docking ring. Straight across from him, a width not all that long considering Callisto's small size, the ring wall broke into individual sections, each one labeled with a name and a number, bright decor popping personal styles from windows, lights, paints and the occasional bot guard standing out front.

Contrast that to the setting on Davin's right and left, with five-story apartment sections layering people on top of one another. Each one proudly displayed its owning company, and Davin saw docking slots for corporate ring-runners, little buses meant to get workers to and from their homes to the right rings every day.

Every spot in the solar system handled its dichotomies differently, and at least on Callisto, it looked like the workers had some modicum of comfort. Some visibility. Most places that Davin had been, anyone not able to pay for the center ring would've been sent to the fringes. Out of sight.

Davin wasn't here to assess Callisto's socioeconomic status, so he kept on moving. Things were both more and less crowded on the main ring's boulevard. Fewer people bothered walking as the distance around the ring stretched into the kilometers, and frequent shuttles forced those who did use their feet onto marked walkways. Davin fell in behind a family whose children spread out across the walkway, moving at their own speed.

Davin could've asked them to get out of the way, but instead he stayed in line. Took the time to observe with the family's shifting bodies and constant chatter as cover. Merc's designated rendezvous point wasn't far off now: Davin caught *Cornucopia*'s silver halo sign after a few minutes, slipping into view as he walked the ring's curve and the slow speed let Davin take in a long look.

As places for an ambush went, *Cornucopia* looked a little too wide open. Fitting into two outer ring sections, the restaurant sprawled up and down five stories, matching its name to its size and the apparent feast on offer. A long, glittery banner above the main entrance declared every item on the menu to be locally grown.

Truly, a sinister joint.

Merc's positioning put the meeting on the third level, right in the restaurant's center. The host bots didn't bother Davin as he brushed by them, though the captain drew eyes aplenty as he moved through *Cornucopia*'s higher-end lunch crowd. Fliers like Davin ought to be in the docking bay, sucking down nutrient goop before liftoff, not dallying here.

Davin made sure to nudge his jacket aside, give everyone a clear look at the sidearm on his hip. If Callisto had any public laws against weapons, Davin hadn't seen any, but those disapproving eyes sure blinked away fast when they caught the sidearm.

"Davin, stop scaring the locals," Merc said, peering down from the chalk-white staircase, its glass-and-silver-railed supports proving a good rest for his elbows. "Keep the sidearm covered. We don't need the attention."

"As if I'm listening to anything you have to say." Davin kept the sidearm visible as he walked up the two stories, though the defiance did nothing to dim Merc's apparent good spirits. "Where's Phyla?"

Davin asked the question as he approached Merc's level, expecting it to be answered with his own eyes. Instead, he found a few taken tables and nobody else paying attention to them. Phyla, if she was here, wasn't in sight.

"We moved her somewhere safer," Merc said. "Somewhere I'd like to bring you."

"You told me to come here."

"So we could make sure you weren't tailed," Merc replied, giving Davin a sympathetic head shake. "We've caught some wind that Eden's after you. That's why I had to go through the whole hostage dance, in case they were tracing our call. "

"Dance? I was talking to Phyla, and then you took her away."

Merc re-created the scene as he led Davin back down and away from *Cornucopia*, stopping for a moment so Davin could snag a sandwich from the grab'n'go counter. Davin would've offered to buy Merc something except, you know, he'd kidnapped Phyla.

Davin might not be able to shoot Merc here in the open, but he'd damn sure use every petty attack he could find.

Phyla had been at *Cornucopia* already, sitting near the window on the upper level and watching for something. The rebels, Merc explained, crawled all over Callisto, and anyone looking a little weird prompted quick attention. The moon served as the primary food source for Jupiter, Saturn and beyond, and nobody thought Eden was above crippling the place to make the rebels suffer.

"I'm starting to think the same way," Davin interrupted between licking the last sandwich remnants off his fingers. "I've never been an Eden fan, but you're pulling me to your side."

"Then you should chat with Phyla," Merc said. They continued along the main walkway, until Merc turned them left, leaving behind the residential and restaurant-dominated primary ring for an industrial one. "She understands our cause."

"Does she?" Davin said. "Because I've never heard Phyla talk about it. Not once. And she didn't seem against getting Eden involved in this adventure before you grabbed her."

"Phyla and I talked about that. Brainstorming, that's all it was. You wouldn't know that, though, because you never ask her what she's really thinking," Merc replied. "Try communicating sometime. It helps."

"That what you and Opal do, communicate?"

"When we can. It's not so easy now."

The industrial ring didn't have the primary ring's decor menagerie, filling its sides with workshops and processing plants instead. Unlike the sprawling factories on Mars and Earth, these had to fit to the curved ring layout, and that meant sending ducts and pipes over and under Davin's feet and head. The grated lines connected the ring's sides, pouring into metal walls fabricated to hold in any possible accidents: Callisto might have a friendly atmosphere, but the rings were too fragile to play with chance.

Merc slowed his walk as they left behind the primary ring and its crowds, swapping them for a bot-driven concourse as materials and refined goods were carted around by machines that took no notice of the two interlopers.

"Truth is, Davin, we're doing all this because we're losing," Merc said. "I'm going to tell you right now that we heard you were running the container, and that the *Zephyr* might be able to make an intercept. Everyone's hoping that what Eden put in that thing could end the war before it starts."

Appealing to Davin's softer side would've worked better if Merc hadn't hidden Phyla, hadn't played this long game first.

"Doubt a single box is going to swing your game," Davin said.

"But we have to try," Merc replied. "This is it. If Eden breaks us around Jupiter, we won't be able to feed our people. We'd lose supplies, what we need to keep our ships flying."

"Merc, take me to Phyla. I don't care about your reasons, your excuses. You want to have a friendly chat about high ideals, it can wait till she's back."

Davin and Merc had worked together for years. Across planets, moons, and space stations. Fought, protected, saved too many to count. In Merc's face, now, Davin didn't see the cocky fighter pilot, but a tired soldier. One whose adventures had finally caught up to him.

In other words, Davin saw himself.

"Yeah, Davin. Okay." Merc waved onward. "I'm just trying to say I'm sorry it worked out this way."

"Me too."

The pair went deeper into the industrial ring, where the bots began to dwindle and the brand names disappeared. Color schemes gave way to a uniform green, the only marker being a white *CI* in a similarly white circle plastered above every door.

Didn't need to be an expert to know that stood for *Caloric Industries.*

Merc finally pointed Davin into a block-wall building, slapping his comm against the security scanner. The door slid open, letting loose refined grain's strong scent, as if Davin had walked into a thick meadow. The smell mismatched with the blue-white glow basking down from ceiling-length lights lining the warehouse top like stripes. From the entrance, Davin could see back to the ring's outer wall, a black expanse lined with shelves and bot-enabled lifts to stock them.

"C'mon, she's this way," Merc said, emotionless.

Merc told the truth this time. Past a couple grain stacks —big, compressed rectangles stacked five high on one another—sat a carved out circular space dotted with a couple tables and a solid comms unit. Uros, along with another fifteen or so rebel soldiers surrounded Phyla and the container.

None looked surprised when Davin walked in, and none moved to stop him when he broke for Phyla, slipping between a couple bodies. Rather than taking his offered hug, though, Phyla shook her head, put a hand on his chest.

"I'm not hurt," Phyla said. "What's important now is the container."

"What?" Davin replied. "I just came all this way because Merc made it seem like they were going to hurt you, and you're focused on the container?"

"Davin, if Merc's right, if there's a weapon in there that they can use," Phyla locked eyes with Davin, and he had to give sincerity's edge to her. This wasn't an act. "Then we have to let them have it."

"But we promised Viola," Davin said, well aware that the whole rebel group was watching, waiting. "I'm not one for breaking promises."

"Some things are more important."

Davin stepped back from Phyla, looked at the rebels. He'd prided himself on keeping away from the bigger fights, power's slow swing from one empire to another. Keep himself and his friends healthy, comfortable, and happy. No matter which thing Davin chose, now, he'd be making an enemy. Merc and the rebels, right here, or the solar system's most dangerous company and Viola, a friend that hadn't tried to kidnap Phyla.

"Sorry," Davin said. "It's my word, and I'm sticking to it."

Phyla, Merc, both of'em opened their mouths as the other rebels went for their sidearms, their rifles slung over their shoulders. All trying to get Davin to change his mind.

They never stood a chance.

**19**

**GOOD BUSINESS**

Eightsix knocked two down and out when she flipped from the grain stacks, barely touching the floor before rolling into a push-off kick that sent another rebel soldier into his ally. The android kept moving, darting in different directions to strike the soldiers in the neck, the arms, the head. All disabling, all keeping the soldiers alive.

As Davin and Eightsix had agreed.

The captain covered the android with precise sidearm fire, zapping raised rifles out of commission. Their owners dropped the burning weapons, diving away before their power packs exploded. Davin let them go.

This wasn't a murder mission, but a rescue.

"What's happening?" Phyla asked, standing still and watching the devastation, listening to the rebel soldiers shouting. "Is that Eightsix?"

"Merc kidnapped you," Davin said, then aimed and shot another soldier in the shoulder before he could blast the android. "I called in reinforcements."

"Merc had a reason!"

"Yup, and I didn't agree," Davin said. He tracked the sidearm around the room as Eightsix continued her rolling rampage, scattering bodies around. "The ends don't justify the means, Phyla."

"You're one to talk."

"I am one to talk, you oughta know that about me by now." Davin punctuated the reply with another shot, hitting the floor next to another rifle-wielding soldier, who danced back and, thus, delayed his own attack. Eightsix took advantage, popping the man in the forehead and sending him, limp, to the ground. "You're not sounding real grateful here."

"Why would I be grateful? Merc's our friend, we should be helping the rebels, not hurting them!"

"Since when did you get all political?"

Phyla went up, made to look like she was going to slap Davin, and when he moved to block it with his free hand, she slugged him in the gut instead.

"Since always, or were you too busy to notice? If the rebels lose, then Eden owns everything, Davin. Guess what happens then? How much freedom are we going to get?"

"Can we have this discussion later?" Davin said, gathering his breath back. Phyla could really lay one on if she wanted to. "When we're not surrounded?"

Davin didn't say that Phyla could use the chance to cool off. He'd never seen her look so angry before. Fists clenched, nostrils flaring, blazing hair flying out as though it had turned Phyla's mood into motion.

The rescue mission wasn't proceeding as planned.

A sidearm's cold end pressed against Davin's neck as he straightened back up, and Phyla's eyes slipped past the captain's, narrowed.

"Call her off," Merc said. "Do it, Davin."

"Merc," Phyla warned. "Put the sidearm away."

Davin started to say that he couldn't call Eightsix off, that he didn't own the android. Eightsix had only agreed, when Davin called her back in the docking bay's conduit, to help on the condition that he give the android the key.

Without Melody, Eightsix could probably just take the key by force once the rebels were down anyway, even if Davin changed his mind.

"She's killing my soldiers," Merc said.

"Not killing," Davin said. "That's not the plan."

Merc only growled, repeated his demand.

Even if Davin could've told Eightsix to stop, there wouldn't have been any point. The android, dodging fire throughout in that kinetic, future-sight way androids could, had combed her way through the rebel force and left a moaning, unconscious group in her wake. As she finished body-slamming the last guard into the ground, Eightsix straightened, the guard's dropped rifle in her hands, and took aim over Davin's shoulder.

"Release him," Eightsix said. "I will not miss."

"She won't, Merc," Davin said. "You know androids don't."

"Please," Phyla added. "This isn't worth dying over."

"You don't know that," Merc said, but, with a final press against Davin's temple, Merc pulled his sidearm away.

Davin stepped aside, turning to give Merc the interrogation the pilot so very much deserved, when a laser flashed and scorched a hole in Merc's chest, sending him to the ground. Phyla shouted and went to Merc's side, while Davin cursed and looked at the shooter.

"Why'd you do that?" Davin yelled at Eightsix. "He was standing down."

"He still held a weapon and presented a threat," Eightsix replied. "There was no other option."

"For you, maybe," Davin waved at her. "Put that rifle down. You don't need it." A look back at Merc, pale on the ground. "How's he doing?"

Merc muttered something that came out whistling, garbled, but Davin could pick out a couple choice words.

"He's alive," Phyla said. "I don't know for how long."

No doubt Callisto would have medical facilities. No doubt taking Merc to any of them would get Davin, Phyla, and Eightsix captured.

"New plan," Davin said, bringing up his comm. "Fournine, you out there?"

"I am enjoying Callisto's airways at the moment," Fournine replied while Davin collected a questioning look from Phyla, another curse from Merc, and Eightsix's blank stare. At least the android put the rifle down. "How can I assist?"

"Bring the *Jumper* to my position," Davin said.

"That will attract the wrong kind of attention."

"We've already managed that. Just do it and tell me when you're overhead."

Fournine blipped a yes and Davin cut the call, joined Phyla next to Merc. The laser burn hit Merc's upper chest, on Merc's right side. Without complications, the hit shouldn't be fatal. Davin said as much.

"Are you making excuses for the android now?" Phyla said. "She shot Merc! Our Merc!"

The accusation hit like hot coffee, shocking and frustrating and staining. Davin tried to find a response, something that would fit the moment, and when the cocky quips offered nothing, when standing over his wounded, former friend didn't spring anything to mind, he found something that did.

"He's not our Merc, Phyla," Davin said. "He left us, remember? After Earth? They all left us."

The Wild Nines had gone with Bosser, their worst enemy, to Earth to try and rescue Viola, to save the solar system from a threat that seemed too large to ignore. And they'd won, dammit. All of them, working together, had done what nobody—Bosser least of all—expected.

Then, at the height of everything, Davin had seen all his friends walk away. He'd cushioned the blow with logic, with nights with Phyla on the *Jumper* as they surfed the planets, telling himself that this was the right call. That he'd had enough excitement for one life.

Except Mox, Viola, Opal, Merc, Trina; they kept on living. Even Erick had found new adventure with his grandchildren. Davin, Davin had shuttled wine to the Moon.

"You think we left you?" Merc said, trying to sit up and letting Phyla push him back down. "We would've had you come with. The rebels would've loved to have you with us. Alissa included. But you wouldn't pick a side."

Because picking a side was bad for business, but Davin didn't say that. Couldn't say that.

"It's bad for business," Davin said. "Can't make an enemy of half the solar system and expect to earn any coin."

"Are you literally talking about coin right now?" Phyla blazed daggers at Davin, who shrugged, turned and pointed his sidearm at one of the rebel soldiers starting to sit up.

"Y'all stay down, nobody's going to hurt you," Davin announced. "We'll be checking out soon, then you can get yourselves on your way."

The rebel didn't fight the threat, laying back down and looking relieved to do so.

"It wasn't always business with you," Merc said, the laser burn making itself known in his taut voice. "You cared before."

Yeah, sure. About Lina and Miner Prime, and when

Bosser wanted to turn the androids into his personal army. Davin had cared plenty about that. But a fight between Eden and the rebels? Davin wasn't a soldier.

His comm beeped and a check confirmed Fournine had pulled the *Jumper* into position. The rescue from the rescue had arrived.

"Hold tight," Davin said. "Eightsix, you're on the container. Fournine, give us an exit. The side wall should do."

Phyla and Merc looked like they had a thousand more things to say, but Davin kept his back turned, watching the rebels and pretending he wasn't at all conflicted about what'd just happened. Life didn't give many easy choices, and this one wasn't any different, Davin only wished he'd come out of some of these looking like the good guy.

Spots on the outside wall appeared, orange glows that expanded and melted away as Fournine delivered *Jumper* lasers into the ring. Callisto's glorious blue sky and sunlight flooded in as the hole expanded high and wide enough for the *Jumper*'s ramp to set down.

"Eightsix, get going," Davin said, turning back to Phyla and Merc's sweaty, glaring face. "C'mon, I'll carry you onboard."

"I'm not moving," Merc said. "Going with you isn't good for my business."

"Yeah, well, it's good for mine," Davin said. "When the rebels come looking for revenge, you can tell them I took good care of you."

Phyla still looked icy-hot angry, but she helped Davin lift Merc to his feet and walk him past the downed rebel soldiers. Eightsix played her role, lifting the yellow-black container and carrying it up the ramp and into the freighter.

Merc didn't fight, and when Davin checked as they

walked, the fighter pilot's eyes had mostly shut. His laser burn looked worse now, too, than when Davin had first glanced at it. Maybe Eightsix had hit Merc with more power than she needed to. Maybe she had been going for the kill.

"You fly," Davin said to Phyla as they reached the ramp's top. "I'll take care of him."

"Can I trust you?" Phyla had one hand on Merc's own, the other on his shoulder.

"Like I said, keeping Merc alive is good business," Davin replied, hating himself as he did so. "The rebels will want him back, and we can make that trade."

"When did you get so cold?" Phyla asked, but she let Merc go and went towards the cockpit.

Davin watched her walk away while the ramp retracted behind them, denial bubbling in his throat.

"He took you, remember?" Davin said. "We got you back. Not my fault he's hurt."

Phyla, though, didn't try to play the game. She shook her head, climbed the ladder, and vanished towards the cockpit.

"I used to admire you," Merc whispered. "Know that?"

"Did that stop before or after you kidnapped my wife?"

Davin, with Merc's arm tossed over his shoulder, hefted the pilot towards the med bay. Eightsix, having set the container down, watched with her frozen face. Merc, never a huge man, managed to get himself strapped onto the sole stretcher as Davin took the room's only launch chair.

It'd been so long since anyone had used the med bay that random junk littered the floor. Erick's old IV stand still held position near the cot's head, tied to the stretcher. Locked, lead-lined metal cabinets stocked with supplies that'd likely hit their expiration dates. The ceiling light flickered as Phyla kicked up the engines and shot the *Jumper* space-ward.

"You hanging in there?" Davin asked after several thrumming seconds. "I'll juice you up once the *Jumper* settles in."

Merc laughed, a ragged thing that had Davin wincing, "You think you'll settle in? Callisto's a rebel moon, Davin. If they're not on your ass already, they will be soon."

## 20

# TURNAROUND

Merc wasn't kidding. Phyla called out the alarm seconds after the atmospheric rumbling ceased, the *Jumper* hitting space getting chased by fighters and bigger ships. A ragtag force emblematic of the rebels' penchant to take anyone and anything offered.

"Buy me some time," Davin shouted back into the *Jumper*'s intercom as he applied a healing balm to Merc's burn, slipped the pilot a pain-killing pill. "I need to get Merc stabilized."

"I can shoot," Eightsix said, appearing in the med bay's door.

"Then shoot," Davin replied. "Take a turret!"

Merc groaned, focused on Davin, "No, don't. We need every last one."

"Then tell your guys to stop chasing us," Davin said, but Merc's eyes fizzled out of focus. The pilot had been dancing along consciousness's edge. Still, there might be a point there. "Eightsix!"

The android poked her head back in.

"Shoot to disable, not to kill."

"That will be difficult."

"Figure it out," Davin said. "I'm thinking we have enough enemies right now."

A five minute procedure turned into ten with Phyla sending the *Jumper* through one maneuver after another, swinging Davin around. Erick, who'd been the Wild Nines's medical officer for a long time, no doubt would've had techniques to keep himself stable. Davin flopped around like a rag doll, using his hands and feet to keep himself oriented and feeling incompetent the entire time.

"There, you bastard, that should keep you alive," Davin said when he rubbed on the remaining balm.

The spot where Merc had been struck by the bolt no longer looked red, black, and puckered. Slathered with a peach-colored cream, the medication had already started breaking down dead skin, freeing other cells to start their repairs. The scanner attached to the med bay's stretcher suggested Merc would make it out okay, provided nobody delivered another shot to the man's chest any time soon.

"Davin!" Phyla said. "They're putting us into a box!"

The captain kicked himself from the med bay, wincing at Phyla's words. The rebels would be coming at the *Jumper* from all angles, cutting off escape routes until, surrounded and without hope, they'd have no choice but to surrender. Escaping a box required either a faster ship than the enemy —unlikely with the rebel fighters—or shooting their way out.

Davin hadn't felt the *Jumper* shudder, though. No blaring alarms saying shields were under fire. The rebels wanted Merc alive. Wanted, perhaps, that container too. If Davin told Phyla and Eightsix to go for lethal, that equation might change. And without a full crew, the *Jumper* wouldn't hold up well in a long firefight.

Maybe it wouldn't have to.

"Eightsix!" Davin shouted. "Ditch the turret and come here!"

The android, with more speed than Davin expected, blitzed up from the bottom turret's hold and joined Davin over his idea: the black and yellow container.

"You want to use it?" Eightsix asked.

"I don't even know what it is," Davin replied. "But if the rebels want it, and Eden wants it, then it has to be good."

"And the key?"

"You don't even care that I'm looking to open it? This thing you're trying to get?"

Eightsix's featureless face didn't react, "My mission is to deliver the container, its contents, and the key. Nothing forbids using it to achieve that mission."

"Point taken," Davin said, then patted his leg where the key sat, hoping they were close enough to Callisto to keep the key from exploding. "Think you can do some precise surgery?"

Eightsix nodded, "Ready?"

"Do it."

Davin wouldn't call himself an expert in surgical procedures, in medicine at all, but he felt pretty confident you were supposed to talk the patient through what was about to happen. That things were supposed to take a little time, work their way through gradually to minimize complications.

Eightsix went for speed.

The android reached out, gripped Davin's shoulder with her left hand to keep Davin steady. The robotic fingers, even coated with skin, dug in tight. Before Davin had a chance to complain, Eightsix's right hand went for Davin's thigh. He felt a painful flash, like a knife's cut, followed by a tug.

"Here," Eightsix said, holding up the bloody key. "Open it."

Instead, Davin pressed a hand on his new wound, felt the warmth as what should've been inside his body leaked out.

"Could've warned me," Davin sighed, relief at his continued existence mingling with the pain of his continued existence.

"I asked if you were ready. You said yes."

Damn androids.

The frustration helped Davin get over the sting, as did Phyla's announcement that she'd run out of room. That she'd have to power the *Jumper* down or destroy someone soon. Neither was an acceptable option, so Davin grabbed the key from Eightsix's hand, tried not to think about how he was holding something coated in his own blood, and jammed the thing into the container's lock.

With a bright chirp entirely at odds with the situation, the container's locks—both seen and unseen—popped open. The lid followed suit, lifting to reveal the secret that'd set Eden agents and rebels after Davin.

A ball. An orange ball with silver circles cut out around it, maybe half a meter in diameter. Davin thought it looked like Viola's bot, Puk, but a different color and without that bot's various tools. No gun barrels, energy packs, or, hell, sharp edges presented themselves.

If this thing was a weapon, Davin didn't know how to wield it.

Eightsix used Davin's hesitation and lifted the object from its container and the protective black foam keeping it safe. The *Jumper*'s engines slowed, shut off.

"Any ideas?" Davin said, already trying to think of ways to spin Merc's injury, Eightsix's attack into something that would convince the rebels to let them live. "Because we're out of time."

"There is a depression here," Eightsix said. "If I press this, I believe the weapon will activate. There is some risk it may destroy us."

"That's always a risk," Davin said. "That thing doesn't look like any bomb I've seen. Press the button."

"Unfortunately, my mission parameters do not give me—"

Davin snatched the orange ball from the android, found it heavier than expected, and managed to get a bloody finger on the button. Pressed it down and heard a click.

The silver patterns on the ball began to move, like sinewy snakes they shifted, crossing each other. The lines moved beneath Davin's fingers and he didn't feel a thing, as if the ball had a transparent shield keeping any touch away. The only place the silver lines didn't brush was the button, which glowed in a blue-white tone.

Davin's chest lit up as the ball's button projected something on it. Squinting, Davin rotated the ball so the projection went straight up. In the cargo bay, looking like a ghostly command, the ball displayed a number ticking down and a demand to turn off all communications.

The counter sat at five. No time to debate.

"Shut the comms down!" Davin yelled. "Don't talk, just do it!"

Phyla would, should know from his voice that this wasn't a test, not something to question.

"Done!" Phyla called back as the counter hit three. "Mind telling me why I just did that? We're getting hailed."

"We're about to find out," Davin said, not yelling, drawn into the silver lines.

The timer hit zero.

The ball didn't explode, didn't shriek or fire lasers around the room. The silver lines stopped moving, lit up bright as if something inside the ball was exploding and Davin felt the object warm up. Almost hot.

Then the glow faded, the temperature returned to its cool standard, and the button Davin had pressed popped back out. The projection disappeared.

Ready to go again.

"What did it do?" Davin said.

Eightsix didn't reply. Didn't move at all. Her static face, normally the only frozen part of the machine, was matched by her immobile limbs.

"She appears to be shut down," Fournine said via speakers. "I'm unclear why."

"Davin?" Phyla called. "You better get up here."

"Keep an eye on things, Fournine," Davin said. "Nobody touches the weapon till we figure out what it does."

"You do realize I have no physical way to prevent anything?"

"Think of something. You're a smart robot."

The captain dropped the ball back in its resting place and jumped over to the ladder, kicking up to the cockpit's entry. Davin stepped through and saw Callisto through the cockpit's windshield, its small blue body sprawling out below. Dark spots, some large and some small, blotted its surface: rebel ships.

"They had us surrounded," Phyla said. "Have us, I guess, but they're not moving anymore. All their lights are down. We're not getting tracked by their systems."

"Open up the comms," Davin said. "See if we can hear anything."

But nothing crossed the waves. Phyla rolled up and down the frequencies, hitting every standard channel. The only traffic they could catch came from docking orders on Callisto's far side. Twenty rebel craft around them, and not a single one bothered with a transmission?

Also, twenty? The rebels must really like Merc. Or want the weapon.

"So they're dead," Davin said. "At least, the ships are. Don't think we would've survived if the people didn't."

Phyla nodded slow, and Davin took a spot in the co-pilot's chair. For once, something seemed to have worked. While Davin didn't understand how, the weapon seemed to have disabled every ship around them.

"If they're down, then we should be getting out," Davin said. "Find a gap and let's get outta here."

"Right," Phyla said, tapping on the console and restarting the engines. "If that weapon can knock out this many ships at once, and it's that small . . ."

"Eden could just mop up the rebels. Any engagement, they could disable—" Davin stopped, thinking back to Eightsix, frozen in the cargo bay. "Fournine, is Eightsix up and running yet?"

"She remains down. I detect no signs of activation."

Davin nodded, rubbed his chin, trying to parse probabilities, "Phyla, are we picking up any energy? Engines, shields, anything?"

The *Jumper* started forward, a slow build as Phyla turned the ship towards deeper space.

"Nothing," Phyla said. "It's like they're all wrecks."

When the *Zephyr* had issued its distress call, Davin had answered. He'd risked the *Jumper* to come to Uros's aid. If the weapon had truly disabled all these ships, they wouldn't have a chance to send that signal. They might not even have life support, and all their crews might be slowly suffocating.

"If we leave now," Davin said slow, as much to himself as anyone. "They all might die."

Phyla asked why and Davin ran out his reasoning, and when he finished the two of them sat silent in the cockpit while the *Jumper* continued to move onward, past the derelict rebel ships.

"I don't think I'd forgive us if we left," Phyla said softly. "I know you don't want to take sides, Davin, but this?"

There wasn't a choice. Not really. Even mercenaries had to find their lines and stick to them.

"Slow us down," Davin said. "Find the closest target, and let's hope they don't kill us when we save'em."

**21**

---

## FOES TO FRIENDS

Manually docking with a dead ship wasn't all that difficult. Phyla lined up the *Jumper*'s hatch, near the ramp on its bottom side, with the nearest rebel hulk and let Fournine handle the precise jetting needed to click things into place. With Eightsix still down, Davin borrowed Phyla's rifle and tried to think up a way to greet the rebels without getting shot.

"Merc?" Davin said, coasting into the med bay. "You awake, kid?"

"Kid?" Merc mumbled, eyes shut. "Since when am I 'kid'?"

"Always have been," Davin replied. "Need your help to save your friends, though."

Davin gave the rundown, saw Merc stiffen as Davin described the weapon and its effects. Davin felt weird asking for help to save his apparent enemies, but stranger things had happened in his life. What had to matter most was whether Davin could stand looking at himself.

The mirror would not show a heartless killer. Not today.

"You want me to stand in front?" Merc said. "Real nice, Davin. Use the wounded man as a shield."

"Hey, it'd be easier to leave," Davin replied. "And the longer you take deciding yes or no, the more chance someone's going to suffocate out there."

That threat proved enough to get Merc, with Davin's help, unstrapped and kick-floating towards the hatch. Phyla gave the green light and unlocked the circular door. With Merc holding onto his side, Davin leaned down, pulled the hatch back. The rifle hovered over Davin's shoulder, its strap tying the weapon to him, but in no position for a fast draw.

The rebels hadn't opened the lock on their side, even though the *Jumper* confirmed a tight seal.

"If they can't open the hatch on their side, this isn't going to work," Merc said.

"Manual releases," Davin replied, easing Merc into the airlock and following. "They'll open up, they just need to know we're here."

A two meter journey between the two ships through the tight, silver lining extending from the *Jumper* and meshing into standard links on the rebel ship brought Merc and Davin to the rebel's hatch. Normally, scanners, alarms, and who knew what else would be blaring a boarding signal the rebel's way, but right now, who knew whether the rebels had any idea what was going on.

For that matter, Davin couldn't be sure the weapon hadn't killed anyone on all those ships. Maybe it wasn't just disabling, maybe it'd done something worse.

"So we're going to knock?" Merc asked.

"You're asking questions like you weren't with the Wild Nines, kid," Davin said. "We always improvised, remember?"

"I remember it got us into trouble more times than it worked."

"Then you and I remember very differently," Davin said, then, bracing against the airlock to prevent every hit from bouncing him back, he knocked on the hatch door. Once, twice, again and again.

Metal thunks echoed through the airlock, but Davin had no way to know whether anyone heard them in the rebel ship. After five solid hits, Davin stopped. Took a breath. Waited.

"Davin," Merc said as they floated together in the silver tube. "Even though this is all your fault, thanks for the rescue."

"Guess that's one way to say it."

"I can't believe your android shot me." Merc looked down at his chest. "Opal's going to be so angry."

"Eightsix isn't mine," Davin said. "She's Eden's."

"Wow. Mister I don't take sides has an Eden android working with him?"

How to explain the events that'd led to Eightsix knocking out a rebel squad and shooting Merc? Davin could either stumble over a mouthful, or take the quick route.

"You stole my container. She offered to get it back."

Merc snorted, "And once she gets that weapon for Eden? Think she's going to walk away and let you live?"

"Hey," Davin said. "Not everyone has to die all the time. Some deals just get done and that's it, you know?"

"Didn't think you were supposed to get more naive as you got older, but you've always proved people wrong, Davin."

Comebacks littered Davin's lips, but before a single one could escape, clicks came from the rebel ship's hatch. A bang as a lock found its way open. Merc and Davin fell quiet, the captain kicking ever-so-slightly behind Merc. Not because he wanted the protection, but because it was the smart thing to do: let'em see a friendly face first.

The hatch opened the slightest crack. Laser bolts didn't come through immediately, a definite win. Not that blowing up the airlock would help either ship much, but it would turn Merc and Davin into vacuum-sealed icicles.

"You're up," Davin whispered.

"It's Merc," the fighter pilot said, speaking up and only sounding a little resentful. "The people that disabled your ship want to save you. So come out, and don't shoot when you do it, because you'll hit me, and I've already been shot once today."

"Merc?" came a distrusting voice from the hatch's other side. "Is this a trap?"

"Not a trap," Merc said. "Not this time, anyway."

The back and forth continued, at one point breaking into a codeword exchange that Davin couldn't follow. The rebels did, finally, open up the hatch. Two, first, joined Davin and Merc in the airlock and confirmed that Eden's weapon had totally knocked out their systems. Not in the way that a simple restart would fix, either.

"A virus," Davin said to Phyla , later, as they flew the *Jumper* to the next ship in line, a small single-person fighter. "That's what they're thinking. Any tech with an open comm in range gets hit by this thing and it erases everything it touches. Just eats up all the data."

"So the computers become bricks."

"Right, it's not that the power doesn't work, it's that the machines don't know what to do when it arrives," Davin said. He wouldn't consider himself an expert on how a modern spaceship kept itself running, but it certainly took more than a simple switch. "They kept trying to reset every-thing, but there wasn't anything to, well, reset."

Davin leaned forward, looked at the little fighter and its pilot as the *Jumper* approached, then the craft disappeared as Phyla swung the hatch into position. Jupiter came into view, its swirling lines running their forever races. How many programs humans relied on were like those storms? Always running, always working. What would happen if they were shut off, erased?

"Eightsix," Fournine said, breaking into the conversation. "She still hasn't activated."

Fournine's usual inflections ran between sarcasm and suspicion at a choice Davin was making. This time, Davin could swear he heard worry. And if his ship computer worried about Eightsix, then it wasn't paying full attention to the docking, or the rebel crews invading the *Jumper*'s hold.

"I'm not Trina," Davin said, "but let's take a look. Think you can handle things up here, Phyla?"

"Pretty sure I can pilot between a bunch of dead ships, Davin, but thanks for the confidence."

"You're welcome." Davin threw Phyla a thumbs-up and received two rolled eyes in return as he left the cockpit.

Eightsix had been relegated to the cargo hold's side while the rescued rebels meandered in its main area. Merc spoke with several, while the others browsed on their comms, grabbing whatever data Callisto's news satellites broadcast. When Davin started down the ladder, a few looked his way, but none approached. No insults or threats flew.

Merc must've spoken to them, laid down the rules. Something the fighter pilot never would've done before. He'd always been the Wild Nines's firecracker, ready to run off into trouble as soon as he found it, and sometimes before. Not someone Davin would've picked out to be a leader, not someone who considered the bigger picture beyond his next target.

Yet here Merc stood, defying Davin's expectations. Could Davin be proud of and angry at Merc at the same time?

Apparently he could.

Zero gravity did have advantages: namely, Davin could tug Eightsix's limp, heavy metal body into the crap-filled workshop without too much effort. The space, dominated by a long workbench with tools built into the wall behind it, had fallen prey to Davin and Phyla's apathy, with random articles purchased or, more often now, won from Phyla's bullet racing, heaped in clusters. Davin had tied them down with cords plugging into magnet clamps, but maneuvering through the space still had him bouncing Eightsix off one stack after another.

"What are you going to do?" Fournine said. "I don't recall you having specific mechanical aptitude."

"I'm going to shock Eightsix a few dozen times, see what happens."

"You're not."

No, he wasn't, but Fournine's attention gave Davin an idea. He looked around the workbench until he spied what he wanted: a connection cable that hooked into the *Jumper*'s network. A dusty console over on the right would let Davin poke around, but, as Fournine pointed out, Davin wouldn't know what to do inside an android's mind.

But Fournine would.

"I'm going to hook you into Eightsix," Davin said, moving the cable around and plugging it into the slot, hidden behind a flap, on Eightsix's neck. After the ball, after Fournine and all the devices Davin had dealt with, he'd learned the obvious spots for buttons. "When you get inside, see if you can figure out how the weapon works, and if you can bring her back."

"What if I copy my own data into her body, Davin?" Fournine said. "I could use Eightsix to regain my physical form, and then enact my long-planned revenge."

"Right," Davin replied, booting up the console and blowing away the dust. "If you wanted us dead, you could just open the hatch to vacuum and let us pop."

"A good idea."

Davin paused, glanced towards the workshop's speaker, "You kill us, never know who's going to take over an empty ship like this one. Bet they'd be jerks and delete you."

"Better the jerks I know then the ones I do not, Davin?"

"Exactly."

The console pointed out that Davin had indeed plugged the cable into Eightsix, but, according to Trina's old diagnostics, the android was dead. No activity, nothing to bring up and dig around in. As if her entire file structure had disappeared. Davin tapped away, bringing up the command to pass the console's ports through to Fournine.

"Okay buddy, you're up," Davin said. "Let me know what you find."

Davin stood back from the console, which, with its rapidly shifting screens displaying programming lingo, indicated Fournine had taken control.

"Davin," Merc said, holding himself in the doorway back to the cargo bay. "We saved another pilot."

"Yeah? Does this one want to kill me too?"

"Not quite," Merc replied. "Have you decided what you're going to do, once you get us all in here?"

"One step at a time." Davin nodded towards the still android. "Trying to get Eightsix back."

"Sure." Merc didn't look like he cared at all, which, considering the android had shot him, made sense. "You might want to move fast."

"You're gonna tell me why?"

Merc slid into an exhausted grin, "Opal's on her way, and when she finds out you got me shot, she's not going to be happy."

Davin winced. People on Opal's bad side tended to end up dead, or worse.

"Davin," Fournine announced as the captain rubbed his temples to stave off an impending headache. "I can save her."

Oh, hurrah.

**22**

---

## THE CAUSE

The secret to restoring Eightsix became the salve to bring back the rebel ships. Fournine copied over the *Jumper*'s core operating systems and, one by one, Phyla and the rebel crews boarded, installed, and restarted their craft. The fit wasn't perfect—a fighter running on a freighter's code wouldn't be so sharp—but the life support came on, the lights glowed, and the engines started. For now, according to Merc, that would be enough.

For Davin, that call would be made by the new arrival.

Opal and her fleet, apparently already orbiting Jupiter and threatening Galaxy Forge around Ganymede, had pulled off to meet Merc and take a look at the captured weapon. Phyla called out as the ships approached, a sturdy collection of captured and, courtesy of the rebel's haphazard shipyard around Saturn, new frigates.

As much as Davin believed he lived in a marvelous time, human technology still had a long way to go to reach the marvels seen in so many movies, read about in so many books. When he joined Phyla in the cockpit, the *Jumper* docked with another disabled rebel corvette, Davin had

Fournine put together rebel ship models based on their radar's data and shook his head.

Nobody would call the *Whiskey Jumper* a beautiful ship. Its bulky cargo bay surrounded by tacked on modules assured its forever association with functionality over form. The same went for most human-built craft, save the svelte-by-necessity fighters. Even with that low bar set, though, the rebel cruisers failed to meet it.

Blocky lumps interspersed with metal, the vessels had obviously been built using material gleaned from Saturn's rings. Large rocks captured and welded together made for cheaper construction than fabricating every element from raw materials, but they didn't do much for looks.

"Think that's hers?" Davin asked, pointing towards the biggest blot on the radar.

"Opal wasn't much for show," Phyla replied. "You think she would put herself on the biggest target?"

"I think your options change when you're a leader, and not a sniper."

Phyla nodded, looked at Davin, "I wouldn't have left them."

The rebels.

"I know," Davin replied. "I didn't want to hurt them, Phyla. I thought they'd hurt you."

"Merc would never."

Wouldn't he, for his cause? But Davin didn't say that. For once, for now, he'd learned to keep some thoughts to himself.

"I'm glad he's going to be okay," Davin said, a lame finish but a safe one. "Are you?"

Phyla reached out, took Davin's hand, "We've been flailing, Davin. Running around. I've been flying bullets, you've been draining glasses. It's not working like before." She tightened her grip. "I made a choice, in that warehouse with those soldiers. They were fighting for something they believed in. And I'm going with them."

She finished the question with her eyes. That iron-willed look that'd always caught Davin from the first time they'd met, when the choices were between where to play, what fantasy to adopt for the afternoon.

Business first. Davin kept calling that his ideology. Chasing the contracts and the deals. But every time fate pressed him on the point, Davin had gone the other way. Europa, Miner Prime, on Earth. If he couldn't stick to a creed, then why bother repeating it?

"Mind if I join you?" Davin asked.

Phyla's slight smile said she wouldn't mind.

"We're being hailed," Fournine announced from nowhere. "It looks like that large ship, one I calculate as more than able to destroy us without effort, is calling."

"Thanks, Fournine," Davin ran a hand through his hair, threw on a cocky grin. "Patch it through."

If Merc had been the Wild Nines's clown, than Opal had been their watchful guardian. She'd come to the mercenary crew after a violent stint with Eden suppressing Martian uprisings, and after the battle on Earth, had swapped sides and joined the same rebels she'd once shot from afar.

When Opal fuzzed in on the cockpit's display, Davin noticed the military vibe didn't suit her. Sure, Opal had her normally frizzy hair pulled back tight, had on some semblance of a rebel uniform—deep red, in contrast with Eden's green—and looked to be standing on a legitimate bridge. Yet, Davin saw her tense shoulders, how her hands, even with her folded arms, looked for something to hold on to. Opal stood a little too straight, as if someone were judging her posture.

For all that, Davin recognized the capable soldier, the brave woman who wouldn't hesitate to dive into a deadly fight for her friends.

"Davin," Opal said. "I'm going to kill you."

So someone had told her about Merc.

"He's fine, Opal," Davin replied. "A little scar. Nothing bad."

Opal's eyes narrowed, "What are you talking about?"

Oh.

"What are *you* talking about?" Davin replied.

"My ships, that you apparently disabled right before we're going to need them," Opal said. "When Merc said you would be coming out this way, I expected trouble, but not this much."

"Good to know I still have a reputation."

"For giving me headaches," Opal said. "I haven't yet caught up on everything, but we don't have much time before Eden gets here. Once you're done cleaning up your mess, and be quick about it, bring the *Jumper* over here. I have questions, and you better have answers."

"Actually," Davin said, "if Eden's coming, I might let you all work it out between yourselves."

Phyla poked his arm. The cause. Right.

Already, Davin was regretting this decision. Opal's slitted eyes didn't help.

"By which I mean, sure. We'll hop right on over."

"Good," Opal replied. "And Davin, if you've hurt my husband, I really will kill you."

ONCE AGAIN, Davin had Merc leading the way. Phyla nestled the *Jumper* into the rebel flagship's lone docking bay—a marker that even though the ship had size, it wouldn't hold up to humanity's larger freighters and Eden's own warships —and the trio, along with a still-setting-up Eightsix, departed. The android carried the weapon container, Eden's ball tucked away inside.

Opal, flanked by two intense-looking guards, waited in the bay. Merc, moving slow, went for an arms-length embrace while Davin watched Opal's reaction go from relief to fury as she noticed Merc's bandaged chest.

"Davin did this to you?" Opal asked the pilot, not bothering to recognize Davin or Phyla.

"Technically, the android shot me," Merc said, jerking his head towards Eightsix. "It's an Eden machine, but the weapon scrambled it so much, it's kind of already dead."

"I suppose I can't be too mad if your team lost to an android," Opal said, then ran a single loving thumb along Merc's cheek. "But I *can* be mad when an old friend decides he'd send in a killer bot against you."

Merc stepped aside, threw Davin a shrug behind Opal's back as the rebel commander reverted her face to solid steel and came his way.

"Hey, Merc took Phyla." Davin reached for another charming expression, settled on disarming and harmless instead. "I had to get her back. Didn't know she'd be safe."

"And instead of asking, you came in with your weapons ready," Opal said, measuring herself up to Davin. She stuck a finger at his chest, a firm jab. "I have a few dozen injured soldiers, both from Callisto and from that weapon right there. I can't afford that, Davin. And I can't afford to lose Merc."

"Don't mean to be a jerk, Opal, but Merc started this whole thing. He and Uros took the container on Deimos. Without that, none of this would've happened."

Opal cocked her head, spoke with ice, "The way I heard

it, you lost a bet. The way I *see* it, you doubled down coming after Merc, and now you're here. Stuck with us. So I'm going to give you a chance."

Better than killing him, at least.

"Eden's coming fast. They won't know we have their weapon," Opal said. "You're going to help us use it and destroy their fleet. We stop them here, and I think they'll talk. You took my soldiers, now you have a chance to give them back."

Sometimes you get the chance to walk away, sometimes you can hold to your principles and leave when someone threatens you. Other times, you have soldiers holding weapons in your face.

"Then let's talk," Davin said.

Planning to take on an Eden force wasn't best done in a docking bay, so the group, along with some of Opal's staff that Davin didn't know, retreated to a briefing room. The flagship's rocky origins made themselves plain in the room's smoothed, but very natural ceiling. Cost-cutting measures showed up too: no carpeting, no art. Every wall-space that could fit it, though, had a screen that, as the group filed in, flipped to show strategic compositions.

Davin hadn't ever been in a military situation like this one, mostly because Eden had been the only game in town for so long. Anyone fighting against that Goliath tended to get themselves swatted before they could assemble anything resembling a military.

The group settled around a long table made from thick glass, one that worked in tandem with the screens to lay out the theater. Opal's rebel ships projected up, a hornet's nest near Callisto's bulk on the table's north end. Opal, Merc, Davin and Phyla sat there while other rebels filled in the rest. They left Eightsix on the *Jumper*, where Fournine could keep rebuilding her code.

The staffers laid out their best guess about the Eden force's size, which came in at so much greater than the rebels could muster that Davin couldn't help but laugh.

"Sorry," Davin said when the eyes turned his way. "There's no way you're winning this one. I didn't think your game was to go up against Eden directly anyway? Aren't you supposed to strike from the shadows or something?"

"We would," Opal replied. "Except the weapon has a chance to deliver us a victory we wouldn't be able to get otherwise."

"Right, the knockout blow," Davin said. "What if it doesn't work?"

"It just took out all those ships," Phyla said. "Why wouldn't it work?"

"No idea, just saying that you're risking a lot that this is going to go as you want it to."

"If I remember right," Opal said, "you used to be a fan of risks."

"Different stakes," Davin countered. "My life, the *Jumper*, that's nothing compared to everything you've got here."

"I'll thank you not to forget me in your equations," Phyla added.

"And I'll remind you to remember your place here," Opal said. "We're going to tell you the plan, and you're going to follow it."

Davin didn't need to ask what would happen if he said no. Opal had a different kind of will in her now. This wasn't a joke, wasn't a contract. She'd adopted the rebel cause, and with it, a willingness to do whatever it took to succeed.

You don't play games with someone like that.

· · ·

AND YET, as he and Phyla sat in the *Jumper*'s cockpit, boosting up the engines with the rebels arrayed behind them, Eden's force coating the radar in front, Davin started wishing he'd picked a different course.

"Ready?" Phyla said, biting her lower lip as she goosed the *Jumper* forward. "They're in range."

"Still love me?"

"Never stopped."

"Then I'm ready," Davin said. "Flip on the comm, and let's see if we can make it outta this one alive."

**23**

---

## TRAPS

**G**oing straight into the fight would've been suicide for the rebel fleet. Opal's flagship notwithstanding, the rest of the ragtag ships lacked Eden's polish and prowess, not to mention weapons. Above all that, the rebel craft that Davin had struck with the secret weapon, about a quarter of their fleet, were only partially functional. Crews now had to manually operate most systems on those ships, which wouldn't work well in a tense firefight.

None of that would matter if Davin and Phyla could pull off their mission. Even half-functional ships would be able to beat disabled ones. Most manual gunners should be able to hit a craft stuck dead in space.

"So you're saying everything depends on us, again," Davin said as the *Jumper* continued to close with the Eden fleet's core.

They'd already performed the initial hail, talked their way through the decided story: the *Jumper* had made it to Callisto as expected, found a rebel ambush, and had taken off under fire and was now on the run and looking for protection.

Yang, the Eden admiral standing tall on the flagship, hadn't looked all that surprised via the comm's hologram. In fact, if Davin had to guess, Yang had seemed so cool about the events, it was like he'd already heard about them.

Amado may have looped Yang in.

"Isn't that where we just said we wanted to be?" Phyla replied. "Right back in the middle?"

"I was personally hoping for a fringe spot," Davin said. "Offer support, have little risk in return."

"Not how it works for us."

"So I've noticed," Davin said. "Those engines ready? If this doesn't play, we're going to have to run like hell."

"For once," Phyla said, "the *Jumper*'s doing pretty good. We haven't taken real enemy fire in, I almost can't believe it, two years Davin. Two whole years."

Since that mishap running proton batteries from Miner Prime to Titan. Davin remembered that, a group of pirates looking for a lone freighter that'd found more than what they expected. The pirates might still be lost in derelict space, drifting in the asteroid belt. At least, Davin hoped so.

"Eden is calling again," Fournine announced. "Shall I put them through?"

"Fournine, you don't and we're probably dead, so yes, put them through," Davin replied.

Yang's visage again formed up in the cockpit windshield. The full hologram option obstructed the view, but Phyla flew more by systems than visuals anyway. Crowded sectors, with craft flowing in every direction, made straight up fly-by-sight a surefire plan to crash into someone, somewhere. Eden had already provided a vector to their main ship's docking bay, so Phyla wasn't even flying at this point: Four-nine had the *Jumper* locked and coasting.

"We've checked out your story," Yang said, giving Davin a dead-set look that could mean anything. "Our sources confirm that you were supposed to be delivering the weapon to Callisto, but you never made contact on the moon. Why?"

"The rebels were waiting. Apparently you've got a leak," Davin answered, staying in truth's broad range. "Next time I take a job from Eden, I'll ask for a premium to make it worth the risk."

"Or perhaps you made too much noise," Yang replied. "Isn't that a fixture for you?"

"Hey, your people chose me. Now let us ditch this device and get our coin, or we can see how much the rebels will pay us for it. Your call."

Yang gave Davin a three second stare as his ship grew near, letting Davin cook in his own words for a breath before issuing a sharp nod.

"You'll dock and then deliver the weapon to the waiting crew. You will remain on your ship until we have dealt with the rebel force, at which point we will debrief you," Yang said. "I am aware of your reputation, Davin Masters, and will not tolerate any deviations from the plan. Should you take any action that presents a risk to my fleet, I will not hesitate to destroy you and your ship."

"Thought you wanted this weapon we're carrying?" Davin asked.

"Tools can be rebuilt. Lives cannot." Yang glanced off camera. "It seems our fight is nearly upon us. We will speak after the battle."

Yang dissolved, his ship taking the hologram's place in the cockpit's center. Behind the Eden fleet, deep space waited. Davin figured they'd hopped around from

Ganymede, choosing to use the moon's rotation to bring the rebel fleet and Davin's own ship towards them while they waited, ready to spring their trap.

Instead, the trappers had become the trapped. Or something.

"There has to be a better way to say that," Davin muttered.

"Say what?" Phyla asked.

"Nevermind," Davin glanced at the console.

The *Jumper* had moved within comm range of nearly the entire Eden fleet. Waiting much longer to deploy the weapon would put them so damn close that, if the weapon didn't work, they'd be very, very dead.

"Guess it's time," Davin said, moving from his chair and reaching behind him, to where the orange and silver ball rested on a tray they'd secured from the kitchen. Not exactly high tech, but it sufficed. "You really want to do this?"

"Try to disable a giant Eden fleet while we're in the middle of it?" Phyla said. "Honestly, Davin, when I said we should fight for a cause, this wasn't really what I had in mind."

"Me either," Davin replied, then grinned. "Want to bail?"

Phyla shook her head.

"Good." Davin pressed the weapon's button, those silver lines lighting up and moving again. "Because now that we're here, I'm really liking what this'll add to my legend. Davin, destroyer of fleets. Sounds pretty good to me."

"You're ridiculous," Phyla said, then tapped away a tight, coded message back towards the rebel fleet to warn them that they'd better kill their comms quick. "We're going dark."

Holding the spinning orb in his hands, Davin felt a little insane, a little whiplash at how fast he'd gone from running random cargo to leading a covert assault on the largest organization in the solar system.

How fast he'd gone from helping to betraying Viola.

That thought stopped Davin cold, while the projected timer over the weapon counted down and the Eden flagship drew ever closer. She'd gone in with Davin over Earth, fired the final shot that stopped Bosser. Now Davin was turning his back on her.

No. He was siding with his other friends, the ones who'd been with the Wild Nines for longer, who'd kept Davin alive through countless missions, ambushes, and disasters. It wasn't Davin's fault that they'd all wound up on different sides.

"You think Viola's on any of these ships?" Davin said suddenly, as the timer ticked through its final seconds.

"Viola?" Phyla said. "Why? Isn't she an engineer?"

The timer hit zero. From the cockpit, the lights adorning the big Eden flagship went dark. If Viola was on there with Yang, she'd no doubt know exactly what'd happened.

"It worked," Davin said. "Viola, I hope your weapon doesn't get you killed. Let's turn and burn, Phyla."

"On it."

The *Jumper*'s pilot wheeled the freighter around, turning back towards a rebel fleet that'd picked up its pace, fighters jolting ahead, followed by the rocky frigates. All racing in towards what had been a deadly force, was now nothing more than dead metal.

"Don't go too far," Merc said when Davin and Phyla turned their comms back on. "We're going to try and cripple the ships. We might need you for captive transport."

The pilot had found himself a fighter, a few injections to push past his wound's pain, and was leading a squad as they flowed around the *Jumper* and in towards the Eden ships.

Davin started to counter that this wasn't part of the deal, before realizing that this wasn't really a *deal* anymore. They'd picked a side, and now they had to play their part.

"Let's not stay too close," Davin said, pointing to the Eden ships that'd been out of range of the weapon, a scatter-shot few trying to converge on their fleet's vulnerable middle. "If the *Jumper* takes any shots, we'll be the ones paying for repairs."

"Agreed," Phyla said, then flashed a soft smile Davin's way. "I know this wasn't easy, so thank you."

"You mean risking our lives and our ship on an all-out assault for a cause I'm not so sure about?"

"Exactly."

"Then you're welcome. And, next place we land, you're buying dinner."

Phyla laughed, "Deal."

The *Jumper* swung around Opal's flagship, Phyla nestling her into the rocky cover. On the radar, they watched the rebel swarm converge on the big Eden blotches. No opposing fighters, no opposing fire. Viola's weapon might really turn the whole war over right here.

On the console, Merc's leading squad broke into strafing runs on the Eden flagship. Davin figured Yang would be on the bridge, yelling at someone, anyone to get the craft back up and running. Without any shields, even smaller fighters would smash through the ship's windows, their structures and vast batteries. One good shot could set off an explosion that'd take the whole ship down.

Phyla tuned the comm into the rebel's broadcast frequency, and they heard Merc announce they'd entered firing range. Heard the call to light'em up.

Silence.

Then shouts. Loud ones, panicked ones, with one word

coming through as rebel pilots called out that the shields, the damn shields were still up and active.

"That's not good," Davin said, low and slow.

The words changed, and Merc's voice came through loud and sharp, "Evasive action! Find your wingmen and stick together!"

"Oh," Phyla breathed. "Look."

On the radar, new blips were emerging. Hundreds, as the Eden ships disgorged their apparently-just-fine fighters. Rebel dots started vanishing as derelict vessels sprang into sudden life, spraying fire at rebel ships not ready for evasive action.

The *Jumper* shook, and Davin saw orange blossom out the cockpit window. Rocks broke against the *Jumper*'s hull as lasers and missiles poured into Opal's flagship, one that'd put itself in position to obliterate a bunch of dead vessels and now found itself surrounded by live ones.

"Get us moving!" Davin said. "This is not where we want to be!"

"How?" Phyla said as she turned up the *Jumper*'s engines and scooted the freighter away from Opal's ship. "What's happening?"

"They knew," Davin said. "They must have known what the weapon could do, that there was a chance we'd use it against them."

That Eden could've built a defense against their own secret weapon didn't surprise Davin too much. That they would've been able to deploy it so fast, that they would've expected Davin to use it when he had? That suggested something else entirely.

A plot. A con. A way to draw the rebels into the open, and crush them.

More debris poured from Opal's ship as it took fire from

all sides. The rebels gave back what they could, and Davin saw several lighter Eden ships break apart, but those were token losses. Yang's own massive cruiser bore down on the rebel fleet, dealing devastation as it closed to murderous proximity.

The rebels weren't going to just lose. Eden would slaughter them.

"Phyla," Davin said as the *Jumper* pointed away, back towards Callisto. "You said you wanted to join a cause, no matter what?"

She nodded.

"Then turn around," Davin said.

"We can't do anything about the fight."

"Maybe not, but we might be able to make sure there's another one."

## 24

## THE BATTLE. THE WAR.

Humanity took to the stars like a dog to its dinner, roaring off Earth through the solar system with profit-seeking abandon. Clashes erupted as would-be homesteaders claimed this moon or that asteroid for themselves, the savvier ones uniting with each other and pooling their ships together to form ragtag fleets. Earth's governments realized, finally, that lawless conflict wasn't the best way forward, and Eden grew from that effort, blanketing the planets with something akin to order.

Now Eden enforced its directive, blasting chunks from Opal's ship in what was, Davin figured, the first big space conflict in human history. And it was as one-sided as battles could get.

With the rebels surprised and in a formation designed to pounce on a hapless enemy, Eden pressed its advantage. Davin saw rebel blips vanish from the radar as Eden declared its intent to take no prisoners, to obliterate every enemy until nothing save space dust remained.

Which, if Davin and Phyla were in a rebel ship, would pose a problem. The *Jumper*, though, aligned with neither side. Its broadcast designation dumped it as neutral, so long as Yang didn't paint a target on their backs.

"He should be thanking us," Phyla said. "We're the ones that set his trap."

"Not a bad idea," Davin replied. "How about we switch sides?"

Phyla shot him the iciest glare, and Davin held up his hands.

"Only joking," Davin said.

"Lotta people are dying while you're joking."

"Then let's make it fewer," Davin said. "Starting right here."

The rebel flagship soaked up Eden fire like a beacon, and Davin figured the ship wouldn't last too much longer. Already, evacuation pods were popping off various sections like seeds, their tiny engines popping out against the laser-filled backdrop as they began their darts towards Callisto.

"Davin, I don't want to switch sides," Phyla said, "but I don't want to die today either."

"Bring us around towards the upper bay, the one near the bridge," Davin said. "We'll hail, pick up any passengers, and then get out before it all falls apart."

An optimistic plan, perhaps, but Davin had that rush again. That adrenaline heat that came with moments made for action. He'd felt it in the Callisto warehouse, coming to rescue Phyla, but beating up Merc killed that fun. Better to get involved when you were on the right side, when you could follow through.

When Davin placed the call to the flagship, Phyla weaving the *Jumper* through the laser-and-debris maze, Opal's fuzzy face appeared. Behind her, the blurred backdrop lit with sparks, and Davin thought he saw at least one small fire. Smoke shrouded her face, which bore a harried expression en route to resigned.

"Davin, please tell me you have another trick to play," Opal said. "If not, I should get back to directing my retreat."

"Don't think you'll have much time for that the way this one's looking," Davin said. "How about you get your crew to your top bay and onto our ship before yours goes up?"

Something rattled the flagship, and Opal's shoulders tightened as she steadied herself. The alarms behind her grew louder, and Davin caught a few bodies making for the exit already.

"Captains go down with their ships," Opal said. "Isn't that how it goes?"

"Only the bad ones," Davin said.

Someone more prone to self-pity might've taken Davin's invitation to bemoan the ambush, to declare that their own bad leadership had caused the disaster. Opal had seen enough war to know victory and calamity were twins, often trading places with each other. You had to take what fate gave you and keep on fighting.

"The top bay?" Opal replied, nodding slow, maybe processing the best path from her current position to the next. "All right. You give us a ride, we'll be there to catch it."

Opal's image fizzled away as Phyla flew up and over the flagship's spine. Up here, Davin could see across the whole conflict, a flashing battleground with Eden's ships marking the borders, hemming in the remaining rebels.

"Merc's still out there," Phyla said. "Near that frigate."

Davin had almost forgotten about the fighters. The small ships swarmed around in pairs and trios, bombing away at larger ships or swirling around each other in snarled dogfights. The rebels, here, had proved more tenacious than their larger vessels, their varied ship and live-pilot assortment doing better against Eden's drone legions.

Tapping on her console, Phyla highlighted Merc's ship, which placed a small green bracket around its dot on the cockpit windshield. The pilot danced his fighter around one laser after another, constantly swirling this way and that as Merc searched and found breathing room by centimeters.

"He can't do that forever," Davin said. "We have a few minutes till Opal gets to the bay. Let's give him some cover."

Spitting lasers at Eden fighters wouldn't do much for the *Jumper*'s current neutrality, but in the blazing battle, anyone would be hard-pressed to tell what shot came from where. More important, Merc was his friend, and Davin owed the pilot this much after getting him shot.

"Eightsix," Davin called through the comm to the cargo bay, where the android sat. "Get to a turret, we're taking on some action."

"I will not." Eightsix's reply came with her usual straightforward nothingness. "I refuse to fire on an Eden ship."

Phyla, who had the *Jumper* moving towards Merc's zone, slowed the engines. She knew as well as Davin that bringing the freighter into a fight like this without both turrets manned would be a bad call. Davin didn't have time to argue with the android, either, which meant a tactical change.

"Find Merc's band and hail him, Fournine," Davin said. "Phyla, take us to the bay. If we can't go in to help Merc, then we'll have to get him out to us."

Phyla curled the *Jumper* around Opal's cratering ship, which now had full sections breaking off and floating away. Fire didn't spread in space, but small bursts nonetheless glittered along the ship as Eden's continued attack chewed it away. Yang's vessel came in for a broadside, one that would give it a clear shot at the bay Opal ran towards.

"Davin?" Merc's voice scattered over the comm. "Now's not the best time."

"Noticed," Davin said. "Need you to come back home. We're picking up Opal before her ship goes bust, and we could use an escort."

"Goes bust?" Merc said, then presumably after checking his scanner, cursed. "Okay, we're coming."

Davin clicked off the transmission as Phyla locked in on the bay. The *Jumper* didn't slow down like it normally would during a normal docking because, well, normal didn't apply when lasers filled the space around you and your target had chunks blowing off and bouncing off your hull.

The bay loomed in front, a blue-lit slit in the rocky flagship expanding as the *Jumper* closed. Yang's flagship opened fire and all the dark Davin could see vanished as lasers filled the air. Opal's ship countered with a pitiful few, and every single rebel shot that emerged seemed to draw a dozen Eden batteries. The bay's blue slit became haloed in orange as explosions rippled across the hull.

Three white streaks lanced in from the right, heading straight for Opal's bridge. Davin didn't hear a sound when they struck, but the light flared bright. The small chunks battering the *Jumper* grew, shaking the ship as the rocks punched through shields designed for laser energy and clanged against the hull.

"That's a big one," Davin said, pointing to a large, whirling slab coming right their way. "Plan on dodging it?"

"We're going too fast," Phyla said. "If I move, we miss the bay, and I don't think we'll have time for another pass."

"The *Jumper* can't ram through debris twice our size," Davin said.

"Abort?" Phyla asked.

And abandon Opal? The hull chunk obscured the blue bay, flipping towards them. Five seconds to adjust.

The sniper had always covered Davin's back. When Fournine had Davin dead on Europa, Opal took the shot.

Four.

But wouldn't Opal want them to live? To save themselves?

Three.

"Davin?" Phyla said. "Need a choice!"

No. Davin would take the chance. He pushed the shields up.

Two.

"Fly straight," Davin said as the debris filled the windshield.

Bright fire burned overhead, the lasers stitching a precise line across the debris's cracking faults. The junk broke apart as the *Jumper* flew through, scraping sounds echoing through the ship, but without alarms, without oxygen leaks, without death.

And on the other side, the blue bay. Still there, still intact.

"What the hell happened?" Phyla said.

"I am not allowed to shoot Eden ships," Eightsix came over the ship's comm, "but I am programmed for self-preservation."

Davin sat back in his seat. Let out the breath he'd been holding for a long moment.

"Eightsix," Davin said. "Next time you shoot earlier. Next time you talk."

"Apologies, Davin. I was not aware you intended to ram the debris. It seemed too stupid an idea."

"You'll get used to those if you're on this ship for long,"

Phyla said. "Davin, get to the cargo bay. I don't think we'll have much time."

The *Jumper* swooped into the flagship's bay, the lights a placid change from the laser show going on outside. A laser-scored gunmetal floor dotted with hasty flight's hallmarks replaced cold space beneath them, and Phyla curled the *Jumper* around as they neared the cluster of people waiting for rescue. Davin spied Opal at the group's head, looking frayed but not frazzled.

"Ice cold, even as she loses the war," Davin said, getting up from his seat and heading to lower the ramp.

"The battle," Phyla called after him. "The war's barely started!"

Sure. If that's what Phyla thought, then more power to her. Davin could count, though, and after today Eden would have at least one full fleet and the rebels would have nothing more than scraps. Ships won wars, and the rebels had none.

Fournine beat Davin to the punch and had the ramp coming down as Davin hit the bay. Opal and her evacuees didn't wait for the ramp to hit the ground; they started pulling themselves on and climbing up as soon as it was within reach. Given the rumbling, crackling noises that poured in as soon as the ramp opened the *Jumper* to outside sounds, Davin couldn't blame them.

He'd have jumped ship long ago.

Fifteen rebel crew clambered on, Opal doing her captain thing and taking the last spot. Davin raised the ramp as she went up it, asking any rebels with gunnery talent to take the turrets. When one asked about Eightsix, Davin told the android to get herself back to the workshop and stay there.

Davin didn't want to draw Eden's attention, but if it

came, he needed someone who'd pull the trigger on the corporate bastards.

"Ready?" Phyla asked as Davin slid back into his seat.

"Very," Davin replied. "Let's get outta here."

Phyla blasted the *Jumper* away as the bay began to break up around them, gasses and fires pouring from vents and broken containers. All around the ship, it seemed like reality twisted as the flagship's core structure splintered and bent, a million forces tearing and pushing the ship apart.

Leaving the bay, the laser lights had died. With Opal's flagship destroyed, Yang's cruiser had gone off in search of fresh meat, not that Davin saw any. The rebel ships capable of fleeing had done so, sprinting far off towards Jupiter and, likely, Saturn beyond. Eden frigates sucked up disabled rebel fighters and anyone who'd launched off to nowhere while evacuating.

Surrounded by debris and away from immediate danger, Phyla slowed down, matching the junk around them and using it as a disguise.

"Now what?" Phyla said. "We leave, and Eden will chase."

Davin, though, didn't answer. He was pouring over his console, pinging through the various blips that he could find. Searching for one in particular.

A crackle came in over the comm, on the rebel band. Close range and targeted, so just the *Jumper* would catch it. The signal coming from a big debris chunk just to port.

"Hey there," said Merc, sounding more exhausted than Davin felt. "Think I could hitch a ride?"

## 25

## NEW PLANS

They drifted in the rubble for a day. Twenty-Four Earth hours spent hugging a fractured chunk the rebels identified as some of their former crew quarters. If you looked hard enough, you could see a picture or two, clothes, and keepsakes littered among the laser-cooked rock. Mementos that'd stay adrift in space for a long time, Davin figured, until Jupiter's gravity well dragged them down.

Eden's fleet finished picking up the leftovers and boosted off. Fournine read the direction and stated the fleet was likely heading to Ganymede for repairs and re-supply, Galaxy Forge doing its level best to help the giant corporation continue the war effort.

"They didn't even try to look for us," Opal said, joining Davin, Phyla, and Merc as they settled into the *Jumper*'s simulators. "I should find it insulting, but I'm only relieved."

Starved for something to do other than stare at each other and think about the disastrous fight, the rebels had helped Davin hook up and repair the *Jumper*'s simulator set to its full capacity. The eight pods gave people a chance to immerse themselves somewhere, anywhere else.

Opal and Merc hadn't wanted to dive in at first. Opal because she thought it wasn't appropriate for a commander, Merc because he would do whatever Opal wanted. Davin wore them down with memories and increasingly outlandish bets about how bad he and Phyla could roast the other pair in a head to head match-up.

"They did turn your ship into floating trash," Davin said as the simulator pod closed over his head, their mics clicking in and syncing up. "What're the odds anyone survives something like that?"

"Davin," Phyla warned.

"Low," Opal said, brushing off Davin's words. "Low odds, and everyone that didn't make it away from that fight is going to haunt me for a long time."

Opal, though, didn't sound sad. She'd spent the day, aside from a medication-aided sleep shift, strategizing with her troops. Rolling up new plans and discarding them in equal measure while Davin checked over the *Jumper*'s systems for damage and Phyla kept the craft from running into any more debris. Rather than wallow, Opal buttressed her grief with action.

Merc? Merc finally had a chance to rest. After getting shot and then being pressed into a fighter's cockpit, the pilot collapsed for most of the time, and nobody cared.

Davin called up the scenario—one he had designed himself—and the simulator's black void faded into a familiar expanse: the crumbling junk heap homes, crowded paths, and a chipping ceiling that marked Vagrant's Hollow on the massive space station Miner Prime.

Davin's home, and he was about to watch it get destroyed all over again.

"But we're not done," Opal said, her voice continuing to come over the simulators. Davin left the comms wide open; the game, this time, wasn't meant to be real. "We're working on more ships. Building up our capabilities. Eden's not going to move on Saturn for a long time, and when they do, we'll be ready."

Davin and Phyla phased in, gliding down a lift towards the wide pad that marked Vagrant's Hollow's connection to the rest of the space station, off limits for this particular adventure. As they descended, words splashed across Davin's vision, outlining the objective:

Find Viola and get her back to the lifts.

Merc and Opal would be seeing the opposite as they stood up in one of several potential spots on the level's opposite side. They had to catch Viola and bring her to a different exit, one that in the real world would lead to Miner Prime's docking bays. In this virtual one, they'd just win the match.

"Ready for what?" Davin replied to Opal over the band. "Eden's going to have more, and better ships than anything you'll be able to carve from those ring rocks. If you try to fight them straight up, you're going to lose."

The lift opened, spitting Davin and Phyla into the crowded level. Merchants and clientele mingled with workers coming and going from shifts. Families looking for food. Entertainers trying to scrape a few coin from the fewer that had it. The hustle sound, so different from the *Jumper*'s general whirring hum, made Davin twitch. The cooking food and unwashed bodies mingled pleasant scents with poor ones, but all pulled Davin home.

Which was why Davin had made the scenario in the first place.

"Someone's not in a good mood today," Merc said.

With nods, gestures, and hand signals, Davin and Phyla advanced from the lift and into the main, crowded, thoroughfare. People bumped into Davin's shoulders, hailed him to buy this and that, or shrank back at his outfit. Both he and Phyla wore the blue-black uniforms of Miner Prime's police force, a group that tended to hurt Vagrant's Hollow every time they visited.

Old habits came back fast, and Davin kept on with the game's second objective: convince Opal and Merc to do the right thing.

"How are you not feeling the same damn way?" Davin replied. "Don't know if you noticed out there, but your asses just got handed to you. If your only plan is to try the same thing again, all you're going to do is litter the solar system with wrecks. Which, speaking personally, makes my job running cargo more annoying."

Davin tapped Phyla's shoulder and jerked his head towards a sturdy overhang. Things were about to get interesting.

"Davin," Opal said. "What are you getting at?"

"Why do you ask?"

Merc's laugh came over the comm, "You always have a plan."

"I wouldn't go that far," Phyla added.

"But in this case, I really do have a plan." Emotions or not, captains had to captain, and Davin didn't want to drag his ship into any more war zones. "You're not going to win in a straight-up slugging match with Eden, and you don't have to."

Vagrant's Hollow rumbled as Davin and Phyla joined a clustered, and very confused, family beneath the overhang. Screams rang out as explosions ripped through the slums, and the first laser flashes started as factions began clashing. Dust and dirt swept up around them as the first buildings collapsed.

The rebel assault had begun.

"I was on Mars after Eden crushed the Red Voice there," Opal shouted over the rumbling. "They didn't let the rebels live. There wasn't peace. It was die or get in line."

Davin gave that remark the solemn second it deserved as he and Phyla broke from the overhang, both pulling their rifles over their shoulders as they advanced deeper. Viola shouldn't be too far ahead, now.

"This isn't Mars. Eden doesn't control your territory, but they will if this keeps up," Davin said as they ducked down a side street, past a several-story tower that had begun a fatal list to the side. Rippling bangs continued, and, back towards the lift, Davin could see the first police reinforcements arriving. "Thing is, I know Eden. They're like me. All about the coin. And we can use that."

Phyla sighed. Davin ignored it.

They reached a broad square, a few bodies already populating the fringes. In the center, looking confused, stood the simulator's version of Viola, a brown-haired woman whose family wealth put her well out of place. Puk, her omnipresent little robot, didn't exist here. Too hard to get the bot's sarcasm right.

She stood talking with two rebels, both projections, though they'd win the scenario for Merc and Opal if they weren't dealt with. In real history, they'd taken Viola with them off the station, prompting the chase that'd led to . . . a lot.

"Guess what Eden's ships are doing when they're fighting you?" Davin said, focusing back on the situation.

"They're not escorting shipments, they're not earning Eden that sweet, sweet coin. All you need to do to get Eden to stop fighting is convince them they'll earn more working with you instead of crushing you."

With a couple gestures, Phyla knelt down to provide cover. Davin went forward, took aim, and fired. The rifle didn't perform like Melody—Davin *would* be getting back to Callisto for that weapon—but, within the simulation, it took out the two rebels with perfect shots.

Merc laughed from wherever the pilot was hiding, "That's what we've been doing, Davin. We're not trying to take over the solar system, just give Eden a bloody nose so they'll leave us alone."

Viola, stunned by the sudden end to her conversational partners, turned to run. Davin reached out, grabbed her arm, and when he touched Viola, a light blue shade went over the woman. As if some switch had been flipped, Viola stopped resisting and started following Davin like a particularly devoted pet.

At a certain point, a game became a game.

"Nope, wrong approach," Davin replied to Merc. "That's a fight, and they'll win a fight. You want to put them into a war. One that's going to last so damn long that it's not worth waging. We get Eden to neutral territory. Hash it out without killing anyone, and turn their minds to money. Talk clear shipping all the way to Saturn and beyond and they'll change. I guarantee it."

Phyla saw them first and squeezed a couple shots over Davin's shoulder. He whirled, keeping up his back-step while trying to find somewhere to aim. A shadow that may have been Merc came and went between two buildings, their alley a dusty haze.

"Keep going," Phyla said, dropping the voiceless act now that they'd hit the game's climax. "I'll cover you."

Davin broke into a run, and Viola's programmed self followed along. Phyla would stay behind, try to buy enough time for Davin's scramble to get to the lifts, or close enough to where it wouldn't matter.

Together, Davin and Viola broke through the side street, hit the main thoroughfare. Other rebel forces and Miner Prime security engaged, now, in a massive firefight that slowly spread through Vagrant's Hollow, filling the air with hot lasers that forced Davin to go slow, to duck and dash between buildings. Viola mirrored his moves exactly, in a way that, really, looked unnatural.

Maybe Davin would change that part when he had time.

Like that would ever happen again.

"I'm surrounded," Phyla said, her voice sounding almost bored. To be fair, the two of them had done this simulation a hundred times. "Hope you made it far enough."

"Almost there. Thanks, love."

After scrambling through some burnt-out houses, Davin and Viola reached the lift pad's edge. Just another few meters and he'd have the game won. Around him, a few security stragglers ran off the pad and into the battle. The dust continued to rise. The crowds and smells Davin remembered from his childhood had been replaced by burned bodies and burning clothes.

Davin didn't see the shot, but he felt it. The simulators didn't give you pain, exactly, but they tweaked his nerves. Sent twinges while his vision flashed red. Davin's legs didn't respond, his arms suddenly flopped, too weak to hold the rifle. Viola watched Davin as he fell, utterly emotionless.

"Damn," Davin muttered as the simulator's vision grew fuzzy, as Opal stepped into view and looked down at him.

With a single touch, Opal turned Viola's blue shading to red. The two women looked at each other, and Opal tapped her chin a single time.

"You know, Davin," Opal said. "You just might be right."

Then she shot him.

**26**

---

## PERMISSION TRANSMISSION

With Eden's fleet gone, they dropped the rebel crew off on Callisto. Heading back to the rings brought Davin problem after problem: first came the demands from local authorities to pay for the damage to the industrial ring Fournine had blown open in the earlier rescue. Opal covered for Davin there, allowing the damages to come from rebel accounts.

"If your idea works and we get that peace," Opal said as Callisto's enforcement left them in the docking bay, "then keeping you out of Callisto's prison will be worth it. If it doesn't work out, then you'll be too dead for anyone to worry about."

"Appreciate the confidence," Davin replied. "Now, if you don't mind, I have to see about Melody."

Opal didn't mind, but she did want to come with. Saying she hadn't seen Davin in a long time, that'd been almost as long since she did something other than issue orders, Opal changed into more casual clothes—one of several outfits still packed away on the *Jumper*, from years ago—and the pair went walking. Merc, Phyla, and Eightsix stuck to the ship, cleaning up debris damage and restocking for what would come next.

"So you've been running cargo," Opal said when Davin finished summing up the last few years. "That's it?"

"That's it?" Davin replied. "Why're you saying that like it's a bad thing?"

"Because the guy that helped save us from an android apocalypse is running packages."

"I've shot enough people in my life, thank you."

True enough. Davin, though, had relished in the adrenaline that he'd felt in the battle overhead. Even in attacking Merc's squad to get Phyla back. Killing hadn't ever done anything for him, but danger? Life lived on a tight line ready to snap?

He still heard that call.

"You could step into shoes like mine," Opal said as they walked along the docking ring, listening for the calls of a certain small salesman. "Trade your rifle for a rank. Save more lives that way."

"You've read me wrong if you think I'm a military man."

"And you've read the rebels wrong if that's what you think we're about," Opal said. "Alissa used to call us the Red Voice, because we spoke up for a free Mars. Now everyone just calls us rebels, and it sticks. We're pushing back, Davin, against the forces that want to trample us."

"Since when did you become an idealist?" Davin stopped at a vendor, transferred a coin to get a fresh, buttered ear of corn. Had to take advantage of his surroundings before returning to nutrient goop, twenty-four-seven. "Wasn't all that long ago you were right with us, taking jobs for coin."

"Because I'd only seen their cause through the end of my scope," Opal said, keeping her mouth and hands butter-free. "If you took up with us, really joined in, you might find you agree."

"But what about my reputation?" Davin winked Opal's way. "I'm Earth's hero. I can't be fighting against her."

"Nobody remembers that except you."

Ouch, but accurate. Time moved forward fast, and Davin's flash-in-the-pan fame hadn't lasted long. Too many powerful people had worked with Bosser to risk giving the case too much attention. Not that Davin minded much: do one talk show and you've done a million.

"Tell you what," Davin said. "If this works out, then I'll join your rebels. Give it a try."

"If this works, there won't be a rebellion," Opal said. "We'd be a state. Like Earth."

Davin shrugged. Opal laughed, shook her head.

"You never change, do you?"

"It's a personal policy," Davin replied, then stopped, listened. "Hear that?"

For all his supposed selling acumen, Mako wasn't what anyone would call the smartest man this side of Mars. The parts seller made noise walking out of a bay in front of Davin and Opal, yelling one thank you after another back into the bay, where a customer must have completed a purchase they were now, no doubt, regretting. Because that's what happened when you dealt with Mako.

"Hello there," Davin said, clapping a hand on Meek's shoulder. "Long time, Mako."

The man didn't jump, didn't start, but instead turned on that greaseball grin Mako had mastered, "Davin! You're back? And not arrested?"

"Connections," Opal said, coming up behind Davin. "Hello, Mako."

"Opal? Are you getting the old gang back together?" Mako asked.

"Just to find you," Davin said. "Where's my weapon?"

"Weapon?"

Punching someone in an open concourse tended to be frowned upon. Tended to attract the wrong attention. So Davin draped an arm over Meek's shoulders and directed the salesman across the ring to a side alcove, one quickly vacated by the two other chatters once Opal caught them in her warning look.

"Don't tell me you haven't seen it," Davin said. "I left Melody inside that passage you showed me. When I went back, after you disappeared, it was gone."

"Lots of people use those doorways," Mako replied. "I didn't take it."

"Mako, we barely survived a bad battle. I'm tired, stressed, and not happy. What'd you do with Melody?"

Mako shook his head, "Look, I ran when that captain put a bad look on his face. Out here, things are wild Davin. They'll as soon as shoot you as say no. You learn to read a room and run."

"It's not that bad," Opal said.

"You don't think so?" Mako shot back. "You try selling parts on this stupid moon."

"Then what happened to it, Mako?" Davin said. "You really don't know?"

Mako shook his head, "No idea, boss. But I can find out. Ask around. People talk to me."

That, Davin believed. Mako had a way of worming into conversations and going unnoticed. Davin didn't want to rely on Mako for anything, but, especially with Opal standing behind him, the *Jumper*'s captain knew he didn't have forever to hunt for a missing shotgun. The solar system's grand future waited.

"Fine," Davin said. "You ask around. Send the *Jumper* a call when you've found it. I'll pay you back if you get it."

"Of course, Davin, of course." Mako weaseled out from under his arm. "Sorry that fight didn't go your way. Better luck next time?"

"Sure." Davin stood up as Mako took the reply as a sign to leave and ducked back into the crowd, tools and parts pack jingling as he went.

Returning to the *Jumper* empty-handed hadn't been part of the plan, but the stop at Callisto had let them get rid of the extra crew. Had let Merc and Phyla get the ship and his fighter into shape. Sometimes you had to take what wins you could.

Alissa Reinhart came first. The Red Voice leader maintained control over the rebel effort, though she'd passed along the hands-on missions to people like Opal and Merc in favor of administrative responsibilities out by Saturn.

Floating off Callisto, Opal keyed in the frequency and started the transmission from the cockpit, all four humans crammed together. Davin had Eightsix on permanent patrol around Eden's weapon, once again locked in its container, the key secured in Melody's weapon locker in the captain's quarters.

The time delay for data to travel between Saturn and Jupiter, often an annoyance in space communications, would be an asset. The four could strategize between every reply, come to an agreement, and send back the perfect response every time. At least, that's how Davin saw it.

Alissa did not.

"You lost our fleet, and now you want me to empower

you to negotiate on our behalf?" Alissa said after they'd laid out the situation.

The distance and signal distortion kept any video out of the equation, but Fournine had enough image data from old files to put Alissa's approximate hologram on the cockpit's windshield. Flame-haired and severe, Alissa packed power into her look. Davin hadn't really met her, but from what Opal said, she was an uncompromising leader. The cause above all else.

"Eden laid a trap," Opal replied to Alissa's accusation with the theory they all accepted. "They fed us the weapon knowing we would use it, and we went right into their net. Without our fleet, and even with it, we would not be able to stand up to Eden, Alissa. We need a new strategy. A new plan. This gives us an opportunity."

Opal sent the signal, leaning forward with her hands on Phyla's and Davin's chair backs. Her dark hair pulled up tight, the sniper and commander showed nothing of the exhaustion that ought to be weighing her down. Davin couldn't imagine what it'd be like to have a loss like that on your shoulders.

But then, Opal had played a part in tragedies before. Maybe she was used to it. Maybe, to lead a force like the rebels, you had to be.

"Opal, I'm impressed," Phyla said as the minutes ticked by between transmissions. "You've really changed."

"Have I?"

"Before, I always thought you were a loner," Phyla said. "You always seemed so lost in your past. Now, you're stronger."

Davin caught the admiration in Phyla's words. Had to agree with them.

"I'm not," Opal said. "I just stopped running from what I had to do."

"That's not easy," Merc added. "Especially when you have to drag along a goof like me."

"I know what that's like," Phyla said, throwing Davin a smile, "but sometimes the goofs are worth it."

"Sometimes they are." Opal reached back, gripped Merc's hand.

Alissa's reply came back, fizzling and cracking, "Provisional authority, Opal. If you manage to get Eden to give us Saturn and Jupiter, then I'll consent. We can share Galaxy Forge. I'll not accept any other deal. We might not be able to win a forever war with Eden, but I won't betray those who've given their lives by surrendering what we've won."

Terms Eden wouldn't accept, most likely, but at least a starting point. Something that could be massaged. Opal agreed, and sent the acceptance, which left Davin hovering over his console waiting to send the next transmission.

"What're you going to say to her?" Phyla asked.

Viola had given Davin the container. Had led them into this mess. If Eden really had meant for the weapon to fall into rebel hands, meant for the device to turn into a trap, then Viola had started all this. The girl that'd left Ganymede clueless about the solar system had turned into a cold killer.

"I can't see it," Davin said. "Viola's not that person."

"She's smart," Opal said. "And it's been years, Davin. Years spent working with Eden. That can change someone."

"Didn't you say," Davin asked Merc, "that the rebels had someone on the inside, and that's how you found out about the weapon in the first place?"

Merc nodded, "I'm sure Alissa's taking care of them. But I guess it's possible Eden didn't have this whole thing planned, then found out we had the weapon and changed tactics."

Either way, there was one person that could answer that question. That could, maybe, find a way to end the war before it took any more lives.

Davin punched the button, and sent his voice flying through the void.

## 27

# NEUTRAL TERRITORY

Outpost X-225, an asteroid-hugging mining base that Eden had built decades ago and left in a minimal state as it drifted through the dark between Mars and Jupiter. Viola suggested the base as neutral territory: it offered zero defenses, zero strategic value, and barely-there facilities that ensured neither party would want negotiations to go on long.

The *Jumper* made the journey in a few days, faster than Viola's climb all the way from Earth. Phyla transmitted the access codes Viola had sent along, and the base opened a docking bay—one of a whole two—for them to land. No human voice greeted them, because there simply wasn't a human living here.

"As if that's a downside," Fournine stated. "I quite prefer it when you're all off this ship. In fact, if Viola kills you all, Eightsix and I might take the *Jumper* for ourselves."

"Okay," Davin replied. "If we're all dead, you've got my blessing."

Despite the base's apparent emptiness, Davin, Merc, Phyla and Opal armed themselves before leaving the

*Jumper*. Their arrival bay had the sturdy, non-gleaming metal finish requisite for bases built years ago, when style had been sacrificed for substance, for cost. The curved bay, built into a hollow on Outpost X-225's chosen asteroid, hummed with clanking, clunking machinery. Air purifiers and more chugging away with ancient noise to keep oxygen around for nobody to breathe.

Getting off the *Jumper* via its ramp, Davin noted racks filled with basic supplies. Old fuel canisters, tools, and a sparse scrap selection. Enough, perhaps, for emergency repairs, but if you came to Outpost X-225 needing something more, you'd be out of luck.

"What a lovely spot," Davin said, leading the group towards the bay's sole exit, a big sliding metal door. The base's loud yellow lighting spoke of bulbs with dirty glass, so while the group could see, everything appeared to have a greasy film. "Might be my new favorite base."

"A good spot for an ambush," Opal said, keeping the rifle she'd borrowed from Phyla raised and ready. "A single entry vector, only one way out from the bay."

"You're paranoid," Davin replied. "Viola wouldn't kill us like that."

Amado would, but Davin had kept silent about the Eden enforcer. Whether that guy or his thugs would show up again, Davin couldn't tell, but this *would* be a ripe spot for Amado to jump out and jam another device into Davin's leg.

"I like it," Phyla said. "Reminds me of home."

"Because it's so dirty and old?" Merc said.

"Exactly."

Merc laughed. Davin couldn't disagree: Vagrant's Hollow had character stuffed into its every corner, but you would never mistake the place for somewhere clean or new.

Outpost X-225 let them inside with a grinding greeting,

the door sliding aside to reveal not a long, dark hallway that Davin expected but instead a wide open ball that would only work on an asteroid like this. Without much gravity, architects could get creative, and Outpost X-225 showcased the early space rush's innovative side.

Handled ladders ran like a spiderweb's tendrils around the central ball, occasionally pairing sliding rails with latched carts for moving larger objects. All the rails converged on a large platform in the center, one that appeared to have a hole in the center. On the platform's sides, tables, chairs and nutrient goop containers sat, opposite each other in every way.

Davin's boots picked up enough magnetism to keep a grip on the ground, one he dislodged with a single step and reach to grab the first hand-rail and pull himself along towards that middle. The effort would've been exhausting on a normal planet, but here it felt no different than walking or swimming. No real weight made for a fluid experience.

Like the docking bay, embedded lights shone their greasy yellow. Every breath flooded Davin's lungs with that combination of stale and purified air, oxygen that'd been recycled and regenerated over who knew how many years. The station's chill represented its limited solar panels and its zero geothermal energy: heat took power the station simply didn't have.

Fournine had recommended bundling up, and Davin, for once, was happy he'd followed the android's suggestion.

Bordering the big room, and linked by those handrails and carts courses, were other side spaces. Crew quarters, lavatories, the second docking bay, and even an exercise room, a requirement to keep bones from turning to mush in a zero G environment.

"Cozier than I thought," Merc said, following Davin on

the hand-rail. "I figured we'd get a squat room, a single table, and a strong desire to shoot each other."

"That last might still happen," Davin replied.

They'd discussed, on the flight over here, the plan. Negotiate, yes, but also try to suss out Eden's appetite for conflict. If the company seemed eager to reach a deal, then Alissa and the rebels could be flexible. Opal figured she could convince Alissa to take a deal that'd keep Saturn in rebel hands while saving enough lives to try again in the future.

What everyone did expect, though, was that Eden would set up something else around the asteroid. A failsafe in case things went negative. A frigate or four coasting nearby to deliver a fatal blow to the *Jumper* if Eden thought things couldn't be saved.

"Look, Davin," Phyla pointed towards the food dispensers as the foursome swung their way to the middle. "Your favorite."

"I'm so in love with this place," Davin said, noting all four nutrient goop flavors on offer. "It's like Viola knows me: old, dirty, and bland."

Nobody disagreed.

Exploring the outpost didn't take all that long as there wasn't, frankly, much outpost to explore. The crew quarters had enough cots for a half dozen members, perfectly made and likely left that way for years upon years. Each room the size of, if Davin was being generous, a bathroom stall. No decorations and a single long ceiling light.

Davin would be sleeping on the *Jumper*.

The supply rooms proved better, and filled with cans and vacuum-sealed provisions, tools, and scanning equipment designed to dig deep into an asteroid and determine its precious metal composition. Artifacts from a time when actual human crews did the analysis as opposed to the drone swarms that coated the asteroid belt now, searching like past prospectors for valuable rocks.

Outpost X-225 didn't contain any hidden ambushes, any dire secrets. Old, dirty, and bland were fitting words, and soon enough they all retreated back to the *Jumper*. The ship's friendlier confines, simulators, and Fournine commentary provided better ways to pass the time. Merc's blast wound healed, and for a little while, things felt like they had before: a crew on an adventure.

"They're here," Fournine announced, broadcast into every *Jumper* room in what was, according to the ship's internal clock and the dead lights, sleepy time.

Davin jerked up from the bed, Phyla doing the same, and scrambled to pull on an outfit.

"How long do we have, Fournine?" Davin said, accidentally kicking himself into the air while trying to pull on trousers. Dressing in zero G had its challenges. "Are they waiting for us, or can we still beat them?"

"They're on final approach," Fournine replied. "I suggest you hurry."

"Then get Eightsix into position," Davin said. "Are Merc and Opal moving?"

"Faster than you."

"Didn't need that, but thanks," Davin muttered.

The *Jumper*'s ramp clanged down, its sound echoing through the ship, and Eightsix's clomping came soon after. The android's inability to fight Eden didn't make her all that useful in open conflict, but Fournine had convinced Eightsix that she could still watch for any signs of danger or duplicity without breaking her programming. In other words, if Viola's crew planned to detonate the asteroid or come in blazing, Eightsix, hanging out in Outpost X-225's other docking bay, would be able to warn them.

"Are you ready?" Phyla said. "Because I'm not so sure I am."

"Way I see it," Davin replied. "We don't have any pressure. Opal and Merc are the rebel reps, Viola and whomever she brought are talking for Eden. We just get to watch, suck on some nutrient goop, and see what happens."

"The day you sit and watch something like this without opening your mouth is a day that'll never come, Davin."

"You're just salty that this rock doesn't have a bullet course."

Phyla laughed, "My ranking is going down because I'm not riding. After this, we have to stop somewhere I can at least get a run or two in."

"Priorities, right?"

"Right."

They met Opal and Merc leaving the ship, and together the foursome went into the outpost's central room. Fournine left the *Jumper*'s ramp down, had the engines active and ready in case they needed to make a quick getaway. While none of them carried rifles openly, they'd stuck weapons around the central room, near where each one stood. Ready to pull from behind a couch, from under a table if tensions rose.

"Everyone cool?" Davin asked, sharing the upright platform with Opal, while Phyla and Merc lounged on the downward side.

"So cool," Merc replied.

"Ready," Phyla added.

Opal just gave him a straight look and the slightest of nods.

"No immediate threats," Eightsix sent through the comm. "They have greeted me politely and are heading inside."

Well, that was something. Eden didn't intend to outright blow them up. Maybe the big company really was changing its methods.

The second docking bay door ground open like the first, Eden's party walking in with the same hesitance Davin and crew had shown on their arrival: every unseen room could hold an ambush, best tread carefully.

"Mox?" Davin said as the big shape resolved into the exoskeleton fighter, one who should've been on the moon. "What're you doing here?"

Mox stood big, not wearing his Centurion uniform but instead sporting an athletic combo that showed off the silver-black bars, wires, and connections coating his muscles. The man's shoulder-length black hair, braided and thick, floated loose in the zero G.

"Viola asked for help. Said she was meeting you." Mox brandished a supernova grin. "Thought I would take some time off, see what mess you had made now."

Without grabbing the handrails, Mox kicked away from the door and floated all the way to the central platform. Davin reached out, caught the man's larger hand in his own and pulled Mox in for a heavy hug.

"As messes go, it's a big one," Davin said, parting and looking Opal's way. "Difference is, this one's not all my fault."

"Opal," Mox said. "It has been a long time."

"It has," Opal replied. "You look good."

Davin faltered at the nervous air suddenly surrounding them before he remembered that this wasn't a Wild Nines reunion. There were sides and serious stakes here, and Mox and Opal weren't partners. Could wind up on opposite ends of a firefight.

Mox kept on with the introductory rounds, chuckling as he dropped through the hole to see Merc and Phyla, while Davin turned back to the entry, and the woman standing there, taking in the outpost's central room with an analytical eye. Floating over her shoulder, as always, was the gray metal bot. Puk's appendages had grown since Davin saw it last, a spindly array that gave the bot capabilities Davin never wanted to test.

"Viola!" Davin said. "Glad you could make it!"

Viola snapped her eyes his way, offered a single raised hand as a greeting. Since Davin had met her as a runaway on Europa, Viola had come along way in knowing the gray lines of life in space. Everything presented both opportunity and disaster, risk and reward. She'd gone from naive to, as Davin saw her now, suspicious.

When Viola went for the handrails, she moved with determined effort as Puk followed along. She reached the center, took Davin's hand to land on the platform, and, as she settled, took a long breath.

"Welcome to the wonderful Outpost X-225," Davin said. "What you see is what you get, I'm afraid."

"Well, Davin," Viola said through tight teeth, looking at Opal. "You're going to get us all killed."

## 28

## FRIENDLY DIPLOMACY

Despite Viola's warning, nobody died right away. Not after a few hours, not after a few days. Reunited with each other, they didn't consider negotiations until the fourth day, when enough drinks had been spilled and nutrient goop meals made to share all the stories that needed sharing.

Davin played ringleader, matchmaker: he set the bunch spinning from one to another, fostering conversation with quippy interjections and suggestions, pulling sets to go to the *Jumper*'s simulators and relive the missions Davin had programmed from their past. So many moments grew from personalities at play, from Merc and Mox tossing insults at one another, to Viola and Davin sharing Eden dirt, and Opal and Phyla digging deep into bullet racing.

Hours burned in Outpost X-225, and by the time both Viola and Opal had received calls from their superiors—Yang and Alissa, respectively—no one had reached their limit. Davin and Phyla had, the night before, talked of parenthood, how these were, in a sense, their children.

The Wild Nines, mostly, had come together on a far flung base, with a mission, as usual, far beyond their scope and skills.

Not that such things had ever stopped the 'Nines before.


Viola entered the outpost's central section with a tired look on the next evening, bearing news and orders from Yang to get going on the negotiations. Fleet movements were pending, and if a peace with the rebels was coming, then there were pirates and smugglers that Eden ships could pursue.

Alissa had said similar things to Opal, declaring that the tantalizing ideal of a rebel controlled Jupiter and Saturn would bring stability, prosperity, and that it was best to get on with it.

"So," Davin said, the two groups on either side of him, sitting in re-arranged couches and chairs. "How do we start?"

"I'll lay out Eden's terms first," Viola said, Puk hovering near her as ever. "You're going to hear these and feel insulted, but Yang said I could give away plenty."

"You're not supposed to say that," Opal replied, smiling. "Lets me know to push you."

"Sorry," Viola replied. "I'm not exactly used to this."

She'd been, so Viola had said to Davin, locked up in Eden's incredible labs. Pushing designs for new tools, ships, and, occasionally, weapons. Whereas Galaxy Forge, her father's immense factory on Ganymede, bent on mass production, Eden wanted marvels, no matter how unique. The massive company could take a workable idea and refine it; Viola had to come up with those ideas.

Viola had been sipping a little too much martian wine—

the *Jumper* had cases of the stuff, bonus payments for their runs—and let slip that Yang and Eden's others had chosen her for this mission because they thought Davin, Opal and the rest would go easy on her. They were Viola's friends, and would see her as a person, rather than as Eden's representative.

"Viola." Opal killed her grin, clasped her hands. "I'm not talking to you as a friend but as a spokesperson for millions who want to live a free life. Let's hear your terms, and then you'll hear ours."

"And, as the moderator," Davin interjected. "I'm hoping we can all clink glasses at the end of this. We're just deciding the fate of the solar system, people. Let's have some fun."

Mox, at least, gave Davin an appreciative snort.

Opal had a couple decades on Viola, but the younger woman didn't blanch at Opal's opening. She straightened, adopted a confident pose that Davin hadn't seen before. The runaway had disappeared inside a professional shell.

"Eden wants all the inner worlds," Viola started. "That shouldn't be a problem for you, as the rebels haven't had a presence there—"

"Since Eden murdered thousands on Mars," Merc interjected, and Opal put a hand on his wrist.

Viola took a breath, went back to it, "Like I said, the inner worlds. Including the asteroid belt and everything in it. We're willing to concede Saturn. Neptune and Uranus should be left open to anyone looking for opportunity."

Who would be bankrolling those opportunity seekers didn't take much intuition: Eden wouldn't hesitate to fund smaller companies to set up outposts on the fringes that, when those companies inevitably needed help, Eden would support and then take over.

Then again, if the rebels were smart, and Davin resisted the urge to stroke his chin as he parsed this in the moment, they'd offer support to those same companies. Claim faster response times from Saturn and leverage Eden's initial investment to expand their own outreach.

A dizzying game of moves and counter-moves that Davin had no desire to play.

Viola continued, breaking down smaller agreements like trade, transport, and the like. Essentially, Eden didn't want borders, didn't want tariffs, didn't want anything getting in the way of the almighty profit.

"We're also taking Galaxy Forge," Viola finished. "Jupiter itself is negotiable. Galaxy Forge is not."

"And that is where we have our sticking point," Opal replied. "Alissa and I agree with your proposed territories. We will make our own laws in our own space, but at first, the borders stay open. Goods flow free. We want Jupiter and Saturn, in their entirety."

"Opal," Mox said. "It is her damn family's factory. You cannot ask for that."

"Galaxy Forge makes the weapons that kill our people," Opal replied. "I can, and will, ask for it."

Phyla looked Davin's way, as if the *Jumper*'s captain had some special insight into what would bridge this particular gap.

"I won't give it up," Viola said. "Ceding the rest of Jupiter and Saturn is a lot when we could just crush you."

"Threats already?" Opal said. "Viola, you have to at least try. If you're not going to—"

Davin whistled, a spitting, sputtery thing. He'd never learned how to get his tongue and lips just right, but the strange noise served to cut Opal's words before they could do any more damage.

"Here's the way I see it," Davin said. "As a neutral runner that stands to benefit from two big customers not killing each other, how about we make a compromise?"

Davin looked between the two parties, caught a mix of suspicious and laughing looks back.

"I'm assuming you have an idea?" Opal said.

"Of course I do," Davin said, realizing in that moment that he did have an idea, one that'd been growing in the back of his mind since Mako lost Melody on Callisto. "Galaxy Forge spends all its time making bigger and better ships and weapons. The rebels are afraid it's going to make Eden unstoppable, while Eden doesn't want the rebels getting their hands on all that production. The place itself is a fortress, self-sustaining and ready to rumble with anyone that tells it what to do."

Nods all around. A good start.

"So here's what I'm thinking. Make Galaxy Forge like me."

Now Davin earned confusion.

"A cocky captain that's constantly in over his head?" Opal said.

"Someone in need of a shower?" Merc added.

"The guy all the criminals trust with their secrets?" Mox said, getting in on the game.

"A welcome friend who, nonetheless, screws everything up?" Viola said, smiling.

"My lovable rogue that I wouldn't trade for the world, unless he makes another stupid deal?" Phyla finished.

Davin shook his head, spread his hands, and flicked his fingers back towards himself, "C'mon, keep the shots coming. I can take 'em."

"No, no," Opal replied. "I think that's plenty. Tell us, oh wise one, what you think we should do with Galaxy Forge."

The key with comedy was using it to set up the serious move. Bring the people in with a little laughter, a little trust and then lay the real play out when they're ready to listen.

"Keep it neutral," Davin said. "It's not a rebel shop, an Eden shop. Galaxy Forge makes what people order, for whomever wants to buy from them."

Opal was shaking her head, "Eden's got more coin. They'll always be able to buy more."

"Except," Merc said. "Galaxy Forge doesn't just need coin. It's a big place on Ganymede, far away from anywhere, except Callisto. Jupiter itself. If we have those, we can supply Galaxy Forge's materials, what they need to survive. They'd have to work with us."

"Exactly," Davin said, pointing Merc's way. "That's rebel thinking, right there."

The logic laid out and the group looked at it. Took a quick break to think it over. Davin found Mox, and the two sipped on some coffee that tasted like bitterness incarnate. The big man didn't look particularly perturbed by anything that'd gone on so far, seeming almost too relaxed.

"Because I don't really care," Mox said when Davin asked. "I'm here to give Viola support, but the Moon and Earth don't have a stake except keeping the peace. Eden's a big player for us, and we'd rather their time and money goes towards expansion, economics, rather than war. But territory squabbles? Nah."

"So after, you're going to head back home, deliver a report, and go on living?"

"Yeah, Davin. What else?"

Davin shrugged, a slow one with a companion hum through closed lips, "I might have some ideas."

"Like?"

"Phyla and I were drifting, man. We were shuttling crap

between crap centers and keeping ourselves afloat, but inside we were dying," Davin said. "We'd ditched the excitement because we thought we wanted to be safe, but instead, that safety was ruining everything."

"Sorry to hear that." Mox finished the coffee with a long gulp. "Some things just don't work."

"Right," Davin replied. "When we ran into Merc and Opal, they brought us into their rebel outfit. It's a cause—"

"Going to stop you right there, Davin," Mox said. "I already have my cause: my Centurions. I am not leaving them again. I have a home, friends, a life not running from one gig to the next, waiting to get shot."

"We're not exactly *waiting* to get shot," Davin countered, but Mox wasn't having it.

Puk announced the precise time the break ended, and the whole crew re-assembled, Davin's recruiting mission a failure. Opal and Viola accepted a neutral Galaxy Forge, at least in the eyes of Eden and the rebels, and with the overarching terms assembled, both sides transmitted the conclusion to their leaders.

"Fast negotiations," Davin said to Phyla as the groups waited for replies from Alissa and Yang. "But I guess that's what happens when you have reasonable people on either side."

"And a good man moderating."

"Aww, you think I'm a good man?"

"Some days, Davin. Some days."

Without the negotiating pressure, the group fell back into its easier attitudes. Carried away for an hour, a second one, before a low-grade concern began floating in everyone's eyes. Opal and Viola checked their comms again and again, called on Fournine and Puk to check if there'd been a reply and they'd missed it.

After half the day had been spent idling, there was no doubting it: Alissa and Yang had gone dark.

And when Fournine announced the *Jumper*'s radar had picked up approaching ships, Davin didn't have to tell anyone that the fun times were over.

## 29

## TIME'S UP

The general response to the incoming ships wasn't what Davin expected. When he relayed Fournine's communication to the gathered group, the overall response was a defined shrug. Opal and Viola both assumed the ships were for their respective sides, even both, coming to deliver additional parties to the negotiations.

"Wait," Davin said to that. "You're saying that our secret talks weren't all that secret?"

"Are you that surprised?" Merc replied. "I bet half of Eden knows what's going on here. And Alissa's probably playing this to keep support from anyone scared of Eden's win around Callisto."

Both sides turned back to their comms and tried to send out messages. Davin caught Phyla's eye and together, the two of them went back to the *Jumper*. Fournine confirmed the ships were closing and reducing to docking speed.

"How many?" Davin asked, slotting his sidearm back into its holster and grabbing one of the *Jumper*'s rifles.

"Three," Fournine said. "All around our size, though

they appear more designed for combat than diplomatic missions."

"Of course they do," Davin said. "Phyla, you hearing this?"

With her own sidearm, a rifle in each hand and a third slung over her shoulder, Phyla nodded, "Sometimes I'd say we're too suspicious, but this time? I don't think so."

Boiled down, there were two types of surprises: good and bad. A birthday present or an unexpected frozen comet pop in the fridge? Good surprises. Unidentified ships sneaking up on your supposedly-secret conference between the solar system's two largest power players?

Bad. Definitely bad.

"Fournine," Davin said. "Keep Eightsix in the Eden bay. Have her sound the alarm if anyone suspicious comes through there."

"Would you like me to do the same in here?" Fournine replied.

"If anyone sets foot in our bay that you don't know," Davin said. "Blast them to ash."

"An aggressive response. I like it."

"I bet you do."

Loaded up with their weapons, grenades and protective vests now included from lockers that'd gone un-raided for a long time, Davin and Phyla returned to the *Jumper*'s cargo bay. Every mission had a certain air before it started, even surprise ones like this, that came with tension, a realization that, no matter how skilled or lucky they'd been before, this could be the last one. The last moment they'd ever share with one another.

"Bet this turns out to be nothing," Davin said as they stood at the ramp's top. "We're getting all spruced up and it'll be, like, a maintenance crew coming to inspect this place."

"Right, definitely that," Phyla didn't match Davin's grin. "Davin, I know we've been scattered lately. I know we've made a lot of mistakes."

"You have, maybe."

"Quiet." Phyla tapped Davin with a rifle's business end. "I'm trying to say that I somehow still love you, and that you better make it out of this alive, because I'm not done with you yet."

Davin fought back the urge to make another quip, because some sentiments were best conveyed without words. A swift, soft moment that served to remind Davin why the fiery woman had been his partner in every way for so long now.

And, if he could damn well do anything about it, for a long time in the future.

"You want to stay on the ship?" Davin said. "Keep the *Jumper* ready to go in case we need a quick getaway?"

"Fournine can keep her warm," Phyla replied. "I'd rather cover your smart ass."

By the time Davin and Phyla returned to the central ring, Fournine announced that the ship trip had arrayed around the outpost. With both docking bays occupied, the ships didn't have an easy way of getting their personnel onto the asteroid. They could've asked for Viola or Phyla to move their ships, but the newcomers hadn't responded to a single hail. Hadn't reached out.

"I'm starting to think there might be something to your theory," Opal said, taking a rifle when Davin handed one to her. "This is feeling less like the next step in our negotiations and more like the sudden end."

Viola, Mox, and Merc were spitting theories about who

might be crashing their party, considering the only ones who knew this whole thing was happening were Alissa and Yang, possibly others at the heights of both organizations.

"In my experience," Davin said, helping Phyla hand over two of her rifles to Merc and Mox. "There's always someone looking to profit from a fight. Can you think of someone who'd want Eden and the rebels shooting each other?"

"Like your dad?" Merc asked Viola.

"He would never—"

Viola's comeback died as the outpost rattled, a shattering boom coming from Eden's bay. The closed door leading back rattled as shrapnel rammed into it, and those yellow lights flickered as the outpost started up a slow alarm.

The Wild Nines hadn't been a team for years, but instincts were instincts. The group snapped into action, Opal and Phyla kicking themselves to opposite sides, opening doorways to the restrooms and outpost quarters to use as cover. Mox jumped near the Eden bay door, hanging off to the side and ready to blast anyone coming through.

Merc went for the *Jumper*, ready to cover both that bay and present another firing line. Viola, and Puk with her, followed Merc, making for the *Jumper* on Davin's recommendation.

The woman was a scientist, and despite putting an end to Bosser, didn't belong in a firefight like this one.

Davin stayed in the center, sat on the couch with the best view of the Eden bay door and drew his sidearm. Keeping the small weapon ready in his hand, Davin settled on a bored look that didn't match, at all, the swirling excitement buzzing his nerves.

He'd felt the verve back in the fleet battle over Callisto, the collision between forces and the second-to-second fight to stay alive. This had that same feel, but over and above that, Davin felt his family. His crew.

He'd wasted years delivering cargo, believing it would keep him safe and sane. But this? This would keep Davin alive.

"Fournine, you get anything from Eightsix?" Davin said over the station's alarms. "That bang didn't sound good."

"She's reporting minor damage," Fournine replied. "She has taken cover behind some debris. One of the ships is docking in the Eden bay now."

"Can't be easy since they just blew it up."

"They are scratching their hull, but they have managed to land," Fournine said. "Eightsix says there are people disembarking."

"Really."

"And they are armed."

"So surprised."

"You don't sound surprised," Fournine said. "My capacity for reading human emotions is rather advanced, and—"

"Fournine?" Davin said, watching the Eden bay door. "Shut it. Tell Eightsix to get ready. If she's able to, we might be able to use a surprise android on our side."

"If only I hadn't destroyed my body . . ."

Davin clicked off the call. Caught Mox's eye. The man didn't have his big cannon locked into his chest this time, so the rifle would have to do. He swept a look around, confirmed Merc, Phyla, and Opal were in position.

The Eden bay door opened.

Amado strode in with all the cocky confidence belonging to someone who thought they were invincible. Flanked by two other agents, all three of them wearing battle suits that looked appropriately high tech, Amado took a look around the room, found Davin, and shook his head.

"Here I thought we were interrupting negotiations," Amado said. "Yet I'm seeing no such thing?"

"Little hard to talk when you're making so much noise," Davin said. "We were making good progress too."

"I'm sorry to hear that," Amado replied, looking over at Mox and his raised rifle. "I see the bodyguard. Where is Viola?"

"Bathroom break," Davin said, not moving from the couch. "Mind explaining why you blew up your own side's ship?"

Davin figured he and Phyla were the only ones who knew Amado, knew who he worked for. The more information he could pass along to Mox, Merc, and Opal via the conversation, the more they'd understand.

"Eden is a large company." Amado kicked forward. Like Mox, the man didn't touch the handrails but glided all the way to the outpost's center platform. Stopped himself on its edge. The two agents kicked along behind Amado, and another two agents followed, facing off with Mox. "The left and right arms, they do not always work together."

"Apparently." Davin checked his comm, let his sidearm linger down, pointing through the platform's central hole. "Are you going to get to the point sometime today? I've got things to do."

"Of course." Amado reached down towards his thigh, where a click-and-a-hiss unlocked a holstered sidearm. He drew it, raised it, and pointed it at Davin, who refused to flinch. "These negotiations are over."

That's what Davin needed to hear. He pulled the trigger on his sidearm and fired, a bolt that went nowhere near Amado, that streaked below the platform and towards the space beneath the Eden bay door. The shot struck a mine Mox had set there, one that fulfilled its responsibility and exploded.

The outpost's core shook as the mine went off, a caustic bang that sent shrapnel shards flying, that bent and broke the handrails from the Eden bay door. The door's platform blocked the boom from shredding Mox and the agents, but Mox knew the boom was coming. The agents?

They bounced off the platform, zero G giving them zero stability, and they floated out into the open. Merc and Mox lit them up. On the central platform, the explosion pushed Amado forward, forcing him to grab onto the couch. His two back-up agents weren't so lucky, with the force pushing them into Phyla and Opal's lethal firing lines.

Davin felt the mine's push too, its heat force shoving him back. Davin caught the couch's back with his non-sidearm hand, used its bolted-down bulk to hold and whip him back, now behind the couch. Perfect cover, thanks to a move made more for action heroes than cocky space captains.

Every now and then, Davin could still bring it.

"How about a surrender, Amado?" Davin called as the mine's ear-ringing effects wound down.

The central room had an eerie tinge after the two second combat, as four charred Eden agents drifted through the air.

"I suppose I should have expected that," Amado said, and Davin peeked over the couch to see the chief agent had adopted Davin's own strategy and hunkered down in the platform's middle. Despite the hole in the center, Amado had decent cover, and now had a sidearm in either hand as he swung his eyes around. "But you're not the only one with surprises."

Davin's comm buzzed. Fournine, no doubt, but he

couldn't risk taking his eyes off Amado. Not when he should be shooting the man.

"I'll take that as a no to the truce, then," Davin said, feinting a move up and over the couch and instead aiming around the side.

Amado fired both sidearms at both spots, burning holes in the couch and getting Davin to jerk back. Amado didn't stop firing, each bolt blazing through fabric that, Davin realized, offered precisely zero protection.

"Any time you want to help!" Davin shouted as he dropped flat, pulled himself towards and over the platform's edge as Amado lit up the air above him.

"We're busy," Opal shouted, and Davin noticed, as he moved that she and Phyla were shooting.

"With what?"

As Davin flipped to the platform's underside, he saw Mox go flying, the man crashing down into the room's bottom curve. With laser bolts following behind her, Eightsix dove right into Mox, grinding the exoskeleton into the wall.

Oh.

Eden's android had come home.

## 30

## TACTICAL RETREAT

Fighting Eightsix in the *Jumper's* narrow confines, with Phyla helping set an ambush, made for far different odds than adapting on-the-fly to the android's turn. Mox, crushed into the central room's floor, served as leverage for Eightsix to bounce towards the center, towards Davin. The move came quick, too quick and precise for a human to track. Opal and Phyla fired, their lasers providing a glittering trail for Eightsix's flight.

Androids truly were the worst.

Davin kicked off the central platform, aiming down. As he fell, Davin crunched up and aimed his sidearm towards where he'd been standing, where Eightsix touched. The captain started to squeeze the trigger, when a different laser struck Davin in the chest, burning into his protective vest and sending that familiar sting along his nerves. A second bolt followed, still hitting Davin's vest, but higher.

Amado would kill Davin in a second, so Davin pushed away the pain and turned his back to the platform. The next stinging shot burned through Davin's jacket and into his back, torching another hole in the protective vest. But Davin wasn't dead.

Not yet.

Eightsix slammed into Davin, pressing him towards that floor just like the android had done with Mox. Her feet pressed into his back's center, conveniently hitting right where Amado's laser had burned Davin's skin. Davin tilted as the floor came up, tucked his head into his shoulder. He couldn't avoid the impact, so he might as well use it.

Davin caromed off the metal tile, the hit juddering along his arm, and rolled to his right. The dive's momentum gave Davin's roll the speed he needed to slip away from Eightsix's feet, to dodge her reach. As Davin swung back around, he aimed and fired, right at the empty air where Eightsix had been a millisecond before.

Opal's shout clued Davin into the android's next target as the machine kept up her bouncing assault, but the rebel leader would have to fend for herself a minute more. Davin's roll, hard to stop in zero gravity, turned him back towards the center platform, where Amado lingered on its underside, setting up another shot Davin's way.

They both fired, Amado's aim made harder by Davin's motion, and Davin's own shot by the same. Both lasers went wide, scoring holes next to their targets. Davin pressed his left shoulder into the floor, stopping his roll. He and Amado stared each other down, sidearms drawn and ready.

You do jobs like these long enough, you get to stare into a lot of different eyes right before they die. Davin had seen fearful ones, those who pushed their luck beyond their limits and, in their final panic, spent those seconds racing back through their lives to find where they went wrong. He'd seen brave ones, who didn't flinch from their choices and faced the inevitable with the courage it required.

And Davin had seen eyes like Amado's, the ones that even from meters away conveyed icy nihilism, a determination to complete the mission because the mission was the only thing that mattered. The contest, the goal, and nothing else.

The ones with those eyes, Davin didn't mind shooting. Mostly because they'd be shooting him.

A little sphere ruined the moment. Popping through the center island's floor with all the precision afforded things with maneuvering jets, Puk zipped next to Amado's head and, as the Eden agent turned to see what stupid thing had interrupted his moment of glory, Puk zapped his face with a stunning blue bolt.

Amado went limp and drifted off the platform. Davin lurched himself up, glanced towards the ongoing firefight as Eightsix danced between Phyla, Opal, and Merc. He wouldn't be much help there, not now.

"Thanks buddy," Davin shouted at Puk. "I owe you one."

"By my count, you owe me several," Puk replied, giving Amado a second stunning zap for good measure. "Also, I don't know how you feel about overwhelming odds, but Eden is swapping out their ships. Fournine, Viola, and I feel we should run."

"Then let's run," Davin said, wincing as he stood. "Time to go, people!"

Easy to call for a retreat when you didn't have an android bearing down on you with whirling hands, feet, and the metal bones behind them. Davin caught Opal jumping away from Eightsix, the android trying to follow but getting chased away by Merc's steady assault rifle fire. Phyla, who looked like she'd taken a kick to the gut, heard Davin's call and kicked herself off towards Merc's gateway.

Mox, though, still hadn't moved from where Eightsix had dumped him.

Normally, Mox did the rescuing. Crunched through enemy forces like a fist through foil, but now Davin had to swap the roles.

"Cover me," Davin said to Puk. "I'm getting Mox."

"You realize I'm a small bot, right?"

"You came into the fight." Davin kicked off towards Mox, Puk floating along with him. "Now you're stuck with us."

"I could fly away."

Fournine had sarcasm, but Davin couldn't do much about it: being a flight computer protected Fournine from, say, a wayward punch or a little laser blast to the bot's face. Puk had no such protections, and only the appearance of more Eden agents, float-running into the room, kept Davin from delivering a Puk-swatting slap to the bot.

"Just buy me a few seconds," Davin said, touching his toes to the floor to slow down as he reached Mox.

Davin holstered his sidearm while Puk, accepting its fate, darted up towards the Eden agents. The spherical bot started yelling random gibberish as it flew, drawing attention and aim away from Merc, from Davin.

Which let the captain slip a grenade from his belt, press the button to arm it, and chuck the blinking ball towards the Eden doorway. The explosive was years-old at this point, so Davin couldn't be sure the thing would work, but he wasn't going to win a sidearm shoot-out with rifle-packing agents, even with Puk's annoying assistance.

The handheld bomb proved its build quality precisely three seconds later, as the agents realized what was coming towards them and made leaps to safety. The grenade exploded in a blue fiery blast, a combination of concussive and magnetic force meant to break bones and shut down electronics in equal measure.

The agents, their leaps not quite fast enough, splayed out and rocketed towards a crunching impact with the room's ceiling. The doorway platform, already splintered from the mine Davin shot at the start of this whole mess, broke apart entirely, shards bursting out in that uniquely zero-G way. The doorway itself crumpled, the actual barrier sliding halfway down and sending out sparks as its motors failed: any more agents would have to crawl to get in.

"C'mon, Mox," Davin said, looking away from his destructive results. "Time to go."

Mox groaned, but, when Davin reached down and gave his face a good slap, managed to wake up. His exoskeleton grip felt strong enough to break Davin's hand, but zero-G helped again when Davin kicked them both towards Merc's door.

The fighter pilot sprayed constant fire from his rifle towards the room's opposite side, where a glance confirmed Eightsix's current location as trapped in the lavatories. Puk beat Davin and Mox to the doorway and zipped out, followed by Opal, who looked to be favoring an arm.

"Thanks for the pickup," Mox said as they flew across the room, his voice mashing the words together. "Bot hit me hard."

"She does that," Davin said. "We make ground, you go for the *Jumper*."

"What're you doing?"

"Protecting my crew."

Merc stretched out an arm, letting his rifle fire get real wide of the mark, to catch Davin and Mox as they reached the platform. Opal waited too, serving as a buffer and then a handoff for Davin.

"Trade you," Davin said, letting her take Mox and grabbing Opal's rifle in exchange.

"Bad deal," Opal replied. "Let's go, buddy."

The two kicked off towards the *Jumper*, leaving Merc and Davin covering a room filling with downed Eden agents and an android. Eightsix took advantage of Merc's distraction catching Davin and Mox to jump away from the bathrooms. She'd stuck herself to the central platform, using its ruined furniture as cover.

"Time to go," Davin said to Merc. "I've got you covered."

"Thought it was supposed to be the other way around," Merc replied as they both scattered bolts towards Eightsix. "Isn't the captain supposed to get away?"

"You've been watching the wrong movies," Davin said. "And your rifle's nearly dead anyway."

Another blast interrupted the conversation, coming back from the Eden doorway. A bigger bang this time, tearing open the half-closed gate. More Eden agents would be coming through soon.

"They don't quit, do they?" Merc said.

"But we do. Get moving." Davin reached out, pulled Merc behind him. "Tell Fournine and Phyla to spin up the engines and the turrets."

"Okay, but Davin?" Merc said as he kicked away. "Don't die out here."

"Not planning on it."

Davin kept up the fire towards Eightsix, kicking back as Eden agents poured into the room. The *Jumper*'s docking bay doorway gave him some cover. The android didn't seem too keen on pressing her luck, so Davin snuck a glance back towards his ship, saw Merc heading up the ramp.

Time to end the party.

He and Phyla both had grenades, and Davin still had

three on his belt. Holding down the rifle's trigger with his right hand, the bolts scattering around the room, Davin unlatched the ammo belt—loaded with power packs for the rifles—from his waist with his free hand and tossed it lightly into the gravity-less air, arming one of the grenades with a thumb press.

Eightsix flipped herself over the platform, her laser-burned body still moving with inhuman perfection. When she saw Davin's grenades, when she saw his deadly smile, the android stopped her move, reversed it, and dove away, back towards the quarters. In that same motion, Davin saw her reach for Amado's floating, stunned body.

Not that it mattered. Davin threw the grenade belt forward into the room, then kicked back towards the *Jumper.*

"Shields aft, get moving!" Davin ordered as he flew towards the ramp.

The *Jumper*'s entry loomed in front, and beyond the big ship's bulk, Outpost X-225's magnetic shield showcased the Eden ships looming outside. Beyond them, space glowed a perfect blue-black, though any starlight washed away in the *Jumper*'s engine glow.

Still, a beautiful view for a last look.

Behind him, Davin felt, then heard the rippling blast as the grenades went off, as they hit the power packs and blew open all that charged energy. He flew towards the ramp, almost touching it, as the heat, the energy washed over him.

Protecting his crew. No better way to go.

## ASTEROID ESCAPE

You get hugged by Mox, it's an experience. You get hugged by Mox as an asteroid outpost blows up behind you, and it's a life-saving one.

Davin hit the ramp and Mox scooped him up, turning as he did so to put that thick exoskeleton back, where the flying shrapnel that squeaked through the *Jumper*'s shields clattered against the metal frame and bounced away. The explosion's heat and electrical energy bounced off the shields, scattered to the rock around them.

"Debt repaid?" Mox said, helping Davin into the cargo bay as the ramp pulled up behind them.

The *Jumper* shuddered into a takeoff, blasting away from the asteroid.

"I'll think about it," Davin said, "but there's a strong possibility."

Mox chuckled, and Davin looked up to see his crew laid out in the *Jumper*'s bay. Or rather, that's what he thought he'd see. Instead, not a single soul beyond Davin and Mox occupied the space, but shouts filled the ship anyhow.

Opal and Merc, calling out targets from the *Jumper*'s

turrets. Viola, voice coming from the engines in back, refining the *Jumper*'s energy distribution like Trina used to do. A function Davin had pushed to the cockpit, but one more precisely monitored from the engines themselves. Phyla and Fournine chimed in with their vectors, the path to escape the asteroids and any pursuit.

Despite the near-death, despite the fireball raging in the outpost behind him, a tear threatened to leak from Davin's eye.

"Like old times," Mox said. "You need patching up?"

"Later," Davin replied. "Once we get outta this mess. Toss me up?"

"What am I, a toy?"

"Just this once?"

Sighing, Mox threw Davin up to the *Jumper*'s second level. Grabbing onto the railing, Davin looped himself over and into the cockpit. Kick-floated his way into the seat besides Phyla. Looked outside the cockpit and saw spinning rocks, bright laser flashes, and two Eden ships turning to give chase.

"Hey," Phyla offered. "Nice of you to join us."

"Got held up."

"I heard."

"Did you?"

"Hard not to," Phyla said. "Is this new you going to blow things up everywhere we go?"

The comment threw Davin until he played back recent history. Ever since Callisto, Davin's destinations did seem to go up in flames: the food warehouse, Opal's flagship, and now the outpost. A disturbing trend.

"You said find a cause. Maybe this is mine." Davin glanced at the console. Opal and Merc continued to deliver hot fire, with the *Jumper* not receiving much in return. "We're looking good?"

"For a rapid scramble away from an ambush?" Phyla said. "Yeah, we're looking good. Viola's dumping our laser power into our engines to get us outta here, so Merc and Opal are mostly shooting for show."

Davin took another look at the console. Still saw only the two Eden ships—the third, seemingly, had been crushed in the outpost's continuing collapse. Both ships matched the *Jumper* for size, but looked to be troop carriers more than battle-ready vessels.

"Why run?" Davin said. "They came after us. We should show 'em that we have teeth."

"Fournine," Phyla said, tilting the *Jumper* down and away in a circle around the outpost's asteroid. A move that would put the rock in between the *Jumper* and the Eden ships. "Switch Davin's console to long range."

The little screen between Davin's hands had displayed a few red blips alongside the big black blotch representing the outpost. Fournine's swap shrank those blips to tiny dots, the asteroid to a thumb print. Out on the console's left, a nasty red swarm that looked a little like a pixelated explosion expanded towards the *Jumper*.

"Those carriers didn't come alone," Davin guessed.

"We've got a winner," Phyla replied. "Fournine, here, didn't think to notify us when the cruiser and its fighters showed up."

"We are in Eden space," Fournine clicked back. "The presence of a cruiser while we are negotiating with Eden representatives did not seem suspicious."

"Maybe Viola can tune his algorithms," Davin said. "All those blips. Guessing those are fighters?"

"We're going to find out soon," Phyla tapped on the

console, swapped the comm to the engines. "Viola, we're outta firing range. Punch the engines till I say otherwise."

"On it," Viola answered, and the *Jumper* sped up immediately.

Zipping through straight space felt like you weren't moving at all. Without gravity, increasing thrust didn't measure on the muscles. Here, with loose rock floating all around, the *Jumper*'s burst had the asteroids blurring by, eyesight telling Davin what the rest of his body couldn't.

"Those carriers won't catch us," Davin said, watching the console, knowing how much coin he'd poured into the *Jumper*'s engines. "Those fighters will, if they want to."

"Depends on how bad they want us dead."

Which was the real question. Amado hadn't given much of an answer: why would Eden want to murder them all? Why try so hard to kill a bunch of cast-offs? Opal had rebel command, sure, but she'd just lost her fleet, and probably her reputation. Davin and Phyla, much as he didn't like admitting it, were worth jack crap on the solar system's power scale.

Mox? Nothing. No Lunar Centurion had value off the Moon's surface.

Merc was a capable bit player.

Which left Viola herself, who was both the daughter of Eden's biggest weapons manufacturer and—Davin thought—a pretty high-up member in Eden's engineering division.

No easy answer.

"Guess we'll just have to make it outta this and figure it out," Davin said.

"What?"

"Just thinking." Davin leaned over the console, flipped the comm to a wide broadcast. "Hey Nines, we've got a fighter wave coming. Opal, I saw that arm. You good to handle a turret when the targets can actually move?"

"The Nines?" Merc cracked back with a laugh.

"Mox and I are swapping," Opal said. "And if you're willing to rescue us, Davin, you can call us whatever you want."

"My team tried to kill me," Viola added. "You all never did. I'm in."

"Off the Moon, this is my crew," Mox said.

"I'm already flying this rocket box, so I guess I don't have a choice," Phyla finished the line-up. "Stay sharp, everyone. Here they come."

Phyla called it right. Twenty red blips neared the *Jumper*, swirling in from behind, above, and below. More than enough fighters to overwhelm the *Jumper*'s shields. More than enough to break Davin's beloved ship and his new crew apart.

Eden's fighters, drone ships flown by calculations rather than human instinct, swarmed. Without the need for cockpits, the craft resembled discs covered in jets and lasers. In constant communication with each other, and able to bounce around in vacuum with precise changes, the damn things were hard to hit even if they lacked the killer instinct a hot-blooded pilot could provide.

Phyla slowed the *Jumper* as the fighters caught up, giving Viola power to shunt back to the turrets. The slower carriers weren't even trying to catch them, a reality that made Eden's goal perfectly clear: no prisoners this time.

Mox and Merc let loose with the turrets as the drone fighters popped into range, gliding around asteroids or weaving in through space's starry backdrop. Lasers splashed into the void as the drone craft dipped and dodged, while growing return fire struck the *Jumper*'s shields.

"There's too many," Phyla said. "And we can't outrun them."

"So we need an idea, or we're dead?" Davin replied.

"Very."

Davin pulled himself from his chair, his burned skin feeling tight and twisted. He kicked away from the cockpit as Phyla pulled the *Jumper* into a spiral that placed a drone fighter into her front cannon's sights. A sustained stream led to a white flash as Davin left the cockpit, the fighter's remnants lighting up in a brief glow before space snuffed them out.

"Where are you going?" Phyla shouted after him.

"After an idea!" Davin replied, reaching the *Jumper*'s cargo bay and looking down at that familiar container. He glanced at his comm, set to broadcast inside the ship. "Viola, please tell me every one of Eden's ships isn't able to block that new weapon."

Nothing for a second, and then Viola's voice kicked in, "We updated everything, Davin. We're making more of those weapons right now. Eden wanted a guarantee that its ships would be safe."

The *Jumper* rattled as a fighter managed a straight on blast. Mox's vengeful shout carried a second later, declaring the offending fighter a dead ship.

Plenty more to go.

"But," Viola continued, "the defense kills systems once the attack is detected, and they'll have to restart. It's not a long delay, but here?"

A few seconds downtime, longer maybe for drones? That could work.

Davin popped the container, pulled out the orange and silver ball. The *Jumper* shook again, and an alarm hissed out a warning, something popped near the med bay. The motion threw Davin into the air, the ball floating away from him.

Phyla spun the *Jumper*, the cargo bay moving around Davin and the ball. Without anything to press against, Davin floated so slowly towards a side wall, towards anything he could use to get some momentum back.

"Need help?" Opal asked, coming from the med bay.

"That ball? Grab it. Press the button," Davin said, pointing.

Opal, ever aware and on, jumped for the floating ball, caught it as the *Jumper* took another hit. Condensed air poured from one of the turret shafts, and Viola shouted that the shields were dead. Merc and Mox called out that fighters were everywhere, and Phyla said she had nowhere to go.

Too many, and too close.

"Fournine!" Davin said. "Cut the comms!"

The projected timer hit zero and those spinning silver bars aligned, flashed, and went dark.

"The hell was that?" cried Mox as Fournine brought the comms back up. "They're all stopping!"

"Shoot now, ask questions later," Davin replied. "Phyla, let's get out of here."

With Opal's help, Davin kicked off a wall and returned to the cockpit as Phyla blasted the *Jumper* from the asteroid range. Viola kept the energy away from the shields, sinking all the power into the turrets and the engines. Mox and Merc blitzed the drone fighters, shredding them as the discs restarted.

As the five remaining fighters burst after the *Jumper*, Opal pulled out the weapon again, punching the button. The timer hit zero, Fournine killed the *Jumper*'s comms, and again the drone fighters went dead, drifting right where Mox and Merc could finish them off.

Eden's weapon had served to defeat Eden. Not a bad turn.

Fournine read off the damage: communication systems had been frayed, the upper turret lacked half its power, and the kitchen's refrigeration unit had been fried when a fighter shot overloaded a power conduit.

"So warm nutrient goop from here on out?" Davin asked.

"You can always vacuum-freeze and thaw," Fournine said. "Though I doubt that will do much for the taste."

Davin leaned back in the co-pilot's chair. Amado's laser burns still hurt, but after a victory, the pain almost felt sweet. They'd torched an Eden ambush, stuffed Amado's smirking face with grenades, and decimated a fighter swarm, all without losing a man or suffering any serious damage.

And he'd gained a crew.

"Nines," Davin said, broadcasting. "Don't know about all of you, but it feels good to be back."

## 32

# REASONS WHY

Phyla kept the *Jumper* ducking and dodging through the asteroid belt for days, angling away from known space stations, from traveling routes, anywhere contact with other human souls seemed the least bit likely. While she flew, Davin dealt with a suddenly full ship.

Not all that many years ago, everyone now milling around the *Jumper* had been on the same crew. The Wild Nines had roamed the solar system hunting good contracts, running security for sensitive cargo or patrolling high risk sights that didn't want to maintain a permanent force of their own. Merc, Opal, Mox and the rest hadn't always been the best of friends, but the coin and the need to trust the person with a rifle at your side served to keep them close.

"That man's an Eden operative." Opal glared at Viola as they tried to eat a nutrient goop dinner in the *Jumper*'s cargo bay—the kitchen was still off-limits for anything more than grabbing a bite and getting out: the damage from the drone fighters had forced Davin and Mox to tear up the floor and play with wires. "You had to know he would be coming."

Puk floated near Viola, hovering over her shoulders like a protective guardian. The bot had saved Opal's life before, but, going by how its pointed implements aimed, any lingering love had been lost.

"Amado doesn't tell me anything," Viola said, glaring right back Opal's way. "I didn't even know who he was until Davin told me the man had shoved a key into his thigh."

"Then you were a pawn."

"Maybe so," Viola replied. "It happens."

"Hell of a way to dismiss it."

Davin, leaning on the railing above the scene, turned to Mox. They'd finished another kitchen bout and were sucking on their own goop tubes.

"How long till I should intervene?" Davin asked.

"When the weapons come out," Mox answered. "Not before."

"Risky."

"I am bored."

In truth, they were all bored. Simulators not-withstanding, drifting from asteroid to asteroid grew old fast, and Davin hadn't rigged the *Jumper* to entertain a big crew. When it was just Davin and Phyla flying alone, they'd been able to kill time with conversation, with movies and shared interests. Now things felt crowded, tensions simmering.

"I'm not happy with what happened," Viola said, marking a mollifying tone. "It seems like Eden didn't care about the negotiations at all, which means everything was a waste."

"Not if you can tell us why," Opal replied. "If you know what Eden's trying to do, why they'd want the war to continue, then I can take that back to Alissa. Use it against them. And with your knowledge of how Eden's ships work, you could give us a huge advantage."

Viola took the statement, the accusatory turned reparatory tone from Opal and frowned. Davin leaned forward a little, curious how the young woman would handle a simple question with not-so-simple implications.

"I don't know who gave Amado's orders," Viola said. "I don't know why Yang didn't warn me they were coming. But Eden is more than those two. The people I work with, the ones who helped craft the weapon that saved our lives, are good people. If I help you destroy Eden ships, then you'll be killing them. Their friends and maybe their families."

Viola looked at her half-full nutrient goop tube as she finished, then kicked herself away from the cargo container serving as a makeshift table. Opal didn't say anything more as Viola floated away, as Viola saw Davin and Mox hanging nearby. She offered a weak smile, then disappeared into the *Jumper*'s crew quarters.

"Nice work, Opal," Davin said, hopping down to the rebel leader's level. "Anyone ever put you in charge of recruitment?"

"No." Opal didn't look at Davin, ate her goop.

"Too bad. Think you'd be real good at it."

"Are you done?"

"Not even close," Davin said. "You really think Viola's some Eden player that actually knows what happened back there? That she could've planned all of this?"

Opal's eyes flashed, she let the goop tube float away, "Davin, if you don't, then you're too naive."

"Or maybe you're too cynical." Davin snatched Opal's half-empty tube out of the air, squeezed some more into his mouth. The stuff tasted like flavored chalk, but calories were calories. "Amado blew up her ship first, remember?"

"Then why won't she help us?"

"Because she's not a damn robot. I didn't help you either."

"Look at where that got you." Opal straightened as Mox kicked down to join them. "What do you think, Mox? You're the most neutral person here. Is Viola telling the truth?"

"She found me," Mox said, crossing his arms. "She could have had an Eden escort, but she chose not to."

Opal nodded while Davin did the double-take, "You're saying she might've known?"

"Vi is not stupid," Mox said. "She suspected something."

"There you have it, captain," Opal added. "Viola's not telling the whole truth. The question is, who is she protecting? Eden, or herself?"

Davin took Opal's question to the cockpit, where he bandied the idea with Phyla and Fournine, the latter of whom said Viola hadn't attempted any outside communication—a moot point anyway, given their long-range transponder had been immolated in the fight. Phyla jumped on Opal's side faster than Davin expected, pulling back the sympathy that Davin had tried to give Viola.

"You spent more time with her than the rest of us," Phyla said. "So maybe you're blinded. But Davin, she's the only Eden person on this ship. The only one, really, at the negotiations. Amado strikes when Viola's not on her ship, when Puk's right there with her."

"Puk, who stunned Amado to save my life."

"They played us once already," Phyla said, ignoring Davin's comment. "They strung us along for the bigger prize. They might be doing it again."

"Eden threw drone fighters our way," Davin countered. "They definitely tried to kill us in that outpost. You can't say it's all some game."

Phyla, though, said nothing. Just gave Davin a look that

said she definitely could see Eden doing something that layered, that covered. And, if Davin really looked at his life and what he'd seen from the massive corporation, he could too.

"Why?" Davin said to Viola, after knocking on her room's door. She was swapping bunk time with Merc, who'd bounced off with Mox and Opal for a simulator run. "Why'd this whole thing happen?"

"You're going to have to give me more than that," Viola said. She looked tired, lying on the cot and staring at the ceiling. Puk had planted itself on a charging pad, looking like a spiked, dead bowling ball. "There's a lot of things happening right now."

"Why us, with the weapon? There had to be other runners you could've asked."

"How many runners do you think I know?" Viola replied, then waved off a response, the hand moving limp. "It's not an exciting story. We made the weapon. Showed it off, thinking Eden could end the war before it really started." Viola rolled her eyes to the side, back towards the cargo bay. "Except the rebel queen over there never let us get close enough to use it. You take one shot with this thing, and everyone knows it's out there. Eden wanted to end it all with one fight."

Connecting the dots between that idea and a lure to get the rebel fleet all mashed together for one big blow-out wasn't all that hard, even if Davin had a few drams in him to cut the lingering laser burn pain. Amado and all the rest had just been pushing the ruse, getting Davin to deliver the weapon to the rebels, where it needed to go.

Puppets, though, had masters.

"You keep saying Eden like it's a person. Who was giving you the orders, Yang?"

Viola squinted at him, "Davin, are you doing Opal's dirty work?"

"I'm trying to figure out who I'm gonna have to talk to."

"Better if you don't worry about it," Viola replied.

"Hey, we took on Bosser."

"Bosser was one man with a crazy idea that almost pulled it off," Viola said. "Eden's not that arrogant. They won't take chances with you."

"Ask Amado how that went."

"Think you killed him?"

"A man can dream." Davin straightened, glanced at his comm. "Phyla's pulling us out of the belt. Guess Merc has her convinced to head to Saturn. You want us to drop you on a rock?"

"So someone can come along and kill me?" Viola said. "No thanks. I'll come along, if you're allowing."

"Suppose I am, you keep those engines running."

Viola flicked a thumbs up, set her head back on the pillow and closed her eyes. Davin killed the lights as he left.

Phyla listened to the info dump with the same passive stare she usually pulled when her mind was parsing some detail Davin hadn't considered. Outside, the *Jumper* stared into dark space, a slight green line vanishing off into the distance showing Fournine's flight plan towards Saturn. Phyla and Opal figured taking a beeline for rebel territory was safer than stopping at any Jupiter moon and risking Eden interception.

They had enough nutrient goop to make the journey.

"So she used us," Phyla said a second after Davin finished. "She knew what would happen." A short head shake. "Does Opal know that part?"

"Haven't told her."

"I wouldn't." Phyla drummed her fingers on the console.

"If Opal finds out Viola essentially destroyed her fleet, killed so many of her soldiers, we might not be able to save her."

"Save her?" Davin said. "You're sounding softer than usual."

"Without Viola tweaking the power supply back there, we might not've made it out," Phyla replied. "I'm a practical woman, Davin, and I don't want to lose someone useful."

"Even if she's dangerous?"

"Everyone on this ship's dangerous," Phyla said. "Including you and me."

Davin could agree with that. He sat back in his seat, watched the stars and let the cosmos melt his brain for a moment.

"What happens when we get to Saturn?" Phyla asked after a while. "We go say hi to Alissa, tell her the story, and she has Viola executed?"

One way to do things, sure. If you weren't playing the long game.

"We've got a ways to fly yet," Davin said. "Which means Viola has a timer. She gets us a reason not to turn her over by the time we get there, then I don't see us having that conversation with Alissa." He sat up, waggled a finger. "In fact, we get the right plan together with our crew and we can deliver the rebels the win they're looking for."

"We can?"

"Sure. We can think of something," Davin said. "We're the Wild Nines. Best mercenary crew the solar system's ever seen. By the time we hit Saturn, we'll have this war won."

## 33

# FREESTAR

A week burned away while the *Jumper* sped out towards Saturn, a blazing fast trip with Phyla dumping every spare energy ounce into the engines. Without long-range communications, it'd dawned on Davin and the rest of the crew that nobody in the rebels might be aware of what had happened on the outpost, that Eden might be setting up a larger assault while Alissa and her other commanders still expected peace negotiations to be continuing.

Rather than hitting one of Saturn's many moons, Phyla aimed for the closest target: Freestar Station. Originally built to serve as the furthest supply center for humanity's fringe explorations and forthcoming moon bases, Freestar changed its purpose as Saturn's moons came online. Transforming from a frontier outpost to a wild vanguard, Freestar kept its far orbit around Saturn and served as a place for those who wanted to avoid normal society and its requirements.

"Like a dirtier version of Deimos," Opal said, joining

Davin and Phyla in the cockpit as Freestar came into range. "Freestar is a stain."

"You're saying that like you don't own the place," Davin replied. "I think it feels like home."

In fact, Davin would say Freestar had a singular advantage over Vagrant's Hollow, the slums on the larger station Miner Prime: there wasn't a hierarchy. Sure, wealth and power gave its usual advantages, but mobility on Freestar came more through exploits than political manipulation. You could become a hero on Freestar one day, a villain the next, and be dead by the third.

Not exactly stable, but Davin couldn't think of a more primal place in the solar system.

"If we'd actually made peace with Eden, I would be cleaning this place up," Opal said. "It's a waste of resources."

"The bullet course is pretty hard," Phyla added her own spin. "If disaster's not imminent, I think I'll sign up for a race."

"I'll bet on you," Davin said.

"Are you two listening to me?" Opal asked.

"Not really," Davin replied, causing Opal to issue one of her trademark sighs. "Phyla, we in range?"

"Ready ... now."

Davin tapped on the console, opened the *Jumper*'s short-range comm and synced with Freestar's docking band. The conversation with a rather tired-sounding traffic controller came short and sweet. The station, though, didn't have any solo bays open anymore: apparently the Eden conflict had driven tourists and civilians from moons with rebel bases to the more far-flung station.

"Guess we're sharing," Davin said once the call closed. "We'll have to put our nice faces on."

"Do we even have those?" Phyla asked.

Freestar, owing to its mercenary nature, kept its docking bays both clean and locked up. Whereas other bays would give free access to supplies like energy and repair materials, planning to bill the ship's account after it left, Freestar operated on a pay-as-you-go model. Davin's first look as he came down the *Jumper*'s ramp, enjoying Freestar's rotational gravity in the process, was at a multi-colored array all around.

As if a clown had exploded, the various purples, reds, blues, greens and yellows coded various components with their prices. Panels splashing Freestar's swooshing blue-and-white logo blinked from everywhere, hawking coin deposits for the products they protected.

Overhead announcements, made by someone who sounded like they'd started a party the night before and, now, were struggling through its aftermath, droned on about offers on this and that. Restaurants, shows, weapons, everything seemed to be on sale.

"Missed this place," Mox said, coming down by Davin.

"As an officer of the law, shouldn't this annoy you?"

"I enforce the laws on the Moon," Mox said. "This is not the Moon."

"Right," Davin said. "Then how about we go have ourselves a good time while the important kids get to work?"

Most of the time, Davin asking that question would lead to the whole crew finding some disreputable establishment to burn the day away parlaying coin for celebration. In practice, here on Freestar, that meant Davin and Mox heading out while Phyla oversaw the *Jumper*'s needed repairs—she insisted Davin and Mox could watch the ship later while she tried out the bullet course. Viola occupied herself tinkering with the weapon, trying to see if she could find a way to get it past the defense Eden built and thus, perhaps, save herself from a rebel execution.

Opal and Merc left the ship quick for the local rebel headquarters, hunting for a way to contact Alissa, to get up to speed on where things were. To ditch the Nines for their chosen side.

Which left Davin and Mox to journey into Freestar.

If Deimos was the luxury retreat for spacefarers and Earth tourists looking for low-gravity fun, filled with glitz and pizzazz, then Freestar embraced the same for its own clientele. Opal called it dirtier, but Davin found the space station a more authentic form of hustle.

Their shared bay turned out to be occupied by a slight star skimmer designed for venture tourism for couples that wanted to blitz around Saturn's moons and enjoy the view. Aside from a couple sections reserved for engines and landing struts, the whole craft had a clear exterior for perfect viewing. This one, though, had chips and scoring everywhere, as if its driver had flown through denser dust. Little bots combed it now, filling in repairs. The owner was nowhere to be seen.

Good thing too: Davin didn't have much patience for people who didn't respect their ships.

The docking bays led into Freestar's outer rings, a structure that mimicked the station's home planet. A map pulled up on Davin's comm confirmed the steadily-growing station's fringes played home to the newest casinos, bars, shops and hotels, while the middle rings were claimed by more rudimentary services for permanent residents. Freestar's core, perhaps the only serious place on the station, held its small government offices and technical centers.

"Now we just have to find the right place," Davin said as they left the docking bays through a wide spiral door.

"Looks like we have options." Mox replied.

Freestar's local time put them in the middle of the afternoon, and the sturdy crowds reflected revelers just getting back to moving after last evening's disasters. Bunches straggled towards coffee bars, low bet limit tables, or lounged on the ad-coated benches interspersed through the ring's middle. Freestar's main attraction came from its transparent ceilings across its concourses, through which, as the station angled itself, you could always treat yourself to a miracle view of Saturn and its rings.

"How about . . . there?" Davin said, pointing at a shaggy restaurant with an uncertain theme calling itself *Gravity Bowl*.

Davin had one particular requirement for their expedition, and that was a place filled with screens that would give them some update on what'd been happening since their venture to the asteroids. Without the long-range comm active, the *Jumper* had been in a silent bubble during the flight out to Saturn, and Davin itched to see how the rebel news played their fleet's demolition.

"Hey," Mox said as Davin started towards *Gravity Bowl*. "See that?"

Mox's hand on Davin's shoulder directed the captain back towards the concourse's center, where a giant holographic image had changed from a new ship advertisement —get the Starkisser 5000 today!—to something that had Davin's stomach lurch.

Opal and Merc's faces, blown up to stretch almost from floor to that transparent ceiling, stared somber at the people walking by. Slashed across their mugs, in jagged text accompanied by blood spatters, were bitter accusations:

*Rebel heroes murdered by Eden!*

Beneath the faces, in bold letters, scrolled an ask to join the rebel forces, to seek revenge and protect their freedoms. And, going by the number of people glancing towards the image, or outright stopping to read the text, the rebels were getting attention.

"Going to be hard to recruit off that ad once word gets out they're alive," Mox said.

"How did they know Opal and Merc were dead in the first place?" Davin asked, watching the image until it reverted to another ad. "We spoke with Alissa before Eden attacked, but not after."

"Maybe they assumed?" Mox said. "If Opal and Merc disappeared?"

Davin resumed the trek towards *Gravity Bowl*. Mox followed, and the two took seats at the bar. Davin ordered fast, water and food that wasn't nutrient goop. Mox copied Davin, a sequence that would've drawn a second look from a human bartender, but *Gravity Bowl* deployed one of those new robots that couldn't be bothered to care.

Most of the screens displayed sports, many still pulling from leagues on Earth and Mars. Davin found one central to his vision, and once the screen found him, Davin synced it up with his comm, used the tiny console to switch the channel. If the restaurant had been crowded, the channel switch would've gone up for a vote from everyone synced to the screen. With just Davin and Mox on this side of the bar, nobody contested.

Talking heads blew up, along with scrolling headlines along the bottom. Davin had chosen an Earth-side station, one that wouldn't be under rebel influence. It took precisely five seconds for the news to hit on the fight between Eden and the rebels, recapping the precarious rebel military situation with the kind of boastful inevitability Eden, honestly, deserved.

"Wait," Davin said as the newscasters switched their tone, adopting outraged looks as they read along the next item. "What?"

"We have a problem," Mox added.

Eden had been ambushed. Their peacekeepers meant to end the war with the rebels had been surprised and killed during the negotiations. Even though the rebels denied the attack, Eden was sure it'd been carried out by rebel forces, a death squad that'd even gone so far as to kill the rebel's own diplomats to cover their tracks.

"Both sides blaming each other," Davin said as the bartending bot dropped the food and drinks. "Not a good recipe for peace."

"But a good one for business."

Davin glanced at Mox, "You know we're not in that work anymore, right?"

"Not us. Them," Mox said, nodding towards the screen.

"Eden? They'll lose billions fighting the rebels instead of trading," Davin said.

Mox took a slow bite of the sandwich, a greasy looking thing. Davin tried his own, savored the lab-grown roast beef and genetically modified toppings. Artificial or not, the sandwich had real texture, flavor, and, most importantly, didn't come from a tube.

"They'll lose nothing," Mox said. "Earth will pay them. Luna too. No one wants the order disrupted. Competition will die as resources go to Eden to win the war."

"Interesting idea," Davin said, turning the situation over.

The rebels were playing up the supposed death of the negotiators too, claiming Eden did it. That would spike fury, sure. Might bring up recruitment. Get some donations from sympathetic parties. But that wouldn't be enough to fight Eden, unless. . .

"Eden doesn't have friends everywhere, do they?" Davin said. "A big company like that must have powerful enemies."

Mox nodded, his face filled with sandwich.

"People, organizations that wouldn't have the means to fight Eden directly, but could dump coin into a rebel force." Davin tapped the counter. "A force that wouldn't need that coin until it lost its only real fleet."

"Both sides want the war now," Mox said. "Both sides will profit, until one or the other is destroyed."

Davin watched the talking heads for another minute, trying to find the angle. If both sides claimed the other had killed the peace negotiations, then both sides could tap the outrage. But if the rebel victims suddenly re-appeared, with Eden claiming the outpost had been destroyed, its people killed?

Rebel sympathy could dry up real fast.

"They need to stay dead," Davin said, putting down his half-eaten sandwich. "If Opal and Merc are alive, then Eden gets to call them liars. Claim they lost people, no matter the real truth."

"A thin premise," Mox said. "On the Moon, when we're investigating a crime, it is about who benefits. I see it, Eden and the rebels only win if they both push that the other side did it and nobody says otherwise."

Davin looked at his sandwich, sighed, "Which means Opal and Merc are about to meet with some people who very much want 'em to disappear."

"Right."

Davin pushed back from the bar, stood up, "So much for our relaxing evening, then."

The sandwich wasn't that good anyway.

## 34

## STATION WALTZ

Opal and Merc didn't respond to Davin's calls. They continued not responding as Davin and Mox went back to the *Jumper* and found Phyla. Davin thought about digging out Mox's big cannon, re-attaching it to the man's armor, but that seemed like it might draw the wrong sort of attention on their walk through the Freestar.

"It's not worth it," Mox said. "We're not planning to mow down an army."

"Can't promise that," Davin said. "If what I'm thinking is really happening, we might have to tear this whole station apart."

"Let's hope not," Phyla said, "because we're *on* this station."

"Guess we'll have to be careful then," Davin replied.

Viola and Puk would stay on the *Jumper* and keep it protected. Not that Fournine, as demonstrated on Callisto, couldn't do a fine job of that itself, but risking Viola's summary execution by some passionate rebel didn't seem prudent. Besides, as Viola put it, she was getting closer to a breakthrough.

"Amazing what you can achieve without all that corporate overhead," Viola said, hunched over the silver-orange ball in the workshop, Puk buzzing around her. "Without a meeting every ten minutes, it's like being a kid again."

"Sure," Davin said. "Just don't go getting yourself killed while we're gone. And don't destroy my ship."

"No promises."

Davin wondered where Viola had picked up that spunk as the trio left the *Jumper* and started into Freestar. The station, which had a delightfully off-kilter edge, now felt more than a little sinister. Davin noticed the spaces between stores had posters calling for rebel recruitment, pictures of Alissa and other rebel 'heroes' that'd raided Eden and caused general carnage.

Other ads blipped up with less violence, showcasing economic and political improvements on rebel worlds. Local governments un-corrupted by Eden's massive influence. Davin had been to many of the moons depicted, though, and the reality had more gray than the pure good depicted on the utopian posters.

The moons around Saturn might have their freedom, but they lacked Eden's supply network. Many had to subsist on locally manufactured materials, or what they could pull from other rebel moons, a scarcity that could have big implications on worlds with thin or no atmosphere, where little leaks could mean the deaths of thousands.

Merc and Opals' faces continued to crop up too, appearing here, there, and everywhere as lauded martyrs. Heroes that gave everything in the struggle against Eden.

"It's creepy seeing them pictured this way," Phyla said as they walked. "The living dead."

"Might be just dead if we don't find them soon," Davin replied.

The obvious destination, where Opal and Merc had gone after leaving the *Jumper,* were the primary rebel offices on Freestar. Davin had the location pulled up on his comm, a large spot two rings in and halfway around from where the *Jumper* had docked.

Freestar's general who-gives-a-damn attitude didn't quite extend to a heavily armed trio walking through its shopping districts, so Davin, Phyla, and Mox went with small arms. They each stuffed a couple grenades beneath the large coats Davin stocked precisely for this purpose: temperature controls on most space stations kept things cool, so it didn't make immediate sense to wear the thick, ankle-length dusters, but when you had to hide the goods, comfort came second.

They drew eyes leaving the docking bay, but the general law of life in outer space held: don't get involved in other people's problems. Freestar's security, no doubt paid on a contract like the ones Davin used to accept, gave the trio some long looks but ultimately made no moves.

"They're all looking at you," Phyla said to Mox. "Nice not to get any attention myself."

"I am used to it," Mox said.

He did stand taller than Davin and Phyla, and wider, that exoskeleton bulging beneath the jacket like some insect worming its way from its cage. Mox took long steps, his face a passive mask that could mean anything, would mean trouble for anyone that interfered. Even the damn bots plaguing places like Freestar's shopping corridor, hawking this and that deal, fell silent as the trio went by, their algorithms unable to place the proper profile.

As they walked, Davin continued to pepper Opal and

Merc with messages. He didn't expect a response—and received none—but the every few minutes query would serve to keep anyone monitoring their comms that Davin hadn't yet decided on drastic action. Especially as Davin laced every message with an ongoing description of the slow meal he and Mox were supposedly enjoying in *Gravity Bowl*.

"Someday we'll get a real vacation," Davin said as they passed by an intriguing theater designed for zero-G performances.

"We've been on a vacation," Phyla replied. "The last few years. It was boring, really boring."

Davin couldn't argue with that. Vacations had to be a break *from* something—when the slow and stable became your life, well, that just didn't work for them.

Freestar linked its rings with shuttles that blitzed back and forth along narrow, magnetic tracks. Each one could hold a couple dozen people, and they went continuously. The trio fell into the line, one that, with one awkward glance and step after another, fell away before them. The next tram whistled through the magnetic shielding and slid to a slow stop.

Four meters high, topped with a white bar bearing Freestar's logo, and filled with balancing, chrome poles for most people, a couple chairs for those who needed them, the trams filled every other space with ads shrieking for attention. The side opposite the three opened first, and passengers coming to start their evening action hurried off, chattering about this and that.

"Bet we're going to ruin all their fun," Davin said.

"Or give them some excitement," Mox replied.

"Everybody doesn't think like we do," Phyla said.

"And that's a good thing," Davin concluded as they found their poles.

Mox turned and looked back towards the doors, and though plenty of people were waiting for a shot back—workers, looked like, at the end of their shifts and ready to head home—none bothered to join them.

"So nice, them giving us the whole tram." Davin smiled, waved.

"Bet it won't be so nice when we arrive," Phyla muttered.

Swinging between Freestar's outer ring and the next wouldn't take long, but Davin would enjoy the view. As the tram departed, a cheery voice warning of imminent death should anyone get caught outside, the station's metal-and-ad array fizzled into a clear tunnel. Saturn hung huge and brilliant above and in front of them, its rings slicing through black space like a razor.

Flying on the *Jumper* offered great views aplenty, but seeing things from the restrictive cockpit couldn't compare to standing, surrounded by cosmic wonder. No Fournine-generated arrow showing the flight path, no sinking realization that the next meal, like the many before, would consist wholly of nutrient goop.

Here, Davin caught his breath with appropriate purpose. This was where he deserved to be, needed to be. Belonged.

"Ready?" He asked as the tram neared the next ring.

The rebel offices weren't too close, too far from the tram's docking station. The Wild Nines trio had drawn enough eyes that, certainly, the rebels had to know they were coming. Were, at least, marching around. Now the question became whether the rebels would act.

Nobody, not a single passenger, waited when the tram rolled in. The second ring held a different class than the first, second tier hotels and businesses not targeting tourism. Offices, higher-end apartments, and a few concessions to real life like grocery stations and schools broke through Freestar's mercenary design, as if to say civilization could still take root, even out here.

Despite the homey environs, Davin moved his hands beneath the jacket to find the sidearm grips. No better place for an ambush than a peaceful one.

The tram doors slid open without enemy fire. Without anyone coming forward and demanding they drop their weapons. Davin caught Mox and Phyla's eyes, shrugged, and led them off the tram.

The second ring wasn't all deserted: far off, people did continue to come and go from where they needed to be, but not with the casual innocence Davin would've expected. They hurried, darting from one door to the next, often sparing a glance at the trio now walking in the center, before hustling even faster to disappear.

"Either we're scarier than I thought, or someone's noticed," Davin said.

Phyla, who spent half the time checking behind them for anyone following, clicked her tongue loud. Davin and Mox turned quick and saw what Phyla had: a full seven rebel troopers that'd poured out of somewhere walking after them. Nobody had appeared up front yet, but when Davin glanced back the way they were going, several more rebels were stepping out from a commandeered office.

"Still think this is our cause?" Davin asked.

"Now's not the time," Phyla snapped. "Plan?"

"Break left," Mox said.

The metal man had spied a glassy front hotel lobby. The *Freestar Five Star* had an obnoxious name and decor to match, dangling shimmering planets and space art around golden trim. As if some kid had blended elementary school astronomy with a billionaire's budget. Normally, a place Davin would avoid and ignore.

Now, a place that looked very, very vulnerable.

"Go," Davin said, and the three broke towards the hotel.

The rebels, previously content to slowly close the gap with weapons ready, reacted with shouts and a sudden charge. Not one of them pulled a weapon and fired. Apparently the initial plan *wasn't* to kill Davin and Co.

But plans could change.

The *Freestar Five Star* had one revolving door, pointing to its inspirations, and a single normal one alongside it. Both glass from floor to ceiling, and both, when Davin arrived and pushed, locked.

"Move," Mox said, and Davin hesitated.

Up to this point, the Wild Nines hadn't really committed a crime. Hadn't done anything to go against Freestar's laws. If Mox shattered the doors the way the man looked like he was about to, well, then they'd lose their standing. Their arguments.

What if the rebels had a different plan? What if Mox and Davin had measured things wrong?

"Wait," Davin said, turning and facing the oncoming rebels. "Hold up."

"Why?" Mox asked,

"Phyla, you said we had to find a cause." Davin drew his hands, empty, from the jacket. "And around Callisto, we took up with this side against Eden. We tried to help them, regardless of how it turned out. If we start shooting now, all that goes away."

"Except they took Merc and Opal," Phyla said.

"We don't know that. Not for sure."

Mox narrowed his eyes, "Are you going soft, Davin?"

The rebels were close now, slowing their runs. One had stepped out in front, his crimson uniform bearing a small, golden version of Saturn on his chest that the others didn't have.

"For once, I'm trying not to shoot my way out of something," Davin replied. "I'm choosing a side."

"You pick the weirdest times to make a stand," Phyla said, but she didn't draw, she didn't start shooting.

Davin went in front of the other two, spread his hands to show he wasn't packing a grenade. Wasn't about to start laying waste. Behind him, Mox and Phyla stayed close, and Davin could feel their eyes on him, could feel them questioning his sanity.

"Hey," Davin offered to the approaching rebel officer. "Nice force you have here. Maybe you can help us? We're looking for our friends?"

"You're Davin Masters, right?" the officer said, ignoring Davin's question.

Always a good sign.

"Depends," Davin replied. "What do you want with him?"

The officer held up a finger, the rebel soldiers around him drew various weapons, from ragtag rifles to sidearms to one with what looked like an old school projectile shooter.

"He was a legend to the rebel cause," the officer said. "So sad that Eden murdered him too."

**35**

---

## PROFITEERS

A legend? Apparently Davin had done well for himself since his demise.

"I'm flattered," Davin said to the raised weapons. "Except this legend has a few things left to do. Officer, I don't know your name, but I do know that if your soldiers fire those rifles, this whole station's going to blow."

The officer froze, his hand raised and ready to deliver that death sentence. What should've been little more than an execution of a wanted group suddenly had high stakes attached. Make the wrong call and now the officer had a hundred thousand souls on his head, in addition to his own.

The best bluffs focused the mark's mind on the consequences.

"Or we could hold off on this laser-lit party and get to what's really important," Davin said, sliding phrases from the ether with all the skill life-ending adrenaline gave him. "I'm looking for your supervisor to deliver a message. Let me do that, and then they can decide if I'm better off slagged. That way, none of this is your responsibility, right?"

And once you had them focused on their own fate, give them a way out.

The officer spent long seconds with sweat beading on his forehead, hand still raised, until one of his soldiers slipped his rifle from his arms and holstered it.

"Sorry captain," the soldier said. "I'm not risking the station on this. My family's here."

"He's lying," said another. "You're falling for it."

"Look, guys," Davin said. "I'm supposed to be dead, right? Yet Eden's whole fleet couldn't kill me over Callisto. Their best assassins couldn't off me in the asteroid belt. What makes you think you're going to do it?"

The officer, at least, didn't have the guts to try. He lowered his hand, shook his head, "Don't fire. We'll take them in." He locked eyes with Davin. "But if you try anything, I will risk this station to put a laser in your skull."

"Blood on your hands, man," Davin said, then glanced back at Mox and Phyla. "Ready to go?"

The officer led them to the rebel center, a wide building that looked to be a converted casino. A place that'd probably moved to the outermost ring as Freestar continued expanding, leaving good real estate for the rebels to occupy. The old signage still hung, though attached flags and posters laying over the dead neon.

Merc and Opal's faces were here too, hanging on the outer walls and calling for recruitment.

People gave the crew space, and since the entire rebel force stayed with Davin, Mox, and Phyla the whole way, the march to and into the old casino had a celebrity feel. Brought back that old fame tingle Davin had felt after stopping Bosser, when the solar system claimed him as a brief celebrity.

Before the whole android story became too complex to

get much traction and Davin had been dropped for the latest movie stars. The newest Eden tech.

Inside the lobby, a two-story thing blazed over in icy blue, apparently in sync with the old casino's theme towards Uranus's chilly frontiers, the officer demanded their weapons. The soldiers formed up around Davin's trio in the center atrium, a constant projection above them showcasing the gas giant's swirling storms. To the right, the lobby gave way to shuttered betting tables now covered in workstations, and to the left, a theater had been repurposed as a meeting center.

"Give'em up," Davin said to Mox and Phyla, when the officer repeated the request for their sidearms. "We're not here to hurt anybody."

The soldiers collecting the sidearms set them on a table near the casino's entrance, its dull gray plastic belying its late addition as a junk catch-all: the sidearms joined backpacks, random gear, and a crimson uniform stack. Davin didn't see anyone secure the weapons, the rebels just left them lying out.

Ripe for a pick-up later.

Left with their fists and feet, the officer dismissed his force and led Davin's trio up with only a couple tagalongs. Eschewing the elevator for a single stair set along the rear wall, a silver riser series with zero decor, the officer brought them into the casino's back halls, the places customers weren't designed to see.

Davin figured Mox could take the rebel soldiers, while he knocked out the officer, but thus far there didn't seem to be a reason to start a fight. Without sidearms and in the rebel's rats nest, a brawl could quickly turn against them, so Davin put on a smile and tried to chat as they walked.

"So what's the mood after Eden kicked your asses?" Davin asked.

"Unpleasant," the officer replied, throwing Davin a rude look. "But the campaigns are working. Nobody here wants to go back under Eden management."

"Hear you there," Davin replied. "Do you think you really stand a chance, though?"

"It's not about winning," the officer said as they turned down yet another featureless white, tiled hallway. "It's about surviving long enough for Eden to think it's too expensive."

"Lotta lives to lose for that."

"Only a mercenary would think that way." The officer reached a closed door that didn't look any different from the dozens they'd already passed, black faux-wood and thick. "We believe in a better future, no matter the cost."

"Sure you do," Davin said, then pointed at the door. "This where the chief's at?"

"Commander," the officer said. "Remember, Davin Masters, that we've made you a legend to the public. But in here? You're just a tool."

"And you're a cheerless bastard." Davin nodded at the door. "Let's go."

The officer grinned at the insult, the most personality the man had shown, and tapped his comm on the lock. The door clicked and swung open, revealing an office that was anything but the drab, soul-sucking space Davin expected.

Space stations had choices to make, and too often they went towards the cheap and efficient. Building thick outer walls meant less energy spent on shielding, on glass thick enough to block cosmic radiation. Those that took the extra expense and put it to good use, though, created environments like this, where the floor and ceiling looked like they were open windows into space.

Freestar's outer ring, cutting through the view with its big gray bulk, couldn't spoil the look.

Neither could the woman turning to look at the new arrivals, her crimson uniform bedazzled with finery showing off some rank and honor that Davin couldn't read. Not that he had to: Davin knew Cassidy plenty well, though he never expected her to last long enough to climb any ranks.

"Get going," Cassidy said to the officer and the two soldiers after a cursory glance, with no discernible reaction, at Davin, Mox, and Phyla. "I'll handle these three."

"You'll handle them?" the officer very much doubted her words.

Cassidy set her hand on the Uranus blue-white desk next to her, gave a slit smile that Davin recognized from icy commanders he'd seen throughout his life, as if the expression came with the promotion.

"You heard my orders," Cassidy said. "If you like, you can wait outside the door to come to my rescue."

"Of course," the officer replied.

Dishing Davin one more glare, to which Davin offered up a wink, the officer and his two tag-alongs left, the door clicking shut behind them.

Cassidy looked far more refined than when Davin had last seen her. She'd joined the *Jumper* for a brief ride after her mercenary outfit fell apart during an assault out on Neptune's fringe. Merc had initially taken her hostage, then Cassidy had swapped sides when it became clear that living longer meant abandoning her commander and his burn-it-down strategy.

"Aren't you all supposed to be dead?" Cassidy said, keeping her hand on that desk. Her voice had a new edge to it too: self-assurance, someone who'd figured out where they stood and what they were worth. "I've been seeing ghosts all day."

"We're notoriously hard to kill," Davin said as they moved further into the room. "Mind if we sweep the place?"

"Go ahead," Cassidy replied. "Tell me if you find anything."

Phyla and Mox split the room, looking it over for weapons, potential ambushes, and cameras. Davin, meanwhile, kept his eyes on Cassidy, trying to figure out her play. At her prompting, Davin laid out the story that'd brought them here, leaving Viola and the weapon's part out of it. No reason, if Cassidy had the inclination, to get rebels sent the *Jumper's* way.

"Well, yeah," Cassidy said when Davin finished. "We can't let Opal and Merc get recognized, though we might've missed that one already. You have any idea how many people are signing up, now that it looks like Eden might take over?"

"Lots?"

"Exactly." Cassidy moved to her desk's middle, tapped it, and a projection shot up. Davin had to read the words in reverse as Cassidy flicked from one program to another, before settling on a short message. "Eden has to pay everyone that fights for it a lot of coin. We don't, because we have morale. People will take our crap salaries, our busted ships and slapdash weapons because they *believe* in what we're doing."

"You think that's going to wear Eden down?" Phyla asked, joining Davin. "Because that's not going to work. Not when they have Earth behind them."

"We have to believe Earth won't pay for Eden's problems forever," Cassidy slid her finger along the desk, spinning the message to face Davin and Phyla. "I have lines to say, stances to take. I believe them too, but not everybody does. Not everyone's in it for the same thing."

The message came from Alissa Reinhart, the rebel leader, and seemed to go to a select few individuals. Though the message was short, it didn't need much. It had two accounts with two figures, one before the war began heating up, and one after.

"Coin," Mox said, coming to take a look.

"Right, my mono-syllabic friend," Cassidy said. "Everyone at the top's taking home more coin now because everyone wants a piece of the war's pie. For every one of us that wants it to end so we can be free, there's another that wants to keep it going so they can cash out on our lives. Alissa and too many of us believe we're not going to win this thing, so they want all the coin they can get before it falls apart."

Viola had said the same thing about Eden. Morals twisting as the profits became more clear. Not that Davin couldn't identify with that: the Wild Nines had been coin chasers, he didn't have some high ground to stand on.

Phyla looked a little ill, like a person who's beliefs had been cracked. She'd wanted a cause and found a poisoned one. A little bit of time, a little bit of cynicism would get her back to normal. Something Davin could help with later.

Right now, he wanted to find his friends.

"Sure, everyone's a corrupt monster," Davin said. "Not my problem. Where's Opal and Merc?"

"That's just it," Cassidy replied. "Alissa and her friends might be corrupt, but I'm not. We have to win this war, Davin, because if we don't, Eden gets everything. If it comes out that we lied about Opal and Merc being dead, we'll lose."

"What did you do, Cassidy?"

Cassidy looked dead at Davin, frowning, sighing, holding firm and shaking her head, "It's too late."

"Merc saved your life. That's a debt you have to repay."

Seeing a person at war with themselves wasn't a pleasant thing. If there'd been something Davin admired about Bosser, it was that the man never seemed to question his decisions. He'd gone forward with his plan to ruin the solar system without a doubt.

Cassidy did not appear to have that confidence. At least not right now.

"Davin, if I tell you where to find them, you have to promise me something," Cassidy said.

"Promise you?"

"Yes," Cassidy said. "Promise that you won't stop fighting till you're either dead, or this war's over, with Eden on the losing side."

"That sounds dire," Davin replied.

"Just promise me."

Davin looked at Mox, Phyla, found no opposition there, "Okay, we'll keep on shooting. Not really sure who we'll be shooting at."

"That's my problem," Cassidy said, and she tapped away on her desk.

The message disappeared, replaced with Freestar's map, showing the rings. Cassidy kept tapping and, deep in the center, a red dot began to blink. The map zoomed in, showing the location as an apparent food storage center.

"You're freezing them?" Phyla blurted out.

"Preserve the bodies, find them when it's convenient," Cassidy said. "Not my idea. If you get there fast, you might be able to save them."

"You can't just call it off?" Davin asked.

Cassidy shook her head, "Sorry, Davin. I have my part to play."

"We are wasting time," Mox stated.

The metal man had it right. If Cassidy wasn't going to make the call from her spectacular office, then they would have to play rescuers.

"Nice seein' you, Cassidy," Davin said as they turned and went back for the door. "Good luck with your mess."

Mox opened the door, showing, to nobody's surprise, the officer and his two soldiers still standing outside. Davin and Phyla followed, the captain pulling on his cocky grin.

"Thanks for waiting," Davin said. "Mind showing us out?"

"Orders?" the officer asked Cassidy, ignoring Davin.

"They know too much," Cassidy replied, with all the casual coldness someone might use to dispatch an insect. "Kill them."

# 36

## MAKING NOISE

There were hints that Davin had learned to recognize. Some were subtle, like the glib way Cassidy had ordered Davin's death. Some were less so, like the presentation minutes ago where Cassidy had broken down the rebel's corruption.

Cassidy didn't need to do those things if she wanted Davin, Phyla, and Mox to end up as smoking corpses.

So Davin popped the officer in the face with his right fist as Cassidy finished her orders. The punch took the Eden man by surprise, knocking him into the hallway's narrow wall. Behind him, Davin felt Mox burst by with the super-natural speed his exoskeleton offered, a huge blur that, going by the simultaneous shouts from the two rebel soldiers, struck hard.

Davin closed with the officer, pinning the man's neck against the wall with Davin's left elbow while reaching and drawing the officer's sidearm with his right. Flicking off the safety, Davin pressed the weapon to the officer's temple.

"You want to be a legend," Davin said, "or would you rather live?"

The officer managed a gulp, managed a nod.

"Then here's what you're going to do," Davin said. "I'm going to follow real nice and close behind you, and you're going to lead us out of this maze. Let us get our weapons back, and take us to the center ring to find our friends. Got it?"

Another nod, coupled with a whole lotta sweat and some wide eyes.

Apparently Davin was scarier than he thought.

Releasing the officer from the wall, Davin set the man straight, keeping the stolen sidearm drawn and hidden by Davin's big jacket. Just to emphasize the point, Davin drove the barrel into the officer's back one more time.

Down the hallway, Mox and Phyla had worked out the other two soldiers. Mox hadn't been as nice as Davin, and had leveled both rebels with strong hits that left them unconscious on the hallway ground. Phyla came behind, stripped their weapons, keeping a rifle for herself and handing one to Mox. Then the big man dragged the two soldiers back to Cassidy's office, where the woman played her act by cowering behind her desk.

"C'mon," Davin said when Mox returned. "Walk us out all nice and calm, now."

The officer, to his endless credit, did as ordered. Moving a little stiff—understandable, given the potential death lingering close behind—the rebel officer took them through the casino's back halls, to the silver and blue stair, and out to the lobby.

Mox, being a giant human with a metal frame pressing out from his body, always attracted attention. Even with his jacket draped over his shoulders, Mox didn't conform to human standards, and eyes went their way as the officer led Davin's trio into the crowded lobby. That Mox and Phyla now carried rifles didn't help any, particularly when some of the same soldiers that'd escorted them in noticed.

"Cassidy didn't want'em dead?" one soldier, sitting with what looked like coffee, his rifle leaning against the wall at his side, asked as the group walked.

"Looks like she armed'em instead," said another, whose own hands went to his rifle. "Don't see that logic."

"Change their minds," Davin whispered. "We start a fight, you're the first one to go."

"Turns out they're friends," the officer said, his voice breaking a little as he spoke. "We had it wrong. They're here to help us."

"Are they?" said the sitting soldier, standing up and staring at Davin. "Well lucky for us, I guess."

"Keep moving," Davin whispered.

Davin couldn't see the officer's face, his hands, but Davin could read a mood. A firefight in a lobby like this, with himself, Phyla, and Mox in the open would end fast.

As more soldiers stood from their drinks, grabbed their weapons and watched, the officer brought them to the table. Davin, Mox, and Phyla snagged their sidearms, though Davin's move was made awkward by his need to keep the drawn weapon hidden. He reached out with his left, picked the sidearm off the table, and tried to bring it to his holster.

Davin's elbow caught his jacket, brushed it back.

And anyone, everyone watching could see the second weapon, drawn and pointed right at their officer's back.

Davin sighed, cursed, and pulled the trigger, blasting the officer with a shot that ought to hurt like hell while letting him live to see tomorrow. Phyla and Mox saw the flash and used it as the signal to raise their own rifles and start firing, forcing the rebel soldiers to dive for cover like so many bugs fleeing from sudden light.

"Run!" Davin shouted, finishing holstering his sidearm and reaching for the grenades they'd left on the table.

He didn't bother picking up the bombs, but reached and activated the first one. The ball began to beep and blink, and Davin joined Mox and Phyla in the scramble towards the door. The officer, wounded, picked himself up from the floor and broke towards the lobby's far side, shouting for everyone to get down.

"You're crazy," Phyla said as they ran into the broad concourse, drawing eyes from an evening crowd changing over from happy hour to late nighters. "Cassidy wanted us to help stop the leaders, not destroy the base!"

"It won't be that bad," Davin said as they ran.

The explosion blew out loud, rumbling and crackling through the station. Davin's feet flew out from under him and he hit the floor hard as screams broke out. The beautiful windowed look at Saturn and the stars disappeared as Freestar's protective measures sent a vacuum-sealing, metal barrier sliding across the glass. Dust flew through the air, fluttering down around Davin and coating him in silver-gray.

On his chest, Davin looked back towards the rebel base, that old casino, and saw absolute rubble where its entrance had been. The windows spanning its front had been blown out, and cracks ran along its silver, swooshing facade. Smoke poured from the inside, as shouts transitioned from panicked to supportive. Calls for medical help, for assistance in getting this and that debris moved off, streamed out.

"Keep moving," Mox said, bending down and lifting Davin up. "You destroyed a building. Do not waste it."

"Always keeping me focused," Davin said, finding his footing. Phyla was already ahead of them, making towards the next tram heading inward. "Think I hurt anybody back there?"

"Yes," Mox replied, "but you saved us."

And what was the ratio there? How many rebel lives equaled the three of them?

The whole 'cause' made everything so much trickier than before. If the rebels had been pirates, or Eden flunkies, Davin wouldn't have sweated taking out a bunch, but now he had to acknowledge that every rebel he hurt today wouldn't be able to fight with Eden tomorrow.

Davin wrestled with those thoughts all the way to the tram, which wasn't moving. Phyla pressed the call button time and again, even though the tram itself was already sitting there. Every press came back with a stern beep and a red flash from the tram's doors.

"Security override," Mox said. "Luna uses the same trams in our subways."

"Because you had to blow up their building," Phyla said, pressing the button again.

"A thank you for keeping us alive would suffice," Davin replied, then raised his comm, tapped through a call.

Security controls had to run from Freestar's network, and if there was one person who would be able to get inside it?

"Please tell me you're not the reason everyone's panicking around here," Viola's voice came back fuzzy. "The entire bay's sealed off now."

"About that," Davin said. "Think you can get inside Freestar's network?"

"Think? I've been inside it for the last half hour," Viola replied, then hesitated. "I got bored, and Fournine gave me the idea. I think it wanted to see if there were other androids here to talk to."

Worrisome. The last thing Davin needed was for his flight computer to go hunting for robot love.

"Then you think you could do us a favor?" Davin said, looking at the tram and finding what he wanted. "We need tram 3-2-A unlocked so we can keep moving."

"You want to go deeper into the station?"

Mox tapped Davin on the shoulder, nodded towards the damaged building back down the concourse, "They are coming."

"No time, Viola," Davin said. "Unlock it, please."

"Okay, fine," Viola said. "Next time, though, I get to go with you. Fournine's driving me insane."

"You're a peach," Davin cut the call, took up a position with Mox near the tram's front. "Phyla, keep an eye on the door. The second it opens—"

"We go, I got it," Phyla said, nodding through the tram's glass to its far side. "You better start shooting."

Mox acted first, stepping around the tram and spraying lasers with his rifle. Davin, watching through the glass, saw the fireworks scatter the oncoming rebel troops. Mox's bolts blasted black chunks from buildings, benches, artwork, and everything else the man hit.

"Not a single casualty," Davin said. "Good shooting."

"I thought we were being nice?" Mox replied.

"Not so nice that we get killed," Davin said, stepping around Mox with both sidearms drawn.

The smaller weapons weren't made for shooting at significant range, but with the right accuracy, even a laser's fading power could be effective. As soon as Mox stopped his barrage, the beleaguered rebels chasing after them popped up from their cover and kept advancing. A couple squeezed shots Davin's way, choosing to keep their friends protected while they pushed on.

Whether because they'd just survived an explosion or had been shot at by a man of Mox's size, the rebel fire went wide. Davin's, aimed right where those laser pinpricks came from, like bright targets, didn't.

One soldier's rifle blew up in his hands when Davin's shot hit, sending him flying back to the ground. The second one ducked away as Davin's shot burned away a centimeter from their chest. The other four making a headlong charge Davin's way now had zero protection.

"We're in!" Phyla called, the tram doors whooshing aside as Davin took aim.

"Leave them," Mox said, pulling Davin inside the tram, the rebels slowing up their run as they realized they weren't catching the trio.

"If they'd been Eden, I would've lit them up," Davin said, holding onto a pole as the tram lurched away towards Freestar's inner ring. "All four. Easy."

"You would've hated yourself for it," Phyla said. "We're not here to kill a bunch of random soldiers, remember?"

Davin knew. He remembered, but in the moment, it was easy to forget.

"Think Cassidy will forgive me for blowing up her base?" Davin said as Saturn re-appeared in the ring gap, a yellow-blue light with Freestar's glow.

"Maybe if you say you're sorry about a thousand times," Phyla said.

"Sounds like a lot."

"I'm sure you are used to it," Mox said.

These two.

Davin holstered the sidearms, pulled up the comm and flipped to Freestar's public map. The spot where Opal and Merc were being kept was one more ring deep, right in Freestar's center. Davin gave them decent odds to get there.

But getting out?

## 37

## COLD CASE

If Freestar's third ring represented the station's middle class, its second dipped into the lives of those grinding out a living in Saturn's shadow. Packed in capsule apartments greeted Davin, Phyla, and Mox as they left the tram, the micro-sized tubes jammed between older factories producing the raw goods required to keep a space station fed and functioning.

Between sedate signage for those apartments, the occasional working-man's bar and diner lit up beneath Saturn's sparkle, creating a cozier, warmer feeling than the modern and high-tech outer rings.

That, and the lack of rebel soldiers or Freestar security when they left the tram, brought a grin to Davin's face.

"Now, this is my kinda place," Davin said, holstering the sidearms. Mox and Phyla couldn't hide their rifles, but they slung the weapons over their shoulders, giving the appearance to the passing pedestrians that death wasn't inevitable. "Strange that they're not closing the ring here though."

"Is it?" Mox said. "Luna would shut down the minimum required. Panic helps nothing."

"And hurts coin," Phyla added. "Where are we going, Davin?"

Phyla had the right attitude: with Opal and Merc potentially turning into frozen food, Davin couldn't linger in the inner ring's ambiance. He pulled up the comm, checked the map, and found one of the sparse trams to the center ring not far away.

"Follow me," Davin said.

"As if we were going to do anything else," Phyla replied, falling in.

Mox brought up the rear as they walked, trying to look as calm as they could. Behind them, the tram unlocked from its berth and sped away, no doubt to pick up pursuing soldiers.

"So are you regretting coming out this way?" Davin asked Mox. "Leaving the moon to get shot at?"

"It would have been nice for things to go according to plan," Mox replied. "But I would not say no to helping a friend, even if I knew this would be the result."

"You're such a nice guy."

Mox laughed, "I know that what counts in this universe is friendship. Coin, employment, and homes come and go, but the people to share the ride with? That is most important."

"Davin, you could learn something from Mox," Phyla said.

"You couldn't?" Davin replied.

Phyla flashed a smile, "Nope, who do you think taught him what he knows?"

This time, Davin joined Mox in the laugh. Felt good, really, to let a little loose even in the middle of a tense situation. Yes, Merc and Opal seemed to be in dire straits. Yes, they were stuck deep inside a space station with a larger force mobilizing to crush them, but the Wild Nines had been here before.

Disaster felt familiar.

Might as well grin through it.

The tram to Freestar's core wasn't as empty—the security alarms hadn't reached this far, and workers kept up constant shifts this deep in the station—but nobody gave their rifles and dusty jackets any second looks. Davin kept expecting a shout, a surprised glance followed by a sudden stampede away as people realized the heavy arms around them.

Then again, back in Vagrant's Hollow, Davin had grown up surrounded by outlaws and people living on society's fringe. As long as the weapons weren't pointing at him or his friends, Davin wouldn't have noticed. Wouldn't have cared.

He had enough problems.

Casual life's last vestiges vanished as the tram entered Freestar's center. The station's initial section had been, by necessity, built with efficiency in mind. Core systems, life-essential production, and scant consideration for luxury. As the station grew, some more minor mechanisms had been sent to further rings, leaving a scattershot old and new blend.

No transparent ceiling graced Freestar's core, though the station's gravitational spindles and antennas, emergency docking arms and more would've blocked the view. The people with them on the tram seemed more depressed now that Saturn had disappeared, their heads buried in comms or quiet conversation with one another.

Nobody talked about dinner dates, the next show they were going to see, or even what the hell the rebels were up to after their molly-whopping at Eden's hands.

"Glum bunch," Davin said as the tram emptied out. "I think I prefer the outer rings."

"You prefer the party to the projects," Mox said, putting his hand on Davin's shoulder.

"No, I prefer to *bring* the party to the projects," Davin replied. "This is going to be the most fun this ring has ever seen."

"You have a strange definition of fun," Phyla said, checking her rifle's power as the last civilians meandered away. "Give me a bullet course over a gunfight any day."

Phyla's desires notwithstanding, no gunfight pounced as they came off the tram. Going by Cassidy's briefing, rebel operatives had brought Opal and Merc this far and farther. Davin didn't understand why they hadn't tried to set up an ambush, but he wasn't going to complain.

"Sorry, Phyla," Davin said, pointing left, towards where the frozen food storage ought to be. "Something says we'll be pulling the triggers a few times before today's out."

"So long as they're shooting at you and not me, I'll be fine."

Davin would've replied, would've unloaded a charming and devastating riposte to Phyla's comment, but his comm started buzzing. Viola's face showed on the little screen. Not the best time for a call, but Viola was safeguarding his ship, so. . .

"Davin, you're not making this easy," Viola said. "They've locked us inside."

"Locked us?" Davin looked around, noted the lack of chains. "We're plenty free."

"The *Jumper*, you moron. Your event on the third ring riled everyone up," Viola glanced off screen. "Fournine scared off the first crew with the turrets, but now they're just sitting outside. Our bay door's been sealed."

"So blow it open?" Davin kept walking, the warehouse appearing up ahead, its curving bulk pressing out into the ring's thinner concourse. "Get outside, then you can swing around and pick us up."

Just like Callisto. Having no atmosphere would make blowing a hole in the wall trickier, but they could figure something out.

"Yeah, that's going to get us killed," Viola replied. "The rebels have fighters stationed outside, waiting for that. Guess you tried something similar on Callisto?"

"Aww, they paid attention to me," Davin said. "Guess you'll have to think of something, then."

"Like?"

As they came closer to the warehouse, the concourse again devoid of people, Mox and Phyla unslung their rifles. Davin drew his sidearm with his right hand, keeping his eyes moving from the comm to the warehouse door.

"Get creative," Davin said. "The sooner you get out of there and cut around to the center ring, the better."

Davin cut the call, slipped his arm down to the second sidearm, as the warehouse's central door, a big double-wide metal thing, slid open. Cold white mist came flooding out, like a fog. Inside, squinting, Davin could make out hanging and stacked shadows.

"Down!" Mox growled, and Davin followed the order on instinct, diving to his left.

Davin rolled as bright blue laser fire poured from the warehouse, a single steady stream from what appeared to be a heavy rifle or worse. The burning glow laced where the trio had stood, with Phyla having gone right, Davin on the floor to the left, and Mox . . .

The big man banged into the ground right near the doorway, that exoskeleton combining with Freestar's loose gravity to give him a long leap. With the fog still pouring out, Mox had decent cover. Enough, maybe, to squeeze off counterfire without getting immolated.

If Davin could buy him some time.

"Find another door!" Davin shouted at Phyla, who went further right, heading along the warehouse.

Freestar, like most space stations, didn't leave gaps between its buildings, but the warehouse stretched far enough that there had to be another way in. One without hot death coming out. Pulling his sidearm and wishing he had Melody, Davin spat a few bolts in the heavy laser's direction, which only served to attract its attention.

The lasers scorched the floor as they seared towards Davin, bubbling up Freestar's tile and leaving no questions to what they'd do if they caught Davin's body. Another dive put Davin far enough left that the warehouse wall gave him cover.

For a hot second.

Davin's mouth dropped as the damn laser kept going, cutting through the warehouse wall and tracing towards him. He started left again only for the heavy gun to anticipate and cut him off, blasting through the wall where, if Davin had been a faster man not wearing a bulky jacket, he'd have been standing.

"Help!" Davin yelped, feeling distinctly unmanly as he did so, and kicked the other way.

Without strong gravity's friction, his boots slipped on the tile with the rapid turn and Davin fell forward, the lasers streaming towards him.

Well, at least the death would be quick.

Davin raised, fired the sidearm one last time as he hit the ground, sending a red bolt back through that fog towards the laser fire. The shot vanished into the fog, the lasers kept coming, and just as Davin started closing his eyes for the fiery end, the blue death shot upward, stitching a black trail on the building across the concourse as the enemy gunner took his aim towards the ceiling before the bolts snuffed out all together.

His shot. That last desperate shot must've saved him.

"I've still got it," Davin said to nobody as the laser fire died out, no death inflicted.

Davin stood up, crept towards the warehouse entrance. Mox had disappeared, likely inside, and down the ring's length, Davin saw a smaller door swung open. Phyla had found her entrance, one probably meant for actual humans rather than the loading doors.

The fog enveloped Davin as he went inside, its freezing chill coating his skin and burning his eyes. Every sniff brought with it chemicals, that hard, unnatural cold. The perforated warehouse wall and its flaking remnants added an ashen tint to everything.

"Mox?" Davin called out. "Tell me you're in here, buddy."

Shadows grew as Davin walked further in, sidearms in both hands. He came close enough to one dark pillar to see the warehouse meet its purpose, the stacked boxes showcasing the various foods insides. None of the labels read nutrient goop.

"Lucky," Davin muttered.

As the stacks thickened, Davin started to wonder how anyone could've shot outside the warehouse with any accuracy. His boots scuffed on icy tile, his hands felt locked on the cold sidearm grips, and Davin had to keep blinking the frost away on his iced over eyelids.

The man came through the fog right towards him, practically flying over the tile. Davin shouted, tried to backpedal, slipped and fell on his butt. Then he noticed his attacker hung limp, definitely unconscious in his crimson rebel uniform.

Mox held the body, laughing to himself, with the heavy laser in his other hand, the big gun looking awfully normal next to the exoskeleton. No sign of a laser burn on the body or the weapon, so Davin decided to keep quiet about his hero shot. No need to brag, after all.

Phyla appeared a second later as Davin picked himself up, smiling and shaking her head.

"You see what this guy did to me?" Davin said, standing. "This is why I broke up the Wild Nines. All this nonsense when we're on a rescue mission."

"The rescuing is done. They are fine," Mox said. "Back there, I broke them free."

As if hearing their names, Opal and Merc came walking up through the fog, both rubbing their wrists and shivering. Opal met Davin's look, gave him a nod. All the thanks he needed.

"All right," Davin said. "That was easier than I thought. Now we just give Viola a call, she blasts us outta here, and we're free."

A grinding noise punctuated Davin's closing word, coming from behind him. Back towards the exit. A door slammed, over to Davin's right, where Phyla had come in. Without anywhere to go, the fog thickened, grew colder.

"Well," Davin said, tapping his sidearm against a stack of frozen fruits. "At least we won't starve."

## 38

## CHILLY RECEPTION

The rebels filled in the holes blown open by their own man. Using thick foam, the kind made for emergency vacuum breaches, they packed the openings and left Davin poking his finger at the stuff while trying to decide if the foam felt soft or if his finger had gone totally numb.

"I thought I'd die in a lot of different ways," Opal said, staring at the shut double door. "Freezing in a food storage locker wasn't one of them."

"Surprise!" Davin said, then coughed as the cold sucked into his mouth. "Whenever things can get worse, they're gonna get worse."

Phyla and Merc helped Mox move to join them by the doorway, the big man barely able to get the exoskeleton to shift with his muscles. Apparently not designed for a deep freeze, the joints didn't work like normal. Didn't fire with much strength.

At first, Davin had suggested Mox simply bash their way out, but when Mox moved to act on that idea, he'd teetered and fallen over. The heavy laser's battery pack was spent, and the rifles and sidearms the group carried had quickly proved just as useless in the cold as Mox's metal.

"Still nothing?" Davin asked Mox. "Can't believe they didn't warn you about this."

"The person who put this on was a criminal running an illegal lab," Mox said. "They did not tell me anything."

"And you still went through with it?" Merc said, chattering through the words. "Wow."

"I had no choice," Mox replied.

"Loving the memories," Phyla said, hugging herself. "But how are we getting out of here?"

Davin had tried yelling through the doors, even knocking out a message using Morse code just in case, but nobody had replied. The security locks on the two doors didn't respond to Davin's button-mashing. Overhead and around them, insulation mingled with the white lighting. No windows, no grates that made for convenient exits.

None of them were small enough to fit through a duct, no matter how much Davin might wish.

"Split up," Davin said. "Take another look around. See if you can spot anything that might work. Who knows, maybe we can use bananas to club our way out of here."

"I'm cold, but I'm not insane," Merc quipped. "Bananas. You're losing it, man."

"Never said I had it."

Davin went straight back, away from Mox and the big door. Opal, Merc, and Phyla broke other directions while Mox performed a statue's role and waited at the entrance. Those dark pillars, stacked frozen food, leered Davin's way, as if whispering that he'd be joining them, awaiting some far future thaw where, alongside the frozen pineapples, Davin would be served up to a hungry space station population.

Spiraling through scenarios where, having thawed, Davin somehow fought his way through the cannibal hordes to a waiting, resplendent *Jumper*, the captain kept shuffling through the warehouse until his foot brushed something on the ground. Staring down, Davin only saw the mist.

He kicked again. Definitely something there.

"Buried treasure?" Davin said, the cold sinking into his mind, his words, his lungs, his everything.

He reached down, felt stiff cloth. Warmth, slight, beneath it. Davin waved away the mist and stared. The unconscious rebel soldier that Mox had thrashed and tossed aside lay on the ground, big ID badge plastered on the man's chest. A badge that ought to open up the doors.

"Hey!" Davin tried to shout, but the call came out a rusted rasp instead. "Need some help here!"

His voice didn't carry all that well at first, but after a few more yells, the effort bringing some life into Davin's body, the others heard and, minus Mox, came around. Between the four of them, bones aching with the effort in the chill, they hefted the body and carried it back to Mox and the front entrance.

Davin stopped before banging the ID against the doorway, even though he wanted nothing more than to open that gate and stumble into Freestar's warmth.

"They're going to be waiting," Davin said. "Which means we need a plan."

"Body shield," Phyla said.

"What?"

"You go first." Phyla pointed at Davin. "But lean their guy against you. They won't shoot right away, and that'll give us a second. Maybe a chance to talk out a truce."

The rebels might just decide to shoot, but after Davin

did another ask around, nobody seemed to have any better ideas.

"Getting burned down by a laser would be better than freezing," Opal added at the conversation's end. "At least that's a quick death."

"Might be the minority here, but I'd prefer no death at all," Merc muttered.

"Then we're taking the chance, because I'm damn cold and tired," Davin said. There wasn't any discussion about who would hold up the body, who would be the target. "None of our weapons work, so don't hold'em. Remember, the idea is not to die."

"A Wild Nines principle," Phyla added.

"Truth." Davin hefted the unconscious, frosted man. Heavy, dead weight, but Freestar's less-than-Earth gravity let Davin drag the man to the double-wide door. "Here goes."

With his fingers numb, his lungs hurting with every breath and his nose seemingly frozen to an icy chunk, Davin thrust the body against the locked panel, jammed that ID badge iced to the man's uniform against the scanner.

The cold had the scanner blink slow, but unlike the rifles and sidearms, the locks here were designed to function in low temps. A drugged beep sounded, and gears turned, sliding back the warehouse door.

Davin took two shuffling steps, attempting to put the rebel soldier's body in front of his own. Davin stood taller but thinner, so with some hunched knees and a tight grip on the rebel's back, he managed to hold the frozen body in place. Davin's numbed hands helped—he knew, could see the frost where his bare fingers gripped, but couldn't feel it.

The freezing mist took its escape opportunity and ran with it, fleeing the warehouse in a cascading silver-white wave. The avalanche flowed out and into the central ring's concourse, washing over at least fifteen or more rebels, all waiting with weapons drawn.

"Davin Masters!" shouted Cassidy, and Davin picked her out, standing in the group's center. "Why don't you have the good grace to die?"

Davin, teeth chattering, tried to figure out how to talk, "Never had grace in my life, good or any other. Never fancied turning into ice either, so how about we make a deal?"

Seeing Cassidy gave Davin a bit of hope, let some of that cocky courage Davin loved so much back into his heart. No way she would have the soldiers gun them down. There'd be some convoluted discussion and then Cassidy would let the 'Nines go.

"A deal?" Cassidy replied, drawing her sidearm and aiming it Davin's way. As she did so, the other rebels raised their weapons too. "I'll make you an offer: let our friend down, and that way, when you die, you'll have one less life to account for."

Hmm. Not quite the deal Davin expected.

"Uh, as compelling as that offer is," Davin said, trying to figure out his play. "I'm going to have to decline. Doesn't sound so good for me."

"Your call," Cassidy said. "Stun first, everyone. Once our man is out of the way, we can finish Davin and his frozen friends off."

A tipping point. Davin stared at Cassidy, trying to figure in her angry face whether this was still a ruse, whether she had changed back—blowing up her base might've been a bad move—or if, somehow, an escape plan hung on her words.

Davin had one more card he could play. He would say what Cassidy had told them in her office, could try and turn the rebels on their own leader. The odds of that seemed low, but better than nothing.

That would be the mercenary tactic. Loyal only to yourself, to your coin and your survival. Davin had tried that the last few years, and it'd failed. He and Phyla hadn't found love or success leaving causes alone. Davin didn't exactly want to die for one, but better that than dying for nothing.

He kept his mouth shut. For Cassidy, for her cause.

"Ready," Cassidy said, raising her sidearm. "Aim."

Davin locked eyes with Cassidy, saw the slightest smile touch her lips.

Freestar went dark.

The lights died. The constant hum from air recycling machines, from heaters and a billion other devices winked out. The station itself kept spinning from momentum, but that was it.

Mox, creaking as he moved, grabbed Davin as the captain put together what'd just happened. Nobody could see in the dark, but Mox ran anyway as rebel soldiers shouted for orders, and Cassidy replied to hold any fire, to not chance hitting a friend.

For a second, as Mox sped with lunging steps, Davin thought they were abandoning Phyla, Opal, and Merc. To say anything about that, though, would call attention to the two of them sprinting through the dark, pounding on the metal floor.

The rebel sounds dwindled as Mox kept moving around the ring, sticking to what Davin assumed was the center of the small concourse. On one of the outer rings, with their decor and statues and ad projectors, Mox would've been smashing through all kinds of junk. In the austere, functional middle? A blind rampage found nothing to destroy.

"Stopping," Mox said, and he set Davin down. "I believe we are clear."

Davin looked around, total darkness disrupting any concept of where anything was. He lifted up his comm, turned it on. Swiveled the little glow around to see Phyla, Opal, and Merc catching up to them.

"How'd you follow us?" Davin asked, trying to parse his thousand questions, how he'd made the leap from certain death to standing on a pitch-black concourse.

"Mox isn't exactly quiet," Phyla said. "Those frozen joints make noise."

"Noise the rebels would not know to follow," Mox said.

"Well, guess you all are smarter than I thought," Davin replied. "But once Freestar gets its act together, they'll catch us again."

The Nines didn't have any weapons to fight with this time.

Davin's comm buzzed. Viola calling.

"Tell me you're behind this?" Davin said as he answered. Freestar's sudden darkness, its utter mechanical failure, had a certain familiar vibe to it. "And that you have a way out for us?"

"Freestar's original docking hatch is close," Viola said. "Get to it, and I promise I'll tell you how much you owe me once you're on board."

On his comm, Davin found the old hatch. Mox had gone, by luck more than anything, the right way around the central ring, putting their exit not more than a few minute's walk away.

"Gotta say," Merc said as they headed towards the hatch. "Did not expect this. Totally thought you were going to bite it, Davin."

"Agreed," Opal added. "Even for us, it looked grim."

"Never count me out," Davin said.

"Excuse me?" Phyla said. "I don't think that escape had anything to do with you."

"Luck's my middle name, Phyla. Without my charm, we would've been toast. Easy."

Davin didn't have to look to see the shaking heads, didn't have to listen to hear the scoffs and sighs.

The old hatch had emergency signs and stickers plastered all over, none of which stopped Mox from breaking off its seal and opening the airlock. Freestar might not have power, but the airlock's purpose meant manual methods were supported, and Mox was nothing if not efficient at turning valves.

The airlock's narrow space, designed for Freestar's early days, could barely fit Mox. At Davin's insistence, Phyla squeezed in with the metal man for the first cycle, whooshing out and into the gray tube connecting, so Davin hoped, to the *Jumper*.

"Hey," Opal said while they sat in the dark beneath the hatch, waiting for its processes to run. "Thanks for coming after us."

"You doubted me?" Davin said.

"Not that," Merc said. "More like we didn't think you'd even know what was happening."

"Your faces were all over the station. Pronouncing you dead."

"We saw that," Opal said. "I thought they'd be thrilled to see us. Instead, we were pulled aside, told we shouldn't have come back, and brought at sidearm-point to that freezer."

"So much for being rebel heroes," Merc muttered.

"To some, you still are," Davin said as the airlock finished its cycle. "Okay, you two next."

"Davin, you're—" Opal started.

"Captain's orders," Davin said. "Get going."

The fighter pilot and the sniper didn't argue, maybe even smiled at the old words. With Mox's opening efforts loosening the hatch up, Opal and Merc made it in without a problem. The hatch closed, the airlock started, and Freestar's lights burst back on.

Davin blinked in the sudden brightness, winced as a thousand different alarms started up as various systems realized they'd been shut down improperly. Doors opened as workers, sealed in as locks died down, flooded the concourse and alternated between panicked questions and realizing they had big problems to solve.

The Wild Nines' captain watched it all at the emergency airlock's base, arms folded, enjoying the tingling warmth as feeling came back to his hands. Pure chaos, but not, for once, targeted his way.

"You coming, or what?" his comm buzzed as Viola asked the question. "Don't think people will let us sit up here unnoticed forever."

The airlock was open, ready and waiting. Davin climbed up the ladder, opened the hatch, triggering more, now-active alarms to add to Freestar's noise, and slipped inside.

## 39

# A MESSAGE

The *Jumper* floated in the nothing space beyond Saturn's rings, outside its moon's orbits and off of any space lane charts. They'd detached from Freestar as the space station came back to life, and with Phyla at the helm, shot out and away before any revenge could be scrambled after them.

Fournine kept tabs on the scanners while the six former-and-current Wild Nines members gathered in the cargo hold, looking at each other with that mix of friendship and surprise at an unexpected reunion.

"So we have a couple runners, a lunar centurion, two supposedly dead rebels, and one Eden engineer," Davin said as they all slurped on some nutrient goop, drank some very stale coffee, tried to overcome the exhaustion from the Freestar adventure. "Not exactly a normal crew."

The message had come in an hour after they'd blasted away from Freestar, well before Davin was calm enough to call their escape a success. A tight beam from Cassidy, it offered an option, a choice.

"Davin," Cassidy's message began. "Thank Viola for the

idea, otherwise I'm not sure I would've been able to get you out of there alive. Before you go running for the other side of the solar system, I hope you think about our talk. The rebel cause isn't dead, but it will die if we don't change its course. We need to understand why Alissa wants coin more than peace, and convince her to end the war. She won't listen to me, but perhaps those that saved her years ago can get her attention."

As messages go, Cassidy made her argument clear.

"Cassidy wants us to fight for the cause," Davin continued to the crew. "She wants us to find Alissa and change her mind, because Cassidy believes this whole thing is about something bigger than a war."

"Because it is," Merc said. "The rank and file, at least, believe we're fighting for our own freedom."

"I would not have joined if I didn't think so," Opal agreed.

"Okay, so the rebels want to fight for the rebels," Davin said. "Fair enough. The rest of us have to choose whether to go along with Opal and Merc, here, or split."

"Davin," Mox said. "Opal and Merc aren't rebels. They are Wild Nines. So are all of us."

"And we don't abandon our own," Phyla said.

Davin nodded, drifted his eyes to Viola, "What do you think, Vi?"

Viola glanced over to the black and yellow container, where the weapon that'd knocked out Freestar was back in storage.

"I think I owe a lot of people their lives," Viola said. "I created that weapon. I ought to make sure it delivers the peace I thought it would."

"You mean you didn't think it'd make your employer want you dead?" Merc said.

"Alissa's using you just as much as Eden's using me," Viola countered.

"Same question for them, though," Phyla said. "Why's Eden after a fight?"

"We have questions, and it sounds like Eden and the rebels will be too busy fighting each other to notice us digging for answers," Davin said. "Viola, if you'll help us, we'll find Alissa first, then go after the big E."

"You're all forgetting something," Puk, Viola's bot, chirped as it hovered over her shoulder. "Both sides want you all dead. Anywhere you go, you'll be hunted."

Davin laughed, "Puk, if there's one thing we're used to, that's it."

Everyone threw up various smiles, ranging from Merc's broad, cocky grin to Phyla's slightly green upturned lips. Opal shook her head, but didn't deny it.

"You're asking me to throw away my career to take up with you all again," Viola said, as if realizing what this all meant. "I had everything. The top scientists, engineers, and equipment Eden could offer. And I get to trade it all for this?"

Viola made a show of looking around at the *Jumper*'s cargo hold and its cluttered confines, the empty nutrient goop tube in front of her, and a crew still thawing from their frosted adventure in Freestar's warehouse.

"That's the deal," Davin said.

"Okay," Viola laughed as she spoke. "I'm in."

*The **WILD NINES'** next adventure is coming soon—read on for an excerpt from STARSHOT, available now!*

# AN EXCERPT FROM STARSHOT
## THE SKYWARD SAGA BOOK ONE

He is described in superlatives. A living weapon. Death incarnate. The last thing you see before your eyes go dark. All of these and more, on a hundred worlds, have been used to whisper about his coming.

More generally, and to himself, he goes by the name he has earned:

Sax.

A single syllable, because he is as of yet a three-letter Oratus. No ship under his command, no army at his beck and call. Not that he needs or wants those; each would take him away from the blood. From the visceral feel of his claws doing the work they're made for.

He's looking at them now. Checking them in front of a broad mirror. All twenty of them. Five on each hand, and he has four of those. They're attached to arms: two on each side, sprouting from a long torso that, due to his gray scales, shimmers like rippling water on a cloudy day. Twin legs, a tail and his head, thick and dominated by his large oval eyes and wrap-around mouth, round out the limbs. Nearly four meters tall, Sax doesn't come in a small package.

As he checks his body's weapons, Sax keeps an eye on the Oratus next to him. Same body, same height, only Bas is closer to rose gold in color. Sax looks at her with a mix of confidence and love, the sort of bond shared by a Pair.

Bas doesn't notice, because she's already started putting on her mask. She presses her left foreclaw—the upper set of arms—into the mirror. At first, it seems like the claw might push through and shatter the thing. Send glass everywhere. Instead, the surface of the glass warps; sucks in her claw and then oozes out over it. Liquid metal.

The mask flows forward over Bas's claw, her arm and the rest of her. Once Bas is completely covered, eyes and all, the mask appears to sink into her skin. Becomes translucent, as though her pinkish scales were covered by a slight fog.

Sax follows her lead. They all need masks; required for missions with a high risk of attack or exposure to vacuum, and this one has both. Behind him, he hears, or rather, through cavities in his skull full of tiny, vibration-sensing antennae, detects the other half of their set laughing. The usual for those two. Go back to the beginning of their fifty mission stretch and you'd find Sax seething at their hissing.

Now, he ignores it.

When the time comes, Gar and Lan won't be laughing. They'll pull the triggers on their miners, same as Sax. Gar would probably shoot first.

The mask is cool, but quickly warms to Sax's skin. It actually burns a little. Increases Sax's body temperature to ideal levels for performance. While the mask is getting to equilibrium, Sax and Bas step back from the mirror to see the next part of the show.

Oratus claws are like diamonds—they can cut through just about anything—but they're not much help against an enemy at range. The mask helps against weapons fire, but pop enough holes in it, and the mask will fall apart too. Better to eliminate the problem.

The mirror helps them with that. With a wave of Sax's claw, the mirror flows up towards the ceiling and reveals blue metal shelves holding an array of deadly tools. Sax moves first, with the confidence of knowing exactly what he wants and how to get it. The target is a pair of black sticks about my height.

Sax calls them batons. He picks them up with his foreclaws and sets them across his back. They stick to the mask, like a magnet.

Next comes a belt for his waist, followed by a variety of fun and games. Things to be thrown, fired, or tasted, depending on the situation. Next to him, Bas makes her own choices, and when they're both done, they take a second to stare at each other. Check the list, make sure nobody's forgotten something.

Neither of them has.

"Evva says this might be the last one," Bas breaks the silence, and while her mouth moves, the sound actually comes through the mask.

The four of them are already connected.

"There are always more," Sax replies, his voice like grinding sand.

"But what if it is?"

"Then we'll have to find something else to kill," Gar joins the conversation, and their group, in the center of the room. There's not much to say to that, because everyone agrees with Gar's assessment. Oratus are like miners—they serve a purpose, and Sax has a hard time thinking of what that might be if not to tear the galaxy's enemies apart. Lan saves him the trouble by joining in, completing their set.

They're ready to go.

*Continue the adventure in STARSHOT, available now!*

# ABOUT THE AUTHOR

A.R. Knight spins stories in a frosty house in Madison, WI, primarily owned by a pair of cats. After getting sucked into the working grind in the economic crash of the 2008, he found himself spending boring meetings soaring through space and going on grand adventures.

Eventually, spending time with podcasting, screenplays, short stories and other novels, he found a story he could fall into and a cast of characters both entertaining and full of heart.

A.R. Knight plans on jumping through to other worlds and finding new stories to tell in the limitless borders of our imagination.

Thanks, as always, for reading!

*For more information:*
www.adamrknight.com

*To Liza*